BROTHERS

BROTHERS

by

Ralph Josiah Bardsley

A Division of Bold Strokes Books

2015

BROTHERS

ISBN 13: 978-1-62639-538-1

This Trade Paperback Original Is Published By
Bold Strokes Books, Inc.
P.O. Box 249
Valley Falls, NY 12185

First Edition: December 2015

Credits
Editor: Jerry Wheeler
Production Design: Stacia Seaman
Cover Design by Gabrielle Pendergrast

To Peg and Carol. Thank you for teaching my soul to dance.

CHAPTER ONE

Jamus flew down the freeway with the windows open, the warm
spring air buffeting his face, a feeling of power and peace enveloping
him. He breathed in, savoring the damp smell of fresh-cut grass from
along the shoulders of the road mixed with the new-car smell of the
Buick Park Avenue. It was June on Long Island, and it was a rare night
without bumper-to-bumper traffic on the Long Island Expressway. For
Jamus, it was his first time outside of the concrete and glass world of
Manhattan in almost a year.

He loved New York City; everything about it was food for his
soul. He loved the crowded sidewalks in the fall, thick with the smell of
roasted peanuts and candied almonds from the street vendors. He loved
the collage of sounds—at any point in the day he could pause and listen
to a chorus of different languages. He loved the towering elegance of
Midtown and the cozy snugness of the Village. The overstimulation of
it all had made the last two years of his life unforgettable.

But Jamus was still a Bostonian, for whatever that was worth, even
if he had lent himself to this city for graduate school. The apartment he
shared with two other students was cramped beyond anything Jamus
had ever thought he could endure, but it hadn't mattered. He had ended
up with little time to spend there anyway. He passed most nights at the
school libraries or at lectures in dingy underground bookstores. It was
in New York that his mind started to open up to all the possibilities of
life, inspired by the variety that surrounded him. It was in New York
that he started to write. And it was in New York that he first fell in love.

In the mid 1990s, New York was alive with an energy that gripped
the entire nation; the Clinton administration had nudged the country out

of its Bush-era rut and into a booming sense of hope. For Jamus, New York felt like the core of that energy. The arts had new momentum, with theatre from Tony Kushner and Jonathan Larson boiling up from the streets; a reimagined music scene with new acts playing every night in tiny dive bars around the city; and a wave of vibrant realism in literature from authors like Chuck Palahniuk and Cristina Garcia. For Jamus, experiencing New York for the first time felt like everything was coming to life just for him, and he wanted to be a part of it all.

First and foremost, Jamus studied and learned. He knew what had been sacrificed for his chance at an education, and the economics and values of his class were deeply ingrained in who he was. He ate Top Ramen and shopped at secondhand stores for clothes and books. He stayed up late and worked weekends to finish assignments and read ahead. He knew how much had been spent on this opportunity and he wouldn't—and couldn't—waste either a second of the time he had been given or a penny of the money it had cost.

He also opened up to the coffee houses and their ceaseless conversations, the parks and their games of chess, and the clubs and their endless nights of glamour. And he wrote it all down. Everywhere he went, he carried his notebook and captured the smells and the sights and the sounds. It was somewhere dancing between all of this life that New York had to offer that he had fallen in love.

But Jamus did not fall in love with the person he should have fallen in love with. That would have been too conventional. He could have fallen in love with the roommate from Indiana whose parents had sent her to school here to learn medicine, or one of the interns at Goldman Sachs with whom he had sometimes stayed up into the early morning hours talking about the stock market and playing drinking games. He could have fallen in love with the guy who worked at the library, or the woman who taught his Theories of Dramatic Structure class. Any of these people might have been the right person for Jamus to fall in love with, but things didn't happen that way.

Instead, Jamus fell in love one night in the back of a club with someone who had tried to sell him a tab of ecstasy. It was at the Limelight, an old church that had been remade into a dance club. Jamus was at first surprised to look up and find himself the subject of a stranger's gaze, the pair of dark brown eyes locked on to him from a few yards away as Jamus stood in one of the stone alcoves with his notebook. It was so comical to Jamus, someone coming up to him, the bookish, silent guy sitting in the corner writing. This handsome stranger with his high cheekbones and beautiful full lips had seen him and thought he would be a good target. That he, Jamus Cork, would want to score some ecstasy. No one had ever looked at him that way.

Jamus laughed at the stranger when he approached. After politely refusing, he then apologized for laughing at him. "It's all right," the stranger said to Jamus, shouting loudly over the blaring music and the noise of the crowd. "I'm probably not going to sell anything tonight, but I thought I'd give it a try."

Love changes people irreconcilably. If it's real, love bends us into something we never knew we could be. Some people grow because of it, others wilt and fade. Love transformed Jamus, and, through it, he grew up. He let it wash over his soul and shift the sand that lay beneath it. Jamus, so closely tied to his Boston roots before he left for school, began to drift away from that life. He kept things from his parents, he let himself get pulled out to sea in everything that there was to be and feel in New York.

Things had changed for Jamus's parents as well. An unexpected pregnancy the year before he had left for New York meant that Jamus was no longer an only child. The Corks, both in their forties, were new parents again. The center of gravity in their world shifted as they struggled to readjust to diapers and cribs and teething. They were overjoyed and exhausted as a new baby boy took center stage at a time in life when they had expected to be golfing and going on trips as just a couple again. Jamus, away at graduate school and on his own, now required less of their focus and attention than this tiny bundle of bawling possibilities.

But that night out on Long Island in the car, it was just the three of them again. And Jamus, outside of the city for the first time in months, was surprised to feel a wave of release wash over him. Even with his parents in the car, his mother beside him in the front and his father in the back, he still felt as if he were flying, even if he wasn't really going all that fast.

He was graduating, he was in love, and he had one more surprise to share with his parents. He had an agent looking at a manuscript he'd been working on. She liked it and wanted to take some more time with it. "Extremely promising" was what she had said. The words had made

Jamus manic with hope. And tonight, at dinner, he was going to share that with his parents. It was his surprise, his way of saying "thanks for believing in me. I won't disappoint you."

"Jamus," his mother patted his forearm, "honey, you can go a little faster. You're only going forty-five and this is a highway." Jamus laughed. It felt as if they were going much faster than that. It had been so long since he'd been in a car that his sense of motion was distorted. And maybe his sense of direction was as well. For a split second, it looked as if a car was coming at them out of the exit ramp. He only had time to glance up and register just the faintest quiver of panic before it was too late.

It wouldn't have mattered what Jamus did. He had no place to go, and no one would have been able to maneuver out of the path of the driver who sped suddenly out from behind a barricade and slammed into the Corks' Buick almost head-on.

Traffic was backed up for hours on the Long Island Expressway that night. "An accident, eastbound," was how it was reported on the news. It seems cold to hear that phrase, but traffic reporters really can't say "the end of two lives and the dramatic turn of another" has brought traffic to a standstill.

But for Jamus, it was more than traffic. The accident brought his life to a standstill. He woke up days later in a green and brown hospital room somewhere on Long Island. The magic of New York City had receded. The vibrant life, the action, and the excitement in which he had existed evaporated suddenly and left him lying in that hospital bed alone. The lover, the studies, the work, the cafés, the libraries, the music and the art; none of it sang any longer. His world had changed, and his family, his roots, were gone save for one small boy.

A month later, he sat alone in his parents' home in Boston with a crying three-year-old on his knee and the help wanted section open on the table in front of him. This is where Jamus's story started; not from the glittering discotheques and literary salons that had been his prequel, not with the strong mother and father who had guided him all his days as a boy. All that he had in the world was a dilapidated brownstone with no heat. All the family in his life was sitting in front of him, peeing himself and screaming he didn't want to eat applesauce. This was the abrupt start of Jamus Cork's adult life.

WINTER 2005

CHAPTER TWO

Jamus woke with a start. The sheets were damp with a thin film of sweat, and he knew immediately that something wasn't right. He lay there for a few minutes listening to the house, trying to figure out what was wrong. Then it dawned on him. It was too quiet.

The sounds of the street were gone. No whoosh of passing cars or the footsteps and chatter of late-night revelers on their way home. He pushed the sheets off and walked to the window, pulling the curtain aside to see the street blotted out in a deep layer of snow. He rubbed his eyes and strained to see in the orange-white glow of the lampposts.

The snow must have started hours ago; it was coming down in heaps, rushing furiously on the wind and whirling to the earth in small angry flakes. It was still too early for anyone to be out shoveling, and the plows hadn't been through yet, leaving an eerily silent world that only slightly resembled his street. He stood watching the snow globe scene for a few minutes before crawling back into bed.

He shut his eyes and tried to go back to sleep, but it was no use. He lay awake in the snowy silence of the morning, listening to the muffled sounds of the street and of the house: the gentle thump of the plumbing, and the hiss of the steam radiator in the corner of the room. He tried to focus on his breathing, tried to feel the rhythm of inhaling, holding, exhaling. And there it was again—so faint he could barely pick up on it…their smell.

He traced the history of the house in his mind, breathing in deeply to trap the scent before it escaped, trying to hold on to it. He opened his eyes and stared at the ceiling, remembering exactly what the room had looked like when it had been his parents' bedroom. Sometimes he still got a sense of them in here, as if they didn't want to leave. He might turn at the top of the stairs and, out of the corner of his eye, see the bureau as his mother had kept it, with a white doily and a set of perfumes and powders surrounding her jewelry box. Or, like tonight, Jamus would catch a whiff of his father's cologne or the smell of his work clothes.

These faint remembrances, mostly faded, sometimes surfaced at the weirdest moments. These weren't the flashbacks. The flashbacks came and went, bringing him back to the night of the crash. They usually happened when he was writing, and they sometimes lasted for hours, sucking him out of real life and stranding him in some past prison of his mind. He moved along, trying not to think of them, instead trying to find the smell again.

But it was gone now. Jamus looked over at the clock; it was two thirty in the morning. He started to make a mental list of the things he needed to do this week, of the things he was doing wrong, of the fears. He eventually dropped off to sleep, the anxiety giving way to exhaustion and releasing him for a few more hours of almost-rest.

At seven, Jamus opened his eyes to a room filled with the silent brightness of a snowy morning. He immediately started preparing mentally for the morning's activities the moment he rolled over in bed. He took a deep breath and weighed the possibility of sleeping in for another fifteen minutes. The stillness of the house would evaporate soon, giving way to shrieks of anticipation and small explosions of activity. He knew from experience that the extra fifteen minutes of sleep wouldn't really be worth forfeiting the few minutes he had to get his day started ahead of Nick. He grudgingly rolled over and swung his legs down onto the floor, almost knocking over the half-empty glass of warm scotch from the night before.

Jamus had suspected a snow day might be in the cards when it started clouding up over Boston the afternoon before. He knew that the ten-year-old in the room down the hall would be up earlier than usual. So he roused himself and searched around his room for some clean clothes. In his top drawer he found a white T-shirt that hadn't been worn yet. The challenge would be pants. That drawer was empty, so he grabbed the cleanest pair of jeans in the monster pile of laundry that sprawled across one corner of his bedroom floor.

He pulled them on, stumbling back toward the bed in the process.

He pushed his hands into the pockets, realizing that these were the jeans he'd worn Saturday evening, the one evening in the last three months he'd managed to go out when Nick had a sleepover at a friend's house. He pulled out a ball of crumpled-up napkins, some with names and numbers on them, and looked at them for a couple of seconds, wondering about the possibilities hidden behind each number before tossing them into the little trash barrel beside his bureau. He rubbed his eyes and snapped himself out of his early morning haze. He had approximately fifteen minutes to get things rolling before Nick woke up. He tiptoed downstairs to the kitchen and put the coffee on.

As the coffee started to brew, Jamus turned on the tiny television in the corner of the room to the local news channel and waited for the list of cancellations. He made a quick trip to the front hall and dug the snow boots and jackets out of the closet before returning to the kitchen to start breakfast. After a few minutes, Jamus heard the stomp and patter of small feet above his head. First was the sound of Nick jumping out of bed and rushing over to the window. The feet stopped for a minute and Jamus pictured the kid staring out at the snowy street. Then the rushed cavalcade of those same feet getting dressed, brushing teeth, and practically jumping down the stairs, stopping in the front hall for a minute, and then bursting into the kitchen.

"Snow day?" Nick asked as Jamus sat sipping his coffee.

Jamus smiled and nodded toward the TV. "Yep, it's official," he said, evoking a squeal of delight from the kid.

"For you, too?" the kid asked.

Jamus nodded. "Yep, for me, too. Nothing is open in Boston today."

Nick launched into his customary snow day dialogue the minute he sat down to the table. Breakfast, which Nick insisted he didn't need, but Jamus insisted he did, consisted of a bowl of instant oatmeal and a banana.

"Toast?" Nick asked, the minute Jamus set the bowl down in front of him.

"You want toast?" Jamus looked at him to try and gauge how real the request was. Nick had fallen into the habit of sometimes asking for things just because they weren't on his plate.

"Yes, please," came the impatient response. "With peanut butter."

"Okay, fine, but you need to eat a little bit of the oatmeal and bananas, too," Jamus said as he put a couple of slices of wheat bread into the toaster oven.

Nick dived into the bowl as he began outlining the activities for the morning, chattering away about all the possibilities. Snow days meant a series of decisions that had to be made before heading out the door. Nick had paused on his way to the kitchen to swing open the oversized front door of the brownstone and evaluate the depth and texture of the snow.

This was important because the first thing he had to decide was which park they were going to. Their neighborhood had a number of smaller parks which seldom had other kids in them, but they were closer to home, which was important for bathroom and snack breaks. And if it had been a heavy snowfall, these parks were better for snowman making. Snowman making was a solitary task, and he and Jamus were better off without any interference from other kids.

Nick had to decide if it was going to be a snowman morning or a snow fort and snowball fight morning. The latter decision meant they would have to go to the bigger park several blocks away. A bunch of kids were sure to be at that park, and with this morning's snowfall, there should be enough to last through at least lunchtime.

Nick rambled through a description and list of these items as Jamus saw to the peanut butter toast and gulped down his cup of coffee. He waited until Nick paused to chew through the first slice of toast. "So what's it going to be? Big park or one of the little parks?" he asked. Speeding up the decision process was an important part of getting Nick out the door any time before nine o'clock that morning.

"Will you be on my team if we get in a snowball fight?" Nick asked, tentatively swallowing a mouth full of peanut butter as he spoke.

"Of course I'll be on your team, Nicky." Jamus sat down in the chair next to him.

"Okay, then I want to go to the big park."

"The big park it is." Jamus smiled. "Finish up your toast, and let's get ready to go. We want to get down there before the big kids get all the good snow. We'll need it if we're going to make our super-awesome long-range-strategic snowball missiles."

Nick let out a giddy laugh. "Yes! I love the super-awesome missile strategic, um…snowball missiles."

Fifteen minutes later, Jamus pulled Nick's small hands through the sleeves of a puffy red coat and wound a blue fuzzy scarf around the boy's head three times, covering his mouth and nose but carefully leaving his eyes exposed. "You need a hat," he said.

"I don't want a hat," came the scarf-muffled complaint. "I'll be hot."

"You can take it off if you get hot," said Jamus, "but you need it to start out. Which one do you want?"

"Can I have the white one?" Nick asked, pointing up to a white woolen hat hanging on the coat rack in front of them.

"Okay, the white hat it is," Jamus said, grabbing it off the hook and pulling it down over Nick's ears. "Red, white, and blue. You look like Captain America."

The streets were mostly empty as they finally swung open the door to find a fresh ten inches of snow. Most of it had fallen during the night, but it was still coming down in solid sheets, blanketing everything in a mystical quietness that held the promise of a morning full of adventure. A few brave shovelers dotted the snow-scaped neighborhood, scraping away at windshields and steps up and down the street.

A couple of them waved as Jamus and Nick made their way down the partially cleared sidewalks of the South End. The two Cork brothers waved back as the crunch and squeeze of snow under their boots marked every slow, deliberate step. Jamus looked around as they walked. Everyone was moving just a little bit more sluggishly than usual, as if the whole world were in some sort of slow motion silent film. The snow really did give everyone an excuse to take the morning off for a little arctic adventure, he thought. He pictured them all in their snug living rooms later that morning, curled up on their sofas, just back from a trek down to the Appleton Bakery for a five-dollar skim latte and a mango-cinnamon scone.

Jamus brushed aside a layer of snow that was starting to stick to his exposed forehead and a few seconds later a frantic yelp of joy jolted him back to the real world. "Jamus, come on." Nick doubled back and yanked on his hand. "They're already starting to use up all the snow and I want to make sure we get some good stuff for our fort."

When the two arrived, dozens of woolen-capped kids of all ages were already strewn about the park. Around the perimeter were several small groups of moms, some with lattes and mochas and others glued to their cell phones, all bundled up and keeping an eye out on the joyful havoc of the snow-day park.

Nick held up well for most of the morning.

The two brothers staked out a patch of snow in the middle of the park and got to work building a solid, semicircular fort directly in between two other forts that a few of the older neighborhood kids had constructed. They had strategically left a large pile of snow untouched behind the fort for snow missiles. Snow missiles, one of Jamus's inventions, were elongated snowballs shaped more like footballs. They let the launcher fire them into an opponent's fort—or into the opponent himself—with a spiral, smashing apart with more impact than the flat kersplat of a normal snowball.

The missiles worked well that day, and Nick and Jamus were victorious in several battles. The sole exception was an intense three-way fight when the two other forts ganged up on the Cork brothers in unison. The Corks' supply of snow quickly dwindled, and soon they were left cannibalizing their own fort to defend themselves. Luckily, about the time they were getting blasted, several of the moms along the perimeter started to get restless and began calling back their own troops from battle, thinning out the field of opponents considerably for Nick and Jamus. The two brothers walked away from their last battle with a little snow edging in around their necklines and cuffs from the bombardment.

"Jamus," Nick said as they were walking back to the house, a little slower now than they had been on the journey earlier that morning to the park. "How come you're the only dad that comes out to the park alone?"

"I'm not alone," Jamus said, pulling down Nick's hat just over the top of his eyes. "I'm with you."

"No." Nick hesitated for a minute, fixing his hat. "I mean how come you're the only dad that comes without a mom."

"Well," Jamus said. "I'm not really your dad, but I am your big brother, and because there's just the two of us, I'm sort of like your dad."

"You know what I mean, Jamus."

"No, Nick." Jamus tried to follow the ten-year-old's logic but he knew he wasn't getting something. "I don't think I know what you're asking?"

"Will you ever get married? Will there be a mom in our house?"

"Oh," Jamus said, taken a little off guard. They had had a lot of these unexpected conversations throughout their seven years living together. Jamus learned early on that kids' minds didn't always work the way grown-up minds did. They always ended up making sense in some less-than-obvious way, but the first taste of kid logic could sometimes be jarring.

"Well," Jamus said, "I might, someday. But I don't know anyone right now that I would marry."

"Me neither," said Nick. "But you might bring a mom home someday?"

"Well, probably not a mom," said Jamus.

"But you're a dad." Nick sounded puzzled. "Doesn't that mean you have to marry a mom?"

"No, not really." Jamus was starting to sweat. Deep down, he had known this conversation would come up some day. If he was honest with himself, it was surprising it had taken so long. "You only ever marry someone because you love them a lot. Not for any other reason. Most of the time, it's a mom and a dad that get married, but sometimes two moms get married and sometimes two dads get married, and that's perfectly okay."

Nick scrunched his nose up for a few seconds while he contemplated the concept. "Two moms or two dads? Really?"

"Really," said Jamus. "It happens a lot. And getting married is not always about being a mom or a dad. Sometimes people get married, and they don't have kids."

"And if you got married, it would be to another dad?" Nick asked.

"Well, let's just say I have no plans on getting married any time soon," Jamus said. "But yeah, it would probably be to another dad."

"But you got a kid without having to get married?" Nick asked.

"Well, yes and no," Jamus said carefully. "You and I, we're brothers, which is a little different than parents and kids. We both have the same parents."

"Just like Robert and Jamie," Nick said, referring to a pair of brothers who went to his school.

"Sort of, except that there are a lot more years between you and me than between Robert and Jamie. And our parents aren't around anymore, so you and I have to take care of each other. And because I'm the big brother, I get to do all the fun stuff like cooking and shopping. You have to do all the hard stuff like making your bed and going to school."

"Except on snow days," Nick said.

"Yes, except on snow days. In which case, we get to blow off the rest of the world and go have snowball fights, and then go home and pig out on grilled cheese sandwiches."

"And soup!" Nick added. "Don't forget the soup."

"Sounds good," said Jamus as they rounded the corner to their street. "Race you to the door? Last one there has to open the can of soup."

"I don't know, Jamus," Nick said, slowing his walk to a saunter before exploding into a run. Halfway down the block, he shouted, "Okay, go!"

Jamus laughed and gave him a few more seconds of a head start, and then he took off to catch up with him, tailing him slightly as they rushed to a sliding stop in front of the door, each panting heavily as they climbed the steps and headed into the house for tomato soup and grilled cheese sandwiches.

CHAPTER THREE

The smash of the car jolted Jamus to life. His eyes flicked open, the screaming still ringing in his ears as the soft bluish-white blur glowed in front of him. The smell was gone, though—that smell of gasoline and smoke mixed with other, more human smells. He struggled to open his eyes, to pull himself out of it. He knew at this point it was a dream, but it was still too real to let go. The blur in front of him started to come into focus as his laptop screen, and he noticed a painful arc across the top of his shoulders and his neck. He had fallen asleep at the table again.

He tried to clear his mind, but this dream had been a bad one. *It smelled,* he thought, *it even smelled in the dream. Who dreams of smells?* He tried to recount the sense of the dream, but whatever linear pattern to it had already slipped away as he came into consciousness. Only the whirl of violent colors and sounds and, this time, smells lingered as a confusing fog over his brain.

He took a deep breath and tried to pull himself away from the dream world he had created. These dreams always started when he wrote. They were part of the flashbacks, he supposed. His imagination was pulling from his memory, but what happened was a fusion of the two whenever he closed his eyes—the horrors of the accident melded and twisted into whatever plot he was working on and consumed him as he slept. The worst thing was the flashbacks and the nightmares actually helped him with his storylines. So it was a twisted, terrifying riddle that both hurt him and helped him to create.

His eyes fluttered as he ran through the basics of the real world in his mind, trying to reestablish some sense of gravity, of balance. "Okay, start with the basics," he told himself out loud. "My name is Jamus Cork, I live on Dartmouth Street in Boston with my brother Nick. I work at a bookstore, and I am a writer." He exhaled. "Or at least I am trying to be."

He sat up and looked at the text in front of him. He was almost done, almost finished. Just a few more rounds of editing, then he could rest, and the nightmares would stop again. Hopefully. Jamus's hands still shook as he closed the lid on the laptop and rubbed his eyes.

This was the worst part about writing, this being in between a world of dreams and a hazy reality. He didn't know what was real and what wasn't at times. It was usually Nick who brought him out if it. This hadn't happened in his first book. It had been a dark book, yes, but not the kind of dark his books were now. He hadn't had to write in a world where he was alone then. The books he had worked on since his parents had died had been terrifyingly difficult. They often lasted longer than he wanted them to and took on a life of their own when he was sitting at the keyboard. The problem was that they consumed him. He went into these worlds, these characters in ways that stole him away from his real life.

Okay, he thought, *back to the basics*. He looked at the clock and saw it was four in the morning. He squeezed his eyes shut and wondered if it was too late to try and get a few hours of sleep. Nick would be up in three hours. He would need to get the boy off to school, get him dressed, fed, and out the door. If he stayed awake, he would be sure not to oversleep, but he had to find some way to fill three hours.

His vision blurred as he looked down at the closed laptop in front of him. He could always go through another set of edits. A few places still needed polishing, needed a little more work to get the exact turn of phrase, to get the words just right. He yawned. He knew he needed the sleep badly. But if he closed his eyes and it didn't come, he would have to deal with the rest of it, all of it flowing through his mind, not stopping, endlessly washing over his brain, like waves crashing onto a failing pier, tearing it down and dragging it out to sea one timber at a time.

"My name is Jamus Cork. I am a writer. I live on Dartmouth Street in Boston. I work at a bookstore." He struggled with the words this time. In a few hours, the sun would come up and that would make it better, this drowning. But relief would only be temporary, and the dark would come again.

"Jamus?" A small voice came from the corner of the kitchen behind where he was sitting. At first, Jamus couldn't tell if it was a real voice or one of the voices reaching out for him from the story. All the stories pulled and tugged at him, jealous of his dual life. Jamus was able to live in two worlds. He could eventually get out of the story, but they could not.

"Jamus, are you okay?"

Jamus shook his head. This time he could place the voice. Nick. It was Nick, come down to check on him. Or was it later than he thought? Was it seven already? Time for breakfast and school? No, not yet. It couldn't be. He searched around the room for the clock. Where was it? He had seen it a few minutes ago. Right, on the stove. He looked up. It was still just a few minutes past four in the morning.

Pull it together, he told himself. "Hey, Nicky," he said, turning around and reaching an arm out for the kid.

"Why are you still up?" Nick asked, sleepy bugs still stuck in the corners of his eyes. He wandered over to Jamus's outstretched arm and leaned into him.

Jamus curled his arm around his little brother, hugging him in. "I'm just finishing up some writing. I got on a roll and wanted to keep going."

"Are you done yet?"

Jamus nodded his head. "I think so." This was good. Nick was good for him, pulling him out of the story, pulling him away from the loss and theft of the book, of the world he had just created. Created was the wrong word, really. Channeled was more accurate. When he was done, he was always a part of the story. "Did I wake you up?" he asked.

"No. I just couldn't sleep."

"How about now? Think you can head back into bed for a few more hours?"

"I don't know. I don't really feel like it. Are you going to stay up?"

Jamus thought for a minute. "I might try and get a few hours of sleep on the couch."

"What if I get the sleeping bag and camp out on the living room floor?"

"Hmm." Jamus looked doubtful. "Are you sure you're going to be able to sleep?"

Nick bobbed his head enthusiastically in agreement.

"Okay." Jamus gave in. "Run and get your sleeping bag."

Ten minutes later, they were both fast asleep, Jamus on the couch and Nick on the living room floor. Each brother provided the safety they both needed for sleep, but in vastly different ways. Nick needed to know Jamus would stand guard against whatever lurked in the shadows of the house, and Jamus needed Nick to help hold him back from whatever it was that lurked in the back of his own mind.

SPRING 2009

CHAPTER FOUR

Sean Malloy sat on the floor of the tiny apartment in western Massachusetts and tossed another stack of books into the cardboard box in front of him. The sun wasn't up yet, but he had already been packing for over an hour. He wasn't normally a procrastinator, but exams and work on his doctoral thesis had kept him busy up until the day before, and he didn't have enough time to do anything else.

He looked around the apartment and frowned. He'd lived here as long as he'd been a graduate student, for both his master's and his doctorate, but that was coming to a close. He was done with the last of his classes, and his degree would be officially conferred on him later that month in a ceremony for grad students.

His ma wanted him to accept the diploma in person, but Sean knew from experience what it would be like: a sweltering hot day in June and thousands of students sitting side by side in the school's outdoor athletics center, parents and friends crowding into the stands above them, everybody sweating and wishing they were somewhere else.

He had already walked for his bachelor's degree and again for his master's degree in teaching. He didn't see the point in sitting through another crowded furnace of a day. The school would mail it out to him sometime that summer, and he would give it to his ma, who would frame it and put it in the living room right above his last two degrees.

He thumbed through stacks of old notebooks, term papers, flash cards, tests, research reports, and printouts. These papers had made up his entire world for the better part of the last decade. "Screw it," he said under his breath, tossing a stack of notebooks into the trash bag next to the cardboard box. His train to Boston was leaving in a couple of hours, and he still had to finish cleaning out this bookshelf and the desk beside it.

Reaching for another handful of papers, he glanced through them and dumped them into the trash bag, causing it to vibrate and ring softly. Sean looked down into the bag to see the dim glow of his iPhone hiding beneath a clump of balled-up term papers. He fished it out and swiped the phone, rushing to answer it without bothering to look at the caller name.

"Hello." Sean clamped the phone to his shoulder and reached down to throw away another stack of papers.

"Sean?" came a distant gravel-like voice on the other end of the line. "Is that you?"

"Dad?" Sean asked quickly. Something was off in the tone of the caller's voice.

"Uh, no…it's Kevin."

"Kevin?" Sean finally recognized his older brother's voice. "God, you sound like Dad. What's up? Where are you?"

"I'm heading home." The line was quiet for a minute. "I'm in Chicago now on a layover, but I should be there later this morning."

"Oh." Sean was trying to put things together in his head. It had been almost a year since he'd spoken to his brother. They had traded emails off and on while Kevin was away in Afghanistan but never more than a few lines at a time. Sean did most of the writing, filling Kevin in about the family or relaying stories about school. Kevin wrote back, but mostly in one or two sentence emails, never talking much about where he was or what he was doing in the Marines. "Are you on leave?"

"Ah, no." Kevin's voice started to break up. Then after a few seconds, "I'm out."

"Out?" Sean echoed his brother. "Out of what?"

"The Marines," Kevin almost shouted.

"Oh." Sean pulled the phone away from his face for a few seconds. "As in for good?"

"Yeah, as in for good."

"Is everything okay?"

"Yes." Kevin laughed. "Don't worry, Seany, it was an honorable discharge. Ma asked the same question."

"I wasn't asking that, Kevin." There was an awkward pause as

Sean tried to think of something to say, but he suddenly found his mouth dry. "You're moving home, then?" he finally managed to get out.

"Yeah, for a little while. Ma tells me you are, too?"

"Yeah," Sean croaked. "Yeah, I'm packing now. Done with school."

"Look, Sean, I'm losing you." The voice was almost all static on the line. "I'm going to go now. See you in a little bit."

"Yeah," Sean sighed. "See you soon." He took the phone out of the crook of his shoulder and stared at it for a moment before hanging up. He placed the phone on the night stand and sat down on his bed. He'd been so preoccupied with school for the past few months, he hadn't thought much about his brother. There had been a time when the two of them were inseparable. Barely a year apart in age, Sean had followed Kevin in everything—school, soccer, even in church. As a child, all Sean had to do to see eleven months into the future was to look at Kevin. Now they hadn't really talked in years and they were both heading home again.

Sean picked up a stack of papers and threw them directly into the trash bag without even looking through them. Sean stood up and walked over to his bookshelf, pulling down a couple of hardcover volumes and tossing them into a cardboard moving box. He winced, remembering that he still needed to somehow get to the post office before he caught his train. What would they have in common now, he wondered.

"Ugh." Sean sighed and looked at the clock on his desk. The morning sun was starting to come through the tiny window above his bed. He forced himself to focus on packing. There would be enough time over the summer to figure out what to do with Kevin. If he missed the train, he would be stuck without a ride to Boston.

❖

Late that afternoon, Sean stepped off the Number 11 bus and dropped an oversized duffel bag on the ground directly across the street from the house he grew up in. The late spring sun was setting over the horizon, bathing all of South Boston in a hazy golden light. The bus roared off down the street, leaving him standing on the curb in a cloud of smoke. He stared across the street at the steps directly in front of him. All he could think of was his brother. He remembered the last time he'd seen Kevin at the house. He'd still been a senior in high school, but Kevin had graduated a year earlier. They had both wanted to escape from South Boston, but Kevin made his move alone, joining the Marines and leaving Sean to fend for himself at home.

Sean swallowed and tried to clear his mind of that. After all, it was six years ago. He didn't hold it against his brother. In the end, Sean wouldn't have joined the Marines with Kevin, so they would've gone their separate ways eventually.

He looked away from the steps for a few seconds, quickly surveying the rest of the yard, taking in the green clapboards, black shutters, and the hollyhocks lining the small garden along the base of the cellar. Nothing had changed since he'd been home over Christmas.

But this time it was permanent, he thought, with no school to go back to. This time, he was home until he found himself a different place to make his own. He stood there quietly for a few minutes, thinking about all the times he had bounded up those steps as a teenager. The second step squeaked and always dipped a little too much if you didn't hit it in just the right spot. The fourth step was always loose, and if you went down it in bare feet, you had to watch out for a particularly stubborn nail head that always managed to pop up just to the left of center no matter how many times Dad hammered it back down.

The rest of the houses on the block had cement steps, but the Malloys still had the same wooden ones that had probably come with the house. Kevin had painted them every other summer growing up; it was somehow always his job. Sean smiled, remembering how much his older brother had hated painting. Their parents always insisted that Sean was too little to paint, until he wasn't. By that time, painting the porch was just Kevin's job and "this house is not a democracy" was Dad's standard response whenever Kevin tried to get out of it. Kevin would give Sean a look at those moments, then shake his head as if the weight of the world rested on an older brother's shoulders.

He hadn't told his parents exactly when he was coming, but somehow she'd known. His mom stepped out onto the front porch and stood watching him, smiling and looking a little bit surprised as if she was waiting for some sign that he was really there. A few seconds later another figure stepped out from the front door and stood beside her. Sean's jaw slackened. Kevin stood tentatively on the balls of his feet, his hands shoved into the pockets of his jeans, grinning slightly to one side. He had a plain white T-shirt on and a blue Red Sox cap over his closely cropped red hair.

The brothers shared the same storybook Irish red hair, freckled faces, and light blue eyes. Many times growing up, strangers had mistaken them for twins. Sean's eyes stayed glued to the porch in semi-disbelief. It was his brother, only something was slightly different about him, something he couldn't quite put his finger on. He was a little bigger, maybe that was it. His shoulders were a little broader and his arms thicker than they'd been the last time Sean saw him on a Marine base in South Carolina. The family had driven down to visit him before he shipped out on his second tour, that time to Afghanistan.

Sean smiled back at them as he picked up the duffel bag and crossed the street to his house. That was the cue they'd been waiting for. His ma threw her hands up in the air and launched off the porch, jogging along the pavement walkway until she reached him and wrapped her arms around him. Kevin followed behind her, waiting until she had let Sean go, then folding his younger brother into a giant bear hug, picking him up off the ground just a little. Sean hugged his brother back, a little uncomfortable at first. They had been close as brothers a long time ago, but even as close as they were, they rarely hugged.

"It's good to see you." Kevin gradually loosened his hold.

"You, too," said Sean, easing back out of the hug and noticing for the first time silent tears were running down the side of his brother's face. Sean put his hands on Kevin's shoulders and pulled him back close and sighed. When he left his old apartment this morning, he hadn't known what it would be like to see Kevin again. He'd been afraid, at some level, of a cold reunion. This was anything but cold, but he was still a little worried. "Really good to see you, man. I wasn't sure you'd make it," he said under his breath so Ma wouldn't hear him.

"You and me both," Kevin said, pulling away this time and wiping at his eyes. "Sorry, I didn't see that coming."

"It's okay." Sean laughed and punched his brother gently on the shoulder. "If you didn't tear up, I probably would have." Sean didn't know if that was true, the emotion was more than he'd expected to ever see out of Kevin, but it made him realize that things had happened to his brother that would never happen to most people. He stood there looking at Kevin.

"Okay you two, in the house." Ma put her arms around them both, corralling them up the stairs. "The last thing we need is talk in the houses. The neighbors'll say we've been fighting."

"Fighting?" Kevin sounded surprised. "They would have heard worse from us before this."

"Yeah, but not for years. Come on in, you both."

"For years?" Kevin arched his eyebrows in mock surprise. "When was the last time you had the girls over for dinner? I'm sure there was enough yelling to catch plenty of ears then."

Ma smacked Kevin gently across the back of his head. "Enough lip." She laughed. "In the house now."

Sean smiled. It was just like his ma to worry about what the neighbors would think. Some things didn't change. He leaned down to pick up his duffel bag, but Kevin beat him to it.

"How did you know when I was coming?" Sean asked the two of them as they walked up the steps.

"I didn't," his mom said without releasing him. "I've just been watching the buses since I knew you were coming today."

"That's a lot of buses." He laughed softly.

"Trust me, I know." Kevin rolled his eyes. "Every ten minutes, we were at the front window."

"Well, I was looking forward to seeing you," she said. "Didn't you have any more bags? That's all you brought from your apartment?"

"I shipped a lot of books. They should be here in the next week or so."

"Watch out." She pulled on Kevin's shoulder as they headed up the front porch steps. "This one's got a nail sticking out."

Kevin smiled. "You have no idea how glad I am to hear that, Ma."

❖

"So what degree is it this time?" Kevin asked. The two brothers sat in the kitchen watching as Ma cracked eggs and gently opened them into a bowl full of flour, chocolate, and sugar. Kevin was perched on the counter next to the ancient lime green Kelvinator refrigerator while Sean sat at the small butcher-block table in the center of the kitchen.

"It's his doctorate in education," Ma said, beaming as she collected the egg shells and tossed them into the rubbish bin beneath the sink.

Kevin smiled and looked directly at his brother. "Doctorate, eh, Seany? That's pretty good."

"He's not walking, though." Ma looked at Sean out of the corner of her eye, he registered the clear disapproval in her tone.

"What do you mean?" Kevin looked back and forth between them.

"She means I'm not going to the graduation ceremony," Sean said, "and she's a little disappointed."

"He's not going to his own graduation." She reached up into one of the white cabinets above her head and pulled down a bright blue Sunbeam electric hand mixer that had been around ever since Sean could remember. "It's like it doesn't even matter to him."

"Of course it matters to me, Ma. I just don't see the need to sit in ninety-degree heat just to walk across a stage and shake the hand of some dean I've never even met before. I got my degree. That's all that matters to me."

"And," she turned her head to Kevin and explicitly addressed him, "it doesn't seem to make any difference if it would matter to me to see him walk across that stage. Nah, he doesn't give that any thought, this one."

"Ma," Sean said, letting out an exasperated sigh. "You got to see me walk two times before. It would just be the same thing over again."

"Except this time, you would be a doctor." Kevin broke in to the conversation. "Her son, Sean Malloy the doctor, would be walking across that stage."

"And it wouldn't have hurt to have my other son, the soldier and hero sitting next to me, watching the doctor walk across that stage." She punctuated her sentence by pointing a blender whisk at Kevin.

Sean looked up at his brother to see a huge grin stretched across his face. He'd hit on it. Their mother was fiercely proud, and she was on full boil now as she shoved the blender whisk into the hand mixer and attacked the bowl full of flour and chocolate and eggs in front of her.

Sean noticed that the blending lasted a little longer than it should have. That was his ma's version of a cooling-off period because she knew none of them could talk over the noise of the mixer. When she finally turned the machine off, testing the consistency of the mixture by dipping a finger into the chocolaty goo, she had calmed down a little bit.

"Doctorate in education and a hero on the battlefield," she said, detaching the two whisks from the blender and handing one to each of her sons. "I'll have you know how proud I am of both of you."

Sean was surprised at how happy the chocolate whisk made him. It was something she had done with them as children, a treat for whoever happened to be keeping her company in the kitchen as she baked. It still made him feel special. "Thanks," he said after a couple of seconds.

"Yeah, thanks, Ma," Kevin echoed. She nodded and reached up again, grabbing a couple of cake pans from deep inside the cupboard.

A few minutes later, Kevin continued the conversation. "So, you've got a job already, I hear?"

"Yes," Ma replied before Sean could speak. "He'll be teaching at a private high school in Cambridge. Something called Hayfield Academy. Very good school, from what I'm told."

"Ma, let him talk," Kevin said as he watched her pour the batter into a Teflon-coated cake pan.

"Yeah," Sean chimed in. "She's right. It's a pretty good prep school. I interviewed with them earlier this spring when I heard they would have a position coming open in the English department."

"And you're moving home for a while?" he asked, leaning his weight forward on the edge of the counter.

"Well," Sean hesitated, "I don't know how long I'm planning on staying."

Ma kneeled down on the floor and started hunting around in the bottom cupboards. "I suppose you'll be here until you save up enough for your own place, Seany."

Kevin shot a confused glance at his brother.

"I don't know when that will be, given what starting salaries are for teachers," Sean explained.

"Ah." Kevin seemed to understand. "All those years of school just to get out and make nothing."

"Well, he's just starting," Ma said from inside a lower cabinet. "Give him a little time." She reappeared a second later with a roll of aluminum foil.

"What are you teaching?" Kevin asked.

"English. Mostly to sophomores and juniors."

"You must be in heaven," Kevin said. "You'll get to live in your books." He hopped down off the counter, took Sean's whisk and rinsed both out in the sink. "Now you'll get to reread all those books you couldn't get enough of in high school. And all those kids." He laughed. "They don't stand a chance with you, Sean. You'll force feed them the ins and outs of Mark Twain and *Oliver Twist*."

Both Sean and Ma were silent for a few minutes as she fussed with the knobs on the stove and gingerly set the two cake pans in the oven on top of a sheet of aluminum foil. She dusted her hands, and then she set the timer at the back of the stove.

"And what about you?" his mother asked Kevin, not taking her eyes off the timer. "What will you be doing this fall?"

"I'm working on a couple of things," Kevin said, still leaning over the sink.

"Such as?" she asked.

"Such as I don't know yet. I've only been home three hours."

"Three hours turns into three weeks to three months pretty quickly," she said. "Trust me, I know."

Sean watched silently from the table.

"You know?" Kevin repeated her words. "What have you been waiting for?"

She gave him a look that told him more than she could have said. "Oh, just this and that," she finally managed to get out. "This and that."

"I'll be out again soon, Ma. I just need a place to land for a little bit while I figure things out."

"You don't have to be out." She reached out and put a hand gently on his cheek. "That's not why I asked you about your plans." She had a way of making it sound so casual.

"Then why did you ask?"

She went over to the sink and started to run the water over the rest of the batter-covered dishes. "Kevin, you're my son. I just want to know that you're all right."

"I'm all right Ma. I was just done with the Marines," he said, turning around and walking out of the kitchen and up the stairs to his room.

The kitchen was suddenly quiet with just the two of them in it. Sean could hear the gas jets from the oven, and out on the street, the whoosh of a car speeding by. Ma stood still over the dishes for a few minutes before she turned to Sean. "Well, don't sit there like an invalid." She brushed the air roughly with a wave of her soapy hand. "Go up there and talk to him."

Sean silently rose from the table. He headed up the stairs without a word to his ma, grabbing his duffel bag on the way.

❖

The second floor of the Malloy house wasn't very big. A short hallway bisected the house, with three bedrooms and a bathroom opening onto it. Sean headed down the hallway and rounded the corner, taking a second, smaller set of stairs to the third floor, where both boys' rooms were. The third floor had been an attic originally, but their dad had converted it to make two small bedrooms and a tiny bathroom nestled into the eaves of the house, giving each brother his own room.

Across the hall at the top of the stairs, a sliver of light showed under the door of his brother's room. A low thud and a scraping sound came from behind the door.

"Need a hand?" Sean asked as he gently pushed the door open, a soft squeal of protest coming from the hinges. His brother stood in the middle of a sea of cardboard boxes, one of them in his hands. The Red Sox cap was off, and his short red hair was sticking up as if he'd been running his hands through it or trying to pull it out. He looked around for a place to put the box he held in his hands.

"Wow," Sean said, looking around the room. "How did you collect so much stuff while you were in the service?"

"I really didn't," Kevin said, pulling a box off the bed and stacking it on top of another one in the corner. "I brought one bag home. The rest Ma and Dad pulled out of the basement and stacked up here when they heard I was coming home."

"When did you get in?" Sean asked as he made his way to the bed to sit down.

"Just a few hours before you did. We mostly just sat in the kitchen waiting for you." Kevin grabbed a bundle of baseball cards out of one of the boxes and set them down on the bureau with a thud. He winced, the sound suddenly obvious to him. "Sorry if I was asking too much down there."

Sean smiled. "Don't worry about it. Honestly, I'm glad you're here, too. It makes it a little less scary to be living at home again."

Kevin let out a soft laugh. "Yeah, me too, I guess." He reached into the box on the floor and pulled out a stack of Celtics tickets. "I really should have just thrown all this stuff out six years ago."

Sean looked down at the boxes sitting next to him on the bed. "What's in them all?" he asked.

"Mostly just stuff from high school, I guess. Some clothes. Nothing that will fit anymore. What'd you do with all your stuff?"

Sean laughed. "You forget I've been here every few months. I get to throw my stuff out in bits and pieces. Every time I'm home, she'll leave one or two small things for me. I'm never sure where she finds stuff. I think she's trying to clear out the basement for a sewing room or something."

Kevin nudged one of the boxes aside with his foot. "Why doesn't she just use one of the girls' rooms?"

Sean shrugged. "I guess for the same reason she didn't use our rooms for anything else. She thinks they might be back."

Kevin rolled his eyes. "Those two aren't coming back. They couldn't get out of here fast enough."

"I guess." Sean sat down on the bed, watching as Kevin darted back and forth between the boxes on the floor and different shelves and drawers. The two bookshelves lining the inside wall of Kevin's room were already packed almost to overflowing, but he managed to slip a few things into the impossibly tight spots.

"So, you home for good?" Sean asked.

"Yep, for good. Two tours is about as much as I can take." His brother looked down at him and smiled in a deep, creases-at-the-eyes way that caused Sean to hold his breath. It had been years since he'd seen that rigid, almost glass-like smile. It wasn't his real smile; it was something different, something shielded.

"Doctorate, huh?" Kevin sighed. "I'm real proud of you, Seany. That's good stuff, bro."

Sean nodded.

"I can't believe you did it," he continued, making Sean's skin tighten a little bit in anticipation. Sometimes he found it difficult to tell where his brother was headed. When they were kids, he could go from hot to cold in a matter of seconds, and this tone of voice was usually the only telltale sign something was about to change. "That's huge." Kevin's smile grew even wider, and after a few seconds, Sean couldn't look straight at him anymore.

"Thanks." Sean glanced down, unsure what to say next. A few moments of uncomfortable silence passed between the brothers as Kevin continued to dig into one of the boxes.

"Do we call you Dr. Malloy now?" Kevin finally asked, moving over to the bed and clearing off the boxes to sit down next to Sean.

"You can," Sean said. "But most of my students will just call me Mr. Malloy or worse. I'll get no respect for that doctorate." He looked up at the ceiling.

Kevin laughed gently, that soft rolling laughter that happens between brothers and is sometimes its own language. Sean relaxed. The tension in Kevin's voice was gone. "Why did you do it, then?" Kevin asked.

"I'm not sure," Sean said. "I guess I didn't really know what else to do."

"So you kept going to school?"

"Well," Sean thought for a minute, "I guess so. I think it will eventually pay off, but I've got to start at the bottom like everyone else."

"Huh," Kevin said. "So, here we are."

Sean looked over at him and raised an eyebrow.

"Here we are," Kevin continued in response to the raised eyebrow, "both of us back at home, starting over at the bottom again. Midway through our twenties."

It was Sean's turn to laugh. "You make it sound so ominous. What else are we supposed to do?"

"Ominous? That means bad, right?" He paused. "Then, nah. That's not how I meant it." Kevin's voice trailed off and a silence attached itself to his words. Kevin looked up at his younger brother, and in the unspoken phrases that passed between them, they both knew it was Kevin who was starting over, even as Sean was just starting out. Kevin didn't say as much. Neither brother would. Sean knew they both wanted the solidarity of being in it together, and so it was best left as it had been said. Both of them were back at home, both starting something new. At least they were not alone.

The room grew heavy around them with the solitude of evening, and things suddenly seemed very quiet. Sean hesitated for a minute, looking down into the box by his feet. "Why did you get out? Of the Marines, I mean. Did something happen?"

"Nah," Kevin said, shifting his legs from where he sat on the bed. "Nothing specific anyway. I just kept looking ahead, and all I saw was more fighting. No matter what I wanted to do, they were going to keep shipping me back to some desert hole to kill people." Kevin shrugged. "I didn't want to do any more of that. I'm kind of done with war." He looked at Sean. "Know what I mean?"

"I guess," Sean said. Then after a few minutes, "How bad was it?"

"Which part?" Kevin said.

"I don't know, the part when you were overseas? The part when you were here?"

"Overseas is a nice word for it," Kevin said. "Soldiers in World War II were 'overseas.' We were stuck in the frickin' desert."

"Where were you?"

"Honestly, I don't know where the fuck I was, and I couldn't tell you if I did. It was pretty much just hell. Whatever version of hell you can think of, triple it, and that's where I was. Iraq or Afghanistan, it's all the same in the end." He paused, a small catch of untold conflict shining through on his face, in the wrinkles of his forehead, the stillness in his eyes. He wasn't quite the same Kevin who had left six years ago. Something more was below the surface. "The stuff you see over there, that shit will fuck you up if you let it."

Sean swallowed. "Did it change you, Kev?" he asked after a few minutes.

Kevin thought for a second before he responded. "A little, I think," he said. "You try not to let it, but in the end you can't help it. There's only so much fire and sand you can take before it all gets pulverized into you, you know?"

Sean stared at his brother and sighed. He didn't know, but the expression on his brother's face told him everything. He knew that face. He had grown up with it. Among his three siblings, he was closest to Kevin. Even though they hadn't spoken much or seen each other more than a couple of times in the last six years, that was still the case. He knew the geography of his brother to the point where he could tell what was behind the lines and creases of his face. Sean sat there knowing, reading in the circles below his brother's eyes that he had seen more than he would ever tell and that it had changed him a little. Maybe even a lot. But he could also see that the core was still there. *Yes*, thought Sean, *he's still my brother, and the part that makes him who he is is still there*. Sean looked at the digital clock on the table by his bed. It was nine. "Beer?" he asked.

"Nah," said Kevin, "I should get this stuff finished and then get to bed. No good in setting myself up for being useless tomorrow."

"Yeah," Sean agreed, standing up and yawning. "You're probably right."

Kevin hoisted himself up off the bed and lazily punched his brother on the shoulder. "Night, bro," he said.

"Night," Sean said, wandering out of the door and across the hall to his room.

CHAPTER FIVE

L ose an hour in the morning, and you'll be looking for it all day."
Mrs. Malloy brushed through the kitchen like a whirlwind, her
heels clicking on the linoleum floor and her large ring of keys jangling
like a line of tiny Christmas bells at the top of her purse as she moved.

Sean and Kevin sat across from each other at the kitchen table,
Kevin with the paper open in front of him, and Sean with a dog-eared
copy of *The Odyssey* held down by the butter dish on one side and
the salt shaker on the other. The clock on the back of the stove said
nine fifteen, and it was late to still be sitting at breakfast in the Malloy
house.

"Either one of you have any plans for the day?" she asked,
scanning the kitchen table littered with glasses, plates, and cups.

"Plans, Ma?" asked Kevin, holding up the want ads section of the
Boston Courier. "This is my plan for the day."

"There's danger in spending too much time in a kitchen," she said
with a frown. "But you lot be sure to clean this up before you go." She
waved at the table and then glanced again at the clock.

"Who are you waiting for, Ma?" Sean asked, looking up from his
book.

"Grace Kinvara. She's coming over and we're going up the
market this morning. Her ma has her doing the shopping these days,
but the girl is late again. God bless her, but she can't be on time to save
her life."

"Grace Kinvara?" Kevin said, setting the paper down and getting
up to make another pot of coffee. "We remember Grace, don't we,
Sean?"

Sean ducked his head back into *The Odyssey*, avoiding his brother's eyes.

"What's wrong with Grace?" Mrs. Malloy asked. "She's a perfectly nice girl."

"Yeah, Ma, I know. We went to school with her." Kevin grabbed the bag of ground coffee out of the cupboard and set it down beside the coffeemaker. The ancient Mr. Coffee was a beige plastic relic from three decades ago, a testament to durability of the 1980s. He tried not to spill coffee grounds on the counter as he filled the machine, stopping for a minute to look at Sean, but his younger brother was still avoiding him.

As if on cue, a loud banging at the back door rattled the entire kitchen. The knock was followed almost immediately by the groan of the back door as it creaked open. "Helloooo," came a bright voice, half inside the house and half still on the back step.

Ma gathered up her purse as she yelled, "Come on in, Grace."

Grace burst through the back hall and into the kitchen with a ferocity that set the entire room into motion. She paused in front of the counter, a shock of red hair in a tightly cinched mid-length dress. The deep forest green of the dress contrasted with her skin and her hair, making her look a little like the heroine of a nineteenth-century Irish poem. The brothers looked at each other, Kevin with a smirk on his face and Sean with a slightly embarrassed expression across his.

"Hello, Mrs. Malloy, sorry I'm late," she said, stopping short of the counter. Then, as she turned toward the kitchen table, her face transformed into a giant smile, beaming at the younger Malloy son. "Sean, you're home?" she squealed, making her way over to the table, arms out toward him, enthusiastically polished nails leading the charge like ten tiny little pink flags.

"Hi, Gracie." Sean pushed his chair back and reached out to meet her embrace.

"Oh my gosh, it's so good to see you," she said, reaching her arms up around his neck. Then looking over to the coffeemaker, she finally noticed the other brother. "And, Kevin, you, too!"

She reluctantly turned away from Sean to Kevin, who had switched on the Mr. Coffee and restored the coffee can to its rightful place in the cupboard. She reached over and squeezed the top of his arm. "I heard you were back from the front," she said. "For good this time?"

"Yes, for good." His face scarcely moved.

"I don't know what the surprise is, Gracie." Mrs. Malloy leaned back against the counter, watching the three of them like a hawk. "I told you they were coming home weeks ago."

Grace rolled her eyes and threw her hands up on either side of her face. "Yeah, I know, but you know me, I can be a complete space cadet. I totally forgot that." A slightly awkward silence fell between the three of them.

Sean sat back down at the table, and Kevin leaned against the counter as the coffee started to brew.

"So, Sean," Grace said, following him with her eyes as he sat back down. "When do you start the new teaching job?"

"Oh, you know." Sean closed *The Odyssey*, squirming a little under her stare. "School doesn't start until September, but I have to go in a little ahead of that, probably sometime in late August. They don't mail us our final contracts for another couple of weeks."

She glanced at the book. "You reading up for it? I'd have thought you already had a pretty good handle on high school lit."

He forced himself to smile. "Yeah, you know, still makes sense to catch up on the syllabus. I want to be fresh when I start teaching these books this year." He slid his chair back from the table and picked up the book. "I've got to get going," he said. "Got to finish unpacking and get a few things sorted out with some background reading."

"Oh, no, Seany, stay and chat for a few minutes. I barely just got here."

Mrs. Malloy sighed impatiently in the background.

"Sorry," said Sean. "I really need to get some stuff moved around this morning. I'll catch up with you next Sunday after Mass."

Grace shrugged, but her face had fallen. The smile was gone, replaced by a thin-lipped pout.

Sean pretended not to notice. The gurgling Mr. Coffee started to spit out dribbles of water into the glass pot, keeping the room from falling into an awkward silence.

"Coffee, Grace?" Kevin asked, opening the cupboard door behind him for a fresh mug.

"Um…" She hesitated, looking up as Sean cleared his plates and dropped them into the sink. "No, thanks. Can't stay," she said, looking up at Mrs. Malloy, who had been watching the scene unfold before her with a raised eyebrow. "We've got a ton of errands this morning."

"Yes." Mrs. Malloy picked up her bag from the counter, the keys jingling loudly. "That we do, missy."

"Great to see you, Gracie," Sean said. He gave her a quick smile, collected his book from the table, and headed out of the kitchen.

"Well, we should, uh…" She dropped her head and moved uncomfortably toward the door.

"You sure you won't stay for a cup of coffee?" Kevin asked.

"No, Kevin, we should get going," Mrs. Malloy said.

"You should stop up at the house after Mass on Sunday if you can," Grace said as they turned to go. "I know my ma and dad would like to see you guys."

"Yeah, okay, I'll do that," Kevin said. "I mean we'll do that, me and Sean. If he's not busy."

"Okay then." She hesitated a few seconds longer. "Bye then." She gave a little wave of her hand as she and Mrs. Malloy headed out the door.

"Okay, bye," Kevin said, shutting the door after her. "See you tomorrow, Grace."

Chapter Six

It's not stupid, it's cool." Nick stood, arms locked on either side of the doorway of the kitchen with a deep frown on his face. His cheeks were flushed red, and he was still in his running clothes and sneakers.

Jamus sat at the kitchen table looking up at Nick over the top of his laptop, a cold cup of coffee still clutched in his left hand. His writing career had taken off in the past few years, and Jamus had used the money to refurbish most of the house except for this room. He loved everything about the room and had left it untouched. It still looked the way it had in the 1920s. A giant porcelain sink stood guard against a naked brick wall, a few wooden cabinets and butcher-block countertop separating it from an ancient gas stove. The heavy pine table sat between two full-length windows looking out on an overgrown alley. Against the third wall stood a gargantuan stainless steel refrigerator, the only modern appliance in the whole room.

"I know you don't see things the way I do about this, but the answer is final. You are not going to see *RocknRolla*. It's rated R, and you are fourteen years old." He had tried to speak to Nick in an even voice with no sarcastic overtones, even though he had wanted to laugh when Nick first asked.

"Jamus, what the fuck?" Nick pounded his hand on the doorjamb.

"Watch the mouth, Nick." Jamus set the coffee cup down on the table, the snap of porcelain on wood punctuating his sentence. A small splash of coffee spilled over the rim of the cup.

"Seriously? Everyone else my age is seeing it."

"I don't care about everyone else your age," Jamus said. "I care about you, and it's a violent movie. You don't need that kind of crap in your head."

"Who are you to say what I can put in my head anyway?" Nick growled.

"Watch it, Nick." Jamus looked up at him, his tone lower, a cross shadow creeping over his face. "You're on thin ice."

"Jamus, come on," Nick said, the edge of a whine surfacing in his voice. "Matt really, really wants me to go see it with him."

"Matt Spence's ma said it was all right for him to see *RocknRolla*?" Matt was Nick's best friend, and the two of them had been inseparable since they met in the third grade.

"He's going." Nick spat out the words, emphasizing each one but ultimately looking away from Jamus. "And he wants me to go, too. I don't want to let him down."

"Uh-huh." Jamus tilted his head and squinted at Nick, picking up on the veiled threat. "His ma said it was okay?"

"Ugh, Jamus!" Nick pounded the doorjamb again and twisted his torso as if in agony. "I don't know what she said. I just know that he's going, and I want to go see it, too." Nick looked at Jamus, pleading with his eyes. "Please, can I go? Come on, Jamus."

Jamus looked at the young man standing in front of him. Somewhere in that teenager was his little brother, the kid he had pulled through the snow-covered streets of the South End just four years ago. Part of the time he still looked like that kid, but his face was changing more and more. He was filling out, not just getting bigger but also becoming more of his own person. His build was overwhelmingly like their father's, but a tinge of their mother was in his face, especially around the eyes. Jamus sighed. "Okay, I'll look at the reviews, and I will consider it."

"Yes!" Nick pumped a fist into the air and jumped into a rock star stance in the center of the doorway.

"I said I'd consider it," Jamus reiterated, trying his best to use his stern adult voice, an expression he had never quite mastered. "Now go and get showered." But Nick was already halfway out of the room on his way to call Matt.

❖

"I can't believe that guy was a fag," said Matt as they walked home after the movie.

"Mmm," Nick mumbled, unsure of what to say. He was starting to think maybe it hadn't been such a good idea to sneak out and see *RocknRolla*. Well, technically it hadn't been sneaking. He had laid low after the conversation with Jamus earlier in the week about it. He figured if he didn't bring it up again, maybe Jamus would forget about it. The approach seemed to work. When Nick told him he and Matt were going to the movies that afternoon, Jamus hadn't even asked him what he was going to see. He just looked up from his laptop and nodded. Nick was prepared for a fight, but it just hadn't happened.

As it turned out, *RocknRolla* threw a little bit of a curve ball at Nick in a character named Handsome Bob. The character was a petty thug that moved throughout the London underworld as part of a cast of drug dealers and thieves. The only hitch about Handsome Bob was he turned out to be gay.

"I mean I didn't see that coming," Matt said as they walked across the Common toward the Corks' house. "Did you?"

Nick didn't respond; he wasn't really listening. He walked along, hands shoved into his pockets as he focused on the sidewalk ahead of him. He was trying to rationalize the vague connection between the gay character and his brother. But too many pieces were missing. Jamus wasn't like that guy in the movie, not only because he wasn't a criminal with an English accent, but because Handsome Bob was sleazy, which was so far away from anything Jamus was.

"Hello, Cork?" Matt said. "Are you there?"

"You know, Jamus is gay," said Nick after a few minutes.

"What?" Matt jumped at first, and then froze. "What do you mean?" He stood stock still as if it was too much to walk and process at the same time.

"Well, I'm not really sure what it means exactly, but I'm pretty sure it means he's not into women," Nick said. "Not that it would matter. It's not like he'll be dating anyone, ever."

Matt had remained still, standing on the edge of the sidewalk. Nick took a few more steps before turning around and looking at his friend. Matt had a wide-eyed, slack-jawed look on his face. "Dude, you can't tell anybody at school," Matt said in a hushed voice. "I mean nobody. You'd get killed. We'd never be able to show our faces in the cafeteria. We'd have to eat our lunch in the library and pretend like we're studying."

"Why?" asked Nick, starting to walk again. "Just because Jamus is gay?"

"What do you mean 'just because'?" Matt exploded. "People would think you're gay, too, because he's your dad."

"He's my brother, not my dad. It's a little different."

"Whatever. You know what I mean. And that's even worse!" Matt practically shouted, then he glanced around to make sure nobody was in earshot. Of course, it was the middle of summer on Boston Common. Hundreds of people were around, but no one took any notice of this fourteen-year-old yelling at his friend. "We'll be social piranhas."

"Pariahs," Nick corrected him.

"What?"

"Never mind." Nick rolled his eyes. "Look, I'm not planning on telling anyone about Jamus, but he doesn't exactly hide it. He'll talk about it if you ask him."

"Seriously?" Matt blushed and seemed to shudder all at the same time. "Ewwww."

"Matt, relax." Nick said. "You're freaking me out a little here. He's not some weirdo, he's Jamus. He just happens to be, you know, gay."

Matt seemed to disappear into himself for the next few minutes, staring ahead into the distance. "How do you know?" he asked.

"Know what?"

"How do you know he's gay?"

"Oh," Nick said. "He told me." The two boys had come to the end of the Common, to the place where they would turn off to go toward Jamus and Nick's house. For a moment Nick wondered if all of this was too weird for his friend and if Matt might peel off and go home. There was even a split second where Matt seemed to stop and turn toward the subway, but he didn't. He stayed in step with Nick, making the turn off the Common up toward the South End.

"All right." Matt grudgingly seemed to give way as they walked. "If you're cool with it, I guess I am, too, but I'm serious about keeping it low key at school. If it gets out, we will be piranhas."

Nick laughed. "You mean pariahs, numb nuts."

"Whatever."

CHAPTER SEVEN

How was your first day temping?" Sean asked as his brother walked into the kitchen and dropped a camouflage backpack on the table.

"Pretty boring." Kevin walked past him, reaching into the ancient Kelvinator and pulling out a Bud Light. "I'm not sure exactly how much brains it takes, but it's actually kind of perfect for me."

"Because it doesn't take any brains?" Sean quipped.

"Ha ha, asshole." Kevin punched him in the shoulder as he sat down next to him at the table.

"Where do they have you working?" Sean sat in front of a slim volume that he had creased open to about the middle of the book. To his left was a pile of mail, one envelope open the rest stacked neatly up for their parents.

"Up to the Hancock Building in Copley Square." Kevin took a pull off the beer. "Some law firm up on the fortieth floor. Real fancy place—all in suits, every last one of 'em, guys and skirts." He let out a short laugh. "I was so lost. You should've seen me trying to get through security in the morning. Place was like a zoo, so many people trying to get up in just a couple of elevators. All I could think of was how was I gonna get out if there was a fire or something."

Sean chuckled. "What were you doing all day?"

"Oh, that's the best part, Seany." Kevin leaned back from the table and spread his arms wide, the can of beer tentatively grasped in between his left thumb and index finger. "I was reading all day."

Sean shot him a look of amused suspicion. "Really? Reading what?"

"Oh, all sorts of things—emails, faxes, personal calendars, memos. You name it. They call it 'discovery' because I'm supposed to be looking for certain words that tie into whatever case they're working on." Kevin took another swig of his beer. "Now, you might be thinking to yourself over there that this is a little boring. And you wouldn't be wrong. But I can handle boring better than most. If you think reading through boxes of email printouts is boring, let me tell you about sitting out in the middle of the desert for months at a time with nothing to do. At least here it's only boring. I get to sit in a nice safe cubicle and not worry about getting shot at."

"Good point," Sean said as he closed the book.

"Is that from your school?" Kevin asked, pointing at the jaggedly opened envelope sitting on the top of the mail pile.

"Yeah," said Sean, no hint of excitement in his voice.

"Is it your contract?"

"Yep." Sean's face was blank.

Kevin shook his head. "And? You've been waiting for this to come for months. What's up?"

"No, it's good." Sean attempted to smile. "I just sort of realized that if I work at this job for the next ten years, I'll make just enough to pay off my student loans."

"Ah," Kevin said.

"Yeah," Sean wrinkled his nose. "'Ah.'"

"Well, come on, bro. You know this is just your first job. It's not like you're going to be doing this forever. Step one. Step two will pay a lot more." He hesitated. "Well, step two will at least pay a little more, right?"

"I guess."

"Hey, if you're having second thoughts, you can always come work with me. I'm sure you're qualified to read through email printouts and look for the words 'hedge fund,' 'Allegany,' and 'transfer.'"

Sean smiled at his brother. "Thanks, I may have to take you up on that if they have a second shift."

"Oh, I forgot to tell you," Kevin said. "I bumped into Grace on the bus today, this morning, on the ride in."

"Oh yeah?" Sean's stomach sank at the mention of her name. He opened up the book again, eyes immediately sinking down to the page.

"Hey, don't do that again."

"Do what? I'm not doing anything," Sean said without looking up.

Kevin put the book down, forcing Sean to meet his stare. "Every time someone mentions Grace, you duck your head into a book or you leave the room. What's up?"

"I do not." Sean grabbed the book back and folded it closed.

"Yeah, Seany, you do. What's going on there?"

"Nothing is going on anywhere." Sean tried not to sound snotty. "I just find her a little difficult to be around sometimes."

"Huh..." Kevin sat back and looked across the table at Sean. "So what's her story anyway? What's she been doing for the past six years?"

"Grace Kinvara?" Sean's stomach tightened into a knot. "Not too much you don't know, really. She graduated with my class in high school. She lives down the street with her parents still. Never went to college. Works at some insurance place down on Broadway, I think. Maybe it's a law firm. I can't remember."

"Not married?"

"Nope," Sean said. "At least not that I know of."

"Not yet anyway." Kevin smiled at his brother, and Sean couldn't meet his eyes.

"What?" Sean tried to deflect the focus. "You interested in her?"

"Doesn't matter what I'm interested in, she's got a thing for you, bro." Kevin paused for a second, as if deciding whether or not to go on. "She always sort of did in high school, too."

"Grace? Having a thing for me?" Sean laughed. "No, no, no. I don't think so."

"Ah, Sean, my brother. I know the look I saw on her face. She was definitely feeling something, and it wasn't for me. It was for you, Seany, and I think you know that."

Sean sat for a few minutes fidgeting with the pages of his book. Kevin was right. Grace had been after him in one way or another since they had been teenagers. The problem in high school had been twofold, though. Not only was Sean not interested in Grace, but Kevin had pursued her relentlessly.

It came to a head when Kevin asked her out to the prom and she declined, sheepishly saying that she was hoping Sean would ask her. Kevin didn't speak to either Sean or Grace for two weeks after that. Of course, Sean had refused to ask her. It was actually easier then because he at least had the excuse he would never do that to his brother. To

Grace's credit, she laid low after that. But all through college, every time Sean was home, she made it a point to be over at the Malloy house.

Sean had done his best to avoid her without being rude, but sometimes it was impossible. Those were the times she would sit as close to him as she could, her breath on his neck and shoulders during a conversation. Those times would be full of made-up excuses for hugs that made him feel like he had a pile of bricks pressing down on his chest. Sean shook his head. The last thing he wanted to deal with was his brother pushing him into a date, especially with Grace.

"So, does she come around often?" Kevin asked.

"Kevin." Sean rolled his eyes at him. "You're always home. You'd know if she came around. I haven't really seen her since that first morning back."

"I mean, did she used to come around a lot?"

"Not sure, really." Sean thought for a moment. "I think Ma and her ma are kind of close." He thought back. "I wasn't home last summer, but over the holidays she seemed to come around a lot. But they both did—her and her ma, that is."

"Hmmm." Kevin rubbed his chin thoughtfully. "We'll just have to see how this turns out."

Sean hated that look on his brother's face. He knew exactly what was happening in Kevin's head. He was poking around, taking in all the information and trying to figure out what didn't fit. He was like a computer in this way. Always had been. "She's just a little much sometimes," he finally said.

"You mean because she likes you?"

"No," Sean said.

"And you don't like her?" Kevin continued to push.

"There's nothing to like," Sean protested.

"Yeah, that's it," Kevin said. "If it wasn't, you wouldn't get that thing between your eyes."

"What thing?" Sean practically shouted.

"That thing," Kevin put his index finger right between Sean's eyes. "It's like a little ditch. You always get it when you get all huffed up over something."

"I don't like Grace Kinvara!" Sean was almost yelling now. "There's nothing there."

"I know." Kevin remained calm. "That's the problem, isn't it Seany? She likes you, and you're not into her. What's the matter? Is she too much of a townie?"

Sean didn't answer. He just sat there staring at the wall behind his brother's head.

"Yeah, okay," Kevin said. "Well, anyway, she said she'd be around at Grumpy's tonight if we wanted to head over."

"I don't know about tonight," Sean said, opening the book again and gluing his eyes on the pages.

"Come on, Sean. There's nothing wrong with Grace. You got to give her a chance." Sean remained silent, buried in the book in front of him. "Can we at least go and celebrate you getting a contract and me starting a new job?"

Sean picked up the page of the contract with his salary listed and turned it around so his brother could see the number.

"Oh," said Kevin. "Well, so what? So you're poor. You still just got your first career job. We should go out and have a drink to celebrate, especially if there's going to be a hotshot redhead down there waiting to say hi to you."

"We'll see," Sean said.

A few hours later, Sean was upstairs in his bedroom buried in a paperback volume of *A Separate Peace* when Kevin poked his head around the doorjamb. "I'm thinking of going down to the pub now, want to go?"

Sean looked up for a few seconds as if contemplating it before shaking his head no. "Nah." He held up the book. "I'm kind of on a roll here."

"*A Separate Peace?*" Kevin frowned. "You've read that, like, a thousand times."

"Twice," Sean said. "I've read it twice, and it's the first book I have to teach this September, so I want to go through it again and freshen up on it. Let's go this Saturday?"

Kevin shrugged. "That's fine, but Grace is going to be down there. I think I'll go and keep her company."

Sean nodded but didn't budge. "Sounds good. Tell her I said hi."

"I will." Kevin bounced his body up off the door frame, pushing it into motion. "But I'm pretty sure she'd rather see you out there than me."

Sean took a deep breath and tried to clear his mind as he picked up the book again.

The house had been silent for hours when Sean's mobile phone buzzed on his bedside table. He put his book down and picked up the phone to see that it was twelve thirty in the morning. It was Kevin's number. He clicked the button to accept the call. "Are you still out?" he asked.

"Is this Sean?" asked a strange voice at the other end of the line.

"Yes," he said. "Who is this, and why are you calling from my brother's phone?"

"Yeah, ah, this is Flynn, down at Grumpy's Pub." The voice hesitated for a second. "Hey, do you think you could come pick up your brother? He's not doing so well, just now."

"Not doing so well?"

"He's wicked drunk," Flynn said. "I'd give it about thirty seconds before we have to throw him out."

"I'll be right down," said Sean, hanging up the phone.

❖

The two brothers sat side by side on the curb in front of their house. Kevin sat with his arms folded across his knees, looking up at the stars. Sean sat next to him, watching his brother.

"Are you sure you don't want to at least sit up on the porch?" Sean asked.

"No." Kevin pulled his knees in tightly to his chest. "I like it here."

The night was relatively quiet, the way that cities are still without being completely silent. Sean could hear the hum of traffic a few blocks up, the rumble of a plane overhead, and the occasional distant scream or siren. But it was still enough that Sean could hear his brother's breathing. Sean shivered slightly as he sat on the edge of the concrete sidewalk. He had left the house in his T-shirt, and he was starting to regret not pulling on a sweatshirt as he was going out the door.

"Do you want to talk about it?" Sean looked at his brother, but Kevin just continued looking up at the stars. After a moment of silence, Sean asked, "What was it?"

"Tonight?" Kevin's voice was distant. Sean knew that look on his face. He was concentrating. He'd get like this when they were younger, when he would be angry at something but knew he couldn't explode, like at church or at school. Kevin would try to keep it all together inside himself, and he'd knit his eyebrows and squint his eyes. He took a breath and slowly exhaled, a little of the tension draining from his face. "It was nothing. It was stupid," he said.

"It wasn't nothing, you were..." Sean stopped and lowered his voice. "They said you were screaming for everyone to get down. They said you were—"

"I know what they said, Sean. I wasn't drunk. At least not that drunk."

"Then what was it? A flashback?"

Kevin shook his head and continued to stare at the night sky. "They call it 're-experiencing.'"

"Re-experiencing?"

"Yeah," Kevin said. "Some guy knocked over his stool." He let out a long, loud sigh and ran a hand through his hair. "It made a huge bang when it hit the floor. I thought...I don't know what I thought."

Sean waited for a minute, but Kevin had clamped up again, his eyes still and hollow. "You thought what?"

"They thought I was doing better. Better enough to come home, at least."

"What do you mean?"

"Sean, I don't really want to talk about this."

"Kevin, you just flipped out at Grumpy's. You started shouting and pulled four people to the floor, including Grace. What is going on? Are you okay?"

"Shit." Kevin pressed his eyes closed. "I forgot Grace was there. When did she leave?"

"I don't know," Sean said. "She was gone by the time I got there. Now, tell me what's going on? Are you okay?"

"Yeah, Sean. I'm fine. It might have been what they call a trigger." He took another breath. "It's part of PTSD or something. It brings you back to something that you experienced. I guess the sound of the stool hitting the ground did it."

"You guess?"

"Okay—it was a fucking trigger. I flipped out. What do you want me to say, Sean? Jesus Christ, I'm trying to get my shit together."

Sean put his hand on Kevin's shoulder. "It's okay," he said softly.

"No, it's not okay," Kevin shouted up at the sky. "If it was okay, I'd still be sitting in the bar having a beer and being normal. But I'm not. I had a breakdown in front of all of South Boston, and they had to call my baby brother to come pick me up. That's not fucking okay, now is it, Seany?"

"It will get better," Sean said. "It'll be okay."

"Will it? What are you, a fucking doctor? They said it would get better by now, but I don't think they believed it. I think they just wanted to get me out."

"They who? Who wanted you out? I thought you were the one who wanted out of the Marines."

Kevin shook his head slowly. "I did. I guess. But I was having trouble keeping it together. I needed to get out. They knew." He paused. "Christ, now I'll never be able to go back to Grumpy's."

"Hey, Kevin. Look at me." Sean grabbed his brother's ear the way they had done when they were kids and they needed to get each other's attention. "It will be okay, I know that. You will be okay." He put his arm around Kevin's shoulders and squeezed. "I'll go to Grumpy's with you next time."

Kevin smiled. "Even if Grace Kinvara is there?"

"Jesus, Kevin." Sean let out a purposefully dramatic sigh. "Yes, even if Grace is there." They both laughed. The laughter was short and uneasy, but Sean was relieved to see his brother smile. They sat on the curb for several minutes in silence.

"Hey, Sean, what's the deal with her? How come you don't like her? Is there something else going on? Did something happen between you two?"

Sean just looked down at the street. "No, there's nothing else, Kevin. She's just not my speed."

Kevin looked like he wanted to say something else, but he just smiled and pulled his brother's ear, the same way Sean had just tugged on his. "I missed you," Kevin said.

"I know you did." Sean was still. "I missed you, too."

"Come on," Kevin said, pulling his legs underneath him. "Let's go in, huh? I got to work in the morning."

CHAPTER EIGHT

Jamus rolled over and sat up. He looked around, trying to identify something—anything—in the room, eventually locking onto the strange orange-colored digital clock beside the bed. It was three thirty in the morning. He let out a soft groan, feeling the thunk, thunk, thunking in his head. It took him a few seconds to remember how the night had started. The stale taste of scotch in his mouth helped to jog his memory. A moment later, he realized he wasn't in his own bed.

"Shit," he moaned softly under his breath, looking over at the snoring body next to him and realizing that it was already Sunday morning. The body didn't budge as Jamus slowly rolled out of the strange bed. He held his breath and winced when the bed creaked under his movement, but he looked back and the body just lay there snoring, oblivious to Jamus's escape. He walked gently around the darkened room, gathering his clothes in one hand and feeling his way with the other.

He got dressed out in the pint-sized kitchen of the brownstone apartment, not bothering to leave a note on his way out. On the street, he breathed in a sigh of relief, recognizing the neighborhood as one very close to his own house. Perfect. No need to try and flag down a taxi. He patted his pockets, double-checking to make sure he still had his wallet, phone, and keys, and then he started off in the direction of his own block.

Each step of the walk, he focused on remembering, straining to relive the moments of the night, focusing until he could hear nothing but the sound of his own footsteps. A sense of guilt slowly began to make its way through the fog of his mind as he remembered drink after drink, the brief conversations at the bar early in the night, then the lingering stares followed by the nod.

Jamus started to walk faster down the sidewalk, tripping constantly over the jagged, uneven bricks, his mind now tightly fixated on the evening before. He had answered the courteous inquiries about job and college and family. The "are you out?" question finally tumbled off his lips after a few drinks, the question that often seals the deal because it leads to the next question: "Do you live alone?" Jamus himself could never answer that question satisfactorily. He didn't live alone; it could never be his place. But that hadn't mattered tonight. And then there was the taxi ride over to the stranger's house. God, he couldn't even remember his name. Jamus walked faster and faster, finally breaking into a jog as the memories of the rest of the night came back.

His head throbbed and his heart pounded by the time he reached the door. He knew Nick wasn't there, it was sleepover night at Matt's house. He wouldn't be back for another eight hours, but still, Jamus felt a desperate sort of betrayal every time he did this. He worried about the kid somehow discovering these one-night stands. He imagined getting caught sneaking in the door late at night or not being there for an emergency call because he was out in some stranger's bed.

How many had there been by now? Not that many. But still, enough to be ashamed of. Jamus almost laughed at himself. He was so brave on the cover of it all. So out and proud of who he was. But he wasn't, really. After all, his need for these nights was one of the things that he hated about himself. The secrecy of it all perpetuated the loneliness he always felt.

He quickly slid inside the house, shutting the door tightly after himself. He sat down at the kitchen table where he had left the laptop yesterday afternoon. He focused on the computer, eventually reaching out and touching the top of it. The smooth cold feel of the aluminum casing jolted him back to Earth. He opened it up and began rereading what he had worked on the day before.

A couple of times throughout that early morning, Jamus got up for a glass of water. It was five before he surrendered to the inevitable fact that he would be up working on this for the rest of the day and finally put the coffeepot on. The writing wasn't better; it was just easier.

CHAPTER NINE

I really could not believe what the *Times* said about her new book," Eileen said, taking a sip of chardonnay. "Don't get me wrong, I wasn't exactly a fan of the manuscript—that's why I passed on it. But the truth is that review sounded more like a personal attack on the author than a fair and honest look at the text." She shook her head. "On the plus side, she's already sold more books than God, so it probably doesn't even matter."

Jamus sat across from his agent. The clang and din of the posh Newbury Street restaurant set his nerves on edge. It was heading toward winter in Boston, and the outdoor tables had been taken in for the season, cramping the inside. Jamus sat with his shoulders scrunched up and his hands tucked between his knees, as if he were trying to make himself smaller.

He hadn't touched a thing on his plate. Usually, that was a sign he'd been talking too much, but not today. He hadn't said two words since they'd sat down. She, on the other hand, hadn't stopped talking, which was a problem. Eileen McKenna was forty-five, just over five-two, gray haired and casually known by many as Attila. She was a woman of few words, most of the time. But today at lunch, Jamus hadn't been able to get a word in edgewise.

She reached for the wine again, and Jamus took advantage of the pause. "Eileen," he said, "about the new outline I sent you last week?"

She lit up. "Ah, yes. 'Gargantuan.' That's the title you're going with, right? Spectacular. Really, it is one of your best," she gushed, lifting her glass of wine toward him in a mock toast. "It shows a little bit of maturity for you. Brings things to a new level." She put her wine glass down on the table.

Jamus sighed.

"Of course, you know I don't mean a word of that," she said. "It's not what we're used to seeing from you, and I'm not sure it's right."

"I know. It's different." Jamus wiped his mouth with his napkin, even though he hadn't eaten anything. "I just want to try something new."

"New is good," Eileen said. "Really, truly it is. But you have to stay with something you know people want to read. Look, Jamus, I've been doing some thinking about your next piece and I wonder if you might consider something a little more mainstream, but still edgy?"

Jamus took a deep breath. He had known her for ten years, but at times he wondered if she knew anything about his process of writing. She was a great partner. She understood what an audience wanted to read, and she had an uncanny way of working with Jamus to hone his novels to perfection. She knew a character instantly. She could tease more out of a protagonist or help him give just the right shape to the plot. But she never got involved, not really. Not in the way Jamus did.

After all, these works were coming from inside him and fact begot fiction, so each new character detail and every plot twist was rooted in something Jamus had been trying to forget. After he finished a manuscript, Jamus took weeks to recover. He often lay in bed for days at a time, not showering and barely eating, only getting out of bed to see Nick off to school in the morning and take care of supper and homework in the evening.

Everything he wrote rehashed his past while the rest of his life was going on around him without his participation. But even though she saw what happened to him after a book, Eileen managed to maintain her aloofness. And Jamus never challenged her. His private horrors were his own. So what if Eileen sold them? She had managed to make him a relatively good living over the past decade. But he seriously doubted that he had another novel like that in him right now.

"Let's be honest," she said. "The six books we've published together have sold well, albeit to a niche audience. But after *Angel of New York*, you had a captive readership. They fell in love with you, Jamus."

Jamus nodded. They'd had this conversation dozens of times.

Angel of New York was his second novel, and it had been a runaway success. It was the story of a New York club kid and drug dealer who tried to crawl out of the life he'd made for himself when he fell in love. Jamus had stolen from his days in New York as a student for the details of the story and reluctantly pulled from the pain of losing his parents as he brought the tragic ending to life. The book struck a chord with critics and audiences; it was his most successful work to date.

"This one," Eileen continued, jolting Jamus out of his thoughts. "If this next book could be something a little more mainstream, maybe focused on more of a suburban world, it could do a lot to expose you to a broader audience."

After *Angel*, Jamus had followed up with a string of moderate successes, each focusing on the stories of the seedy side of nightlife. They took place in cities—mostly New York—and his characters existed on the fringes of society. They were seldom altruistic, and they often battled drugs, alcohol, abuse, or prostitution. The results had captivated readers. People called him edgy and daring. They liked the anger and the "grit" in his voice as a writer. He had laughed at the time, when he read the comment about "grit" in his voice. Jamus had spent most of his life nowhere near grit. Unlike his characters, he'd had to go looking for it.

He fidgeted with the cloth napkin in his lap. "I don't know, Eileen." She was talking about a broader audience that frankly bored him. He wasn't interested in writing one of the housewives' thrillers that so frequently topped the *New York Times* best sellers list. "I want to try something that's more of a departure."

"But, Jamus," she said, swigging the last of her wine in frustration. "Why, honey? We're making money on these novels, and that's not something that happens that often in this industry."

"Eileen," he sighed. "I just need some time off from writing about everything that went wrong in my life. I've spent my last six novels writing about all the pain I've ever experienced. I need a break from that. I want to focus on something that doesn't remind me that I lost everyone and everything in my life."

She looked across the table at him. "Well, not everyone, right? I mean Nick has got to count for something, doesn't he?"

"Of course he does, Eileen." Jamus poked at a cold French fry on the edge of his plate. "But you're missing the point. For one project, just one, I need to get away from a world where everything hurts. This project is about the beginning of the Big Dig. I've been doing a lot of research, and I think there is some really rich content to pull from."

She stared at him and pressed her lips together. "You really want to try something different, huh?"

"Yes, Eileen. Just one project. Then I'll do your suburban drama. I've already sketched out a few ideas for that."

This seemed to grab her attention. She pursed her lips, giving her mouth a small and greedy appearance. "You have?"

"Yes." He shook his head slowly. "But I'm not sure I should share them just yet."

"Well, you can at least tell me what you're thinking about the project. There's no harm in that, is there?"

He inhaled slowly and then pressed his napkin to his lips again before folding it and placing it on his plate of uneaten food. "Sure, why not. It's called *The Rancher's Wife*. The characters are a little bit older than they have been in the last few books. Think suburbs, PTA meetings, exercise classes. These are the kind of people who make casseroles and laugh at the jokes that TV actors tell on sitcoms."

"I'm listening," Eileen said quickly. "I can't wait to hear the Jamus Cork twist on this one."

"*The Rancher's Wife*," he continued, "is the story of a family—of how it came together in dark times and how, as a unit, they kept each other safe and secure in a world that seems to want to tear them apart as their kids grow up."

"Go on." She nodded cautiously.

"The two kids are desperate for freedom. They want out of this suburban world they think is so fake, but they're torn. As much as they want to be rebels, they're really not. They're really just like their parents. *The Rancher's Wife* is about them figuring out their own lives despite what their parents do to them."

She was staring at him. "I love it. Sort of like a modern-day *Breakfast Club*," she said. "And you'll give me this if you can take one book off to focus on some nonfiction, hardcore political navel-gazing thing?"

"Yes, Eileen," he said. "I will give you all the suburban housewife drama you can handle."

"What the hell, even Stephen King took one book off. Okay," she said, "but hold off on the tunnels project for a little bit. Let me see what I can figure out."

The waiter came to clear their plates. He stacked Eileen's dishes on a carefully extended arm, and looked down at Jamus's untouched plate. "Are you still working, sir, or shall I take your plate?" he asked after a couple seconds. Jamus nodded, and he continued to stack the plates. "Any dessert?" he asked.

"Not, for me," Eileen smiled up at the waiter and they both turned to look at Jamus but he was silent, still staring off into the distant corners of the restaurant. "That's a no for him. Just the check, please," she said.

She pulled out her wallet while the waiter walked away from the table. "How is Nick?" she asked.

Again silence. Jamus stared down at the place on the table where his plate had been. She put her wallet down heavily on the table and the thud pulled Jamus's focus. Obviously, it was his turn to talk, but he had been so lost in his own head he didn't know where to begin, not even enough to fake it. "I'm sorry," he said, "I was thinking about the story."

"Of course you were," she said. "No worries. I was just asking how Nicky is doing."

"Oh," Jamus laughed, "don't let him hear you call him that. He's Nick now. Just Nick. Too old, too mature for Nicky."

She smiled. "He always could get a little serious."

"Yes, I suppose he could. He's doing well, though. Started his first year at Hayfield Academy. It seems to be going okay," Jamus lied. This was part of what he didn't want to think about. The two fights Nick had already been in this year when he had never been in a fight before was worrying to Jamus. "He's running on the cross-country team."

"Cross-country? I thought he liked soccer?"

"Oh, he does." Jamus suddenly remembered the numerous soccer shirts, ball nets, and shin guards that Eileen had given Nick as Christmas and birthday gifts over the years. "That's still his first love, but Nick isn't much of a team guy when it comes to playing sports. He could spend all day watching soccer, but he needs something a little more independent when it comes to actually getting out there."

"I wonder where he gets that from," she said, looking directly into Jamus's eyes.

He ignored the barb, because he figured it was probably meant as a compliment. "I will let him know you were asking after him."

"So, do you think you might be able to work on a few chapters for *The Rancher's Wife*? I mean while I try to line something up on the nonfiction side of things?" she asked.

"Sorry?" Jamus asked. "Chapters? Eileen, it's just a concept right now."

"Please, Jamus? I promise I will make it worth it on the other side."

"All right." He shrugged. "I can work up an outline and a couple of chapters. Give me another month."

"Brilliant. I can't wait to see it, Mr. Cork." She smiled and he laughed. "And you won't regret holding out for a couple of weeks on the nonfiction project. I promise."

He smiled back at her. This was their dance.

CHAPTER TEN

Jamus Cork stood on the steps of the church looking out over the top of the hill at the gleaming glass and granite buildings of Boston's new waterfront. A cool September breeze blew in from the bay, a distant reminder of the muggy August heat that had started to lift over the past week. All the same, it was a clear day, and Jamus could feel the sweat starting to bead on his forehead as he stood in the sun finishing his cigarette and thinking about the day ahead.

He took a final drag and let the cigarette drop on the gray stone beneath his feet before crushing it out with the heel of his shoe. He savored the warmth; a month from now it would be the middle of October and the mercury would be dropping, quite possibly into the forties or even below.

Anyone looking at Jamus's face in that bright September sun would have seen the blueprint of an island. His pale skin was the milky translucent color of the generations who had come before him, venturing forth from that starved island of mist-shrouded fields and cold gray rocks. It was a skin that held in it a series of struggles that had burst forth into hopes, marching across the seas to places like Boston and New Orleans and the eastern provinces of Canada. Caught in just the right light, like the light of the sun on that September morning, Jamus's face was the face of those who had come before him, who had looked very much like him. Their story was in his eyes.

South Boston was full of faces like his, full of Jamus Corks. But his family had come later than most. His parents had landed in this part of Boston less than forty years ago and settled here for some time before deciding they needed more space between themselves and their native Ireland. Ireland haunted every corner and every dank back porch of this place. They wanted out, but even they had stayed here in spirit, coming back to this church long after they had moved to a different part of the city.

He glanced down at his watch. It was 11:30 already. He would have to go soon if he was going to get back to the house before Nick got there. He leaned back against the wrought iron railing of the churchyard and reached into his breast pocket for the pack of Luckys he was almost never without. He pulled another one out and lit it, inhaling deeply as smoke drifted up, shrouding his ice blue eyes from the crowd starting to gather around the church.

Mass was over, and they were filing out in pairs and little groups of three or four, some chatting loudly and others silently staring down at their shoes as they spilled out of the building and down on the sidewalk and the small church lawn. The church was unique in South Boston in that it had a patch of grass in front of it. Most buildings in this outpost neighborhood sat squarely on the sidewalk, whole streets without a patch of green.

"Not too bad a day, is it?" Jamus felt the air move behind him and caught a flash of bright red hair out of the corner of his eye.

"Could be worse, I guess." He turned to the blue button-down shirt and khakis standing next to him. The church was almost empty now, so the man must have waited a while after Mass before getting up to leave. He was scanning the crowd around the front of the church, squinting his blue eyes to take in all the faces in front of him, pale pink lips pressed into a slight frown. He had the mild look of someone being hunted.

Jamus strained to place the stranger, mentally flipping through the faces of people he could remember from church. Jamus knew he was part of one of the regular families. He'd seen him before, but not very often. Sometimes he'd come to the holiday services and once or twice toward the end of the summer. "You looking for someone?" Jamus asked.

The stranger nodded his head, continuing to look out over the crowd. "Sort of," he said.

"Well, what do they look like?" Jamus asked. "Maybe I can help. I've been standing out here for a while."

"Pretty, red hair, freckles, big black bag over the shoulder."

"Mmm, no. Haven't seen him." Jamus was deadpan.

The stranger smiled. "Her, actually. Her name is Grace."

"Ah," Jamus said. "Nope, still haven't seen her."

"Oh, that's good then. I'm actually looking to avoid her." He turned toward Jamus and smiled. "Someone I'm supposed to talk to but really rather wouldn't."

Jamus let out a laugh. "Avoid someone? At this church? Good luck with that."

"That's true enough," the stranger said. "But I don't think we've met before."

"No, I don't think we have. I'm Jamus." He thrust his right hand out.

"Sean," he said, shaking Jamus's hand. "Sean Malloy." He had a good grip, and his hand was dry and warm. Jamus noticed that he hesitated just a tad too long, letting the handshake linger. Jamus looked down at their hands and then up at the stranger's face. His eyes had gone blank, and he looked just a little confused, but still he didn't let go.

"Sean?" A woman's voice floated up from the street in front of them, bringing the handshake to an abrupt end. "Sean, there you are."

Jamus glanced down the sidewalk. About fifteen yards away from them stood a woman in a gray wool suit jacket smoking a cigarette. The coat was a little heavy for the season, but belted and smartly cut just below the knees. She had a green skirt on underneath, the hem of which came down just below the bottom of the coat. She was stylish for Southie, Jamus thought, except for the heavy, shapeless black bag she had draped over her shoulder.

Sean looked over and waved at the voice. "And that's her," Sean said softly to Jamus. "Gotta go, nice meeting you."

"You, too." Jamus watched as the woman approached. Sean was already walking toward her, and she shifted her glance from Jamus to Sean and then back. He nodded to her and walked up the street toward the subway that would take him home. He could walk and often did, but not today. He was running short of time.

Jamus loved and hated Sunday mornings. It was the only time all week that he had for himself. It wasn't that he never got to spend time alone. He worked alone most days from his kitchen table, but his mind wasn't his own then. He was focused on something, some story or some chapter. Sunday was his all alone. He could let his mind wander wherever it wanted, guilt free. But sometimes the solitude of Sunday was too much, even for the brief hours that it lasted. The trouble with church, he thought, was that it gave his mind too much freedom to wander, to think on and see things about his life that he was trying to forget. He was glad to be out of Mass, liberated in the fresh Boston morning.

❖

Sean watched her as she walked toward him, continuing to wave. He couldn't avoid her now. They would have to have the obligatory walk home, and then who knows how long he might have to hang around chatting either at her house or at his. He pointed at the cigarette and cocked his head to the side. She hadn't smoked for years.

"Hi, Sean," she said, dropping the cigarette to the sidewalk and quickly pressing it out with the toe of her shoe.

Smile, he told himself as he forced his lips into a pursed grin. "I thought you quit," he said, moving slowly down the church steps.

She smiled wide and shrugged. He noticed she had lipstick on now. She hadn't had it on earlier in church. "I did," she said to him. "But you know how it is. Hard not to pick it up again when all your family does it. What can I say? I had a little relapse. I'm only smoking a tiny bit though, just two or three cigs a day."

Sean moved like molasses down the steps, and she took a step toward him, as if she wanted him to move faster. "Walk me home?" she asked.

"Sure," he said, resisting the urge to run, "but I've really got to get moving pretty quick. I've got some work to get done this afternoon ahead of the week."

"Sure you do." She shook her head. "That's why you took so long getting out of your seat today, huh?"

Sean felt his face start to go red, but before he could say anything, one of the last of the small sidewalk groups broke up and he noticed the old priest making his way up behind Grace. He moved slowly, with a little bit of a limp and a stiff wobbling motion that made him look a little like a Weeble. "Father Richards," Sean said, raising a hand slightly in a wave. "So nice to see you this morning. Beautiful day for this time of year, isn't it?"

The priest looked around, taking in the cool autumn sun, and smiled back at him. "Sean, it is indeed a wonderful day, so good to see you, and you, too, Gracie," he said, finally reaching Grace and taking her hand. "Every time I see you these days, you remind me of how old I am."

Grace's face flushed as red as Sean's had just been. She smiled widely and held the priest's hands. "Father," she said, "stop it, you're not that old."

"That old." He chuckled. "Gracie, I remember when you started coming to church. Such a pretty little girl, and loud—very, very loud. You used to call me Father Riches, because you couldn't say Richards."

She smiled at him. "That's too funny," she said. "I don't remember that."

"Come down here, Sean." The priest motioned to Sean and he made his way down to the two of them at the bottom of the steps. "I was thinking about you two the other day," he said, putting his hand on Sean's arm as he reached the bottom of the steps.

"You were?" Sean asked.

"Yes, I was." The priest tilted his head in the direction of the side of the church. "Would you two walk me back to the cottage?" The cottage was a small apartment attached to the back of the church where both priests lived. It had been a separate house at one point, but through the expansion of some of the church offices, it was now connected as one big building. Grace and Sean took up position on either side of the old priest, helping to steady him as they started the long, slow wobble back toward the cottage.

"I was thinking," the priest continued, "how lucky we are to have young people like you two in our fold."

"Oh?" Grace raised an eyebrow as the three of them shuffled in synch.

"Yes. I look at the two of you, and I think about how much you have in front of you and it makes me smile."

Sean looked over at Grace out of the corner of his eye and he could see she was smiling back at the priest. "That's nice of you to say," she offered. "Don't you think, Sean?"

Sean, a little unsure of what to say, simply shrugged.

"Are you two getting along all right?" the priest asked. "Everything working out between you?"

"Working out?" Sean echoed the old priest's words.

"Yes, I know it's sometimes hard for young people these days. So many things to do in the world. You want to put off things like getting married and starting a family, but it's not wise to put them off too long."

Sean suddenly realized where this was going, and the skin on the back of his neck turned cold. He fought the urge to drop the priest's arm and run. Instead, he took a deep breath and continued to shuffle along.

"Why are you so worried about this, Sean?" the old priest asked after a few more steps.

"Worried, Father?" Sean gulped. "I'm not worried."

"Now, Sean, I've been your priest since you were born." Sean wondered if Father Richards remembered he had been gone for the past six years. "And I can tell that you're worried about this, but don't be."

The priest stopped for a moment to rest, Grace and Sean buffering him on either side. He took a raspy breath and seemed like he was about to say something but decided not to. After a moment, he looked over to Grace. "Gracie, could you wait for us up front? I want to have a word with Sean here."

"Sure, Father," she said, looking up at the priest and then over to Sean. "I guess I'll just be up at the front of the church."

"That's a good girl," the old priest said. "I'll be seeing you next Sunday, then."

Grace shot a look at Sean.

"No worries if you need to go," Sean said. "I don't want to hold you up if you've got to be somewhere."

The priest tugged at Sean's sleeve, then turned to face Grace. "He'll meet you up front in just a minute or so, Gracie."

"That sounds fine," she said with a smile. "I'll wait for you by the street," she said to Sean.

He nodded and looked back down at the priest.

"Father, I'm not sure—" Sean started to say once Grace was out of earshot, but the priest cut him off.

"Don't say anything," he said. "You think I'm a doddering old fool, here to meddle in your business, but I'm not. It's none of my affair what you and Gracie are up to, but I get the feeling you're afraid of it."

Sean didn't respond.

"I've watched you, Sean Malloy, as a child. You and your brother both, and the two of you couldn't get out of here fast enough. You wanted more of the world than what you saw on the streets of your own neighborhood. This place wasn't enough for you."

"No, Father, that's not it at all," Sean protested. But the priest put up a hand to silence him.

"No, it's all right, Sean," the priest said. "You don't have to try and explain it to me. It's in your blood. The Irish are always looking for a brighter future. You come from a past like ours, and you know how bad things can be. I can see by the way you're looking at me that you think I'm being silly. You're wondering if I even noticed you were gone off to school for the better part of the last few years. I notice, Sean. And I watch.

"We're such a romantic bunch, the Irish, wouldn't you say? We're convinced that a happy ending is out there for us, a brighter journey, greener pastures, no?" The priest looked over at him and put a gnarled old hand up to his face. "But you don't have to make that journey alone, Sean."

"Father?"

"That girl loves you. I know you're afraid, but it will be all right. Don't be scared to start thinking about a family."

"Father, it's..." He couldn't think of any words.

"It's okay, Sean. I know you want to see the rest of the world, get out of this place. But you can do it with her, eh? I've seen people wait too long, Sean. They wait too long thinking they'll miss something and instead they lose everything. The price they pay is a high one. It's loneliness. Maybe not today, maybe not for a while, but they're alone in the end, and it's very, very sad."

"I guess," Sean said. After a few moments of silence, they resumed their shuffle down the cement walkway to the cottage.

"I can manage from here, Sean." The priest released Sean's arm at the door of the cottage. "I'll be looking for you next Sunday, then."

"Yes, Father. See you then," Sean said softly. He turned back toward the front of the church. Grace was waiting for him on the sidewalk, as she said she would be. He'd half expected to catch her smoking again, but she wasn't. She was just staring up at the door of the church, a bored expression on her face.

"What did he want?" she asked when Sean rounded the corner of the building.

"Just wanted to let me know that it's okay to stay in Southie,"

Sean said, trying his best to look casual. It wasn't a lie, he told himself, just a portion of the truth. He closed his eyes to clear his head. "So, walk home?" he asked her.

"Sure," she said. "I'd like that. Maybe grab a coffee along the way?"

Sean took a deep breath. "Okay. Sounds good."

CHAPTER ELEVEN

"We find the family we are meant to have."
Nick read the words over again for the hundredth time. They were printed in red ink on a thin strip of white paper that he had stuffed into his pocket two nights ago. It came from a fortune cookie he'd cracked open after a meal of take-out Chinese food at Matt's house on Friday.

Nick was a little over a month into his freshman year, and he felt like he should feel a lot more grown up. He felt that things like fortune cookie fortunes shouldn't matter to him, but something about this one did. Nick rolled the fortune cookie paper back and forth between his thumb and his forefinger a few times, and then stuffed it back into his pocket.

The subway car screeched to a slow stop and the doors slid open with a ding. The muffled voice of the Red Line PA system announced they were at the Harvard Square Station. He had a few more stops to go. Nick sat hunched over on the cool plastic seat, putting his hands under his legs to keep them warm. The air conditioner was still on in the car even though it was September. It had started to turn cool, so the train was frigid. His shaggy mop of greasy blond hair stuck out from underneath a green and white John Deere cap too big for his head. Baggy jeans and a puffy green sweatshirt completed the look, giving the appearance that Nick was being swallowed up by his clothes.

The T was virtually empty on Sunday mornings, and the only other person in the car with him was an elderly Chinese lady with four shopping bags overflowing with what looked like lettuce, beets, cabbage, and other assorted vegetables.

Nick hated Sundays. It was the one day of the week when everything was over and all that was left was to get ready for the next week. He pulled one hand out from underneath his legs to look at his watch. Eleven thirty. Hopefully, he would make it home before Jamus. The first thing that Jamus would make Nick do was homework, and that was the last thing that Nick wanted to do. If he beat Jamus home, that would buy him some time. Jamus would have to get settled, and he'd do some of his own work. With any luck, it would be about an hour before he thought about getting Nick to do homework. Jamus was cool, but Nick knew he had to keep a couple of steps ahead of him or else he could be a hardass.

The train bumbled to a halt, and the doors slid open. A prerecorded voice came over the speaker, the words scratchy and barely distinguishable, "New England Medical Center, doors open on your right." The next stop was Back Bay Station, South End, his stop.

Nick stood up, grabbing the backpack out of the seat beside him as he made his way to the subway door and waited for the train to rattle into Back Bay Station. He'd been in the same clothes for two days. Jamus had put out a change of pants and shirt for him on Friday morning, but he'd forgotten to take them when he left the house. The car rumbled to a stop and Nick bounded out of the door as soon as it opened, almost running over an older gray-bearded guy with glasses and a newspaper tucked under his arm.

"What's the rush, young man?" the bearded guy shouted at Nick as he passed.

"Trying to beat the crowd," Nick called out as he bounced past him, the only person getting off the train. He ran through the platform and up the escalator into the concrete hall of the station.

Nick frowned as he pushed his way through the station's revolving door out onto Dartmouth Street. A bank of clouds had moved in that morning, and the early sun had turned to a dull bluish glow floating over the late-morning city.

Back Bay Station sat at the edge of Boston's South End neighborhood. The South End was different from South Boston. Though the names of the two neighborhoods sounded the same, they were worlds apart. The South End was crowded with quaint little parks and elegant brownstone town houses crammed together one on top of the other. To Nick, nothing was more obnoxious than this part of town.

He hated the false charm of the brick sidewalks, the planted window boxes, and the wrought iron railings. To him, it was all so fake—the snobby coffee shops, the trendy bars, and the hipster boutiques. Not to mention all the salons. They had salons for haircuts, for facials, for pets, and for massages. Nick even saw a salon just for blow-drying hair. Everywhere he looked, he saw something he didn't like, something that grated on his sense of reality. Of course it didn't help that the kids at Nick's school made fun of him for being from this part of town, Boston's *de facto* gay district.

He hadn't always hated it. When he was younger, it wasn't so bad, with Jamus cheerfully dragging him around to the cafés for cups of hot chocolate in the winter or a Coke in the warmer months. But now, Nick tried to spend as much time away from the South End as possible. Jamus still made him come home every night of the week, though, except Saturday. Saturday was his night to spend over at Matt's house.

In Nick's eyes, Matt existed in a teenager's paradise. He lived in a giant house with tons of space, including a rec room with all kinds of stuff: a pool table, ping-pong, and a huge TV that he watched soccer and pretty much everything else on. His mom was a little odd, though. She was Italian or Greek or something and was always making weird food with olives and tomatoes and stuff like that. She was always trying to push something to eat down Nick's throat, but it wasn't his thing.

Living with Jamus wasn't any sort of treat, but at least he cooked normal food like potatoes and beans and steak and that kind of stuff. And Nick had to admit it was more fun to watch soccer with Jamus. He'd get up and yell and scream at the players and the refs. Matt's family was much more subdued, and they weren't allowed to yell at the television.

The first time Nick had done that at Matt's house, he got scolded and told that the neighbors would hear him. How they would hear him through two sets of walls and a backyard as big as a basketball court, Nick couldn't imagine, but he let it go and kept his cheering to a whispering minimum for the rest of the game. Despite the super-cool house, if Nick wanted to watch footy the way it was supposed to be watched, it had to be with Jamus, in front of the tiny television in the kitchen of their cramped South End home.

Nick knew Jamus hated TV. He would never watch anything except soccer matches or news, and then only in the kitchen, sitting at the table in the uncomfortable oak chairs with no cushions. They had another small television in the living room, but Jamus never watched anything in there. To Nick, he was practically a monk. He never did anything fun except smoke, and that was only fun because both Jamus and Nick knew they shouldn't be doing it.

Jamus's favorite team was Manchester United. Nick's team was the Revolution. Even if they did suck, Nick liked the idea that he had a New England team to root for, not some stupid foreign team from England, at least that's what he said when he wanted to drive Jamus crazy. Nick smirked thinking about it.

Nick slowed to a walk and reached into his bag for the pack of Marlboros he had bought this morning at the Alewife T station convenience store. He knew the woman behind the counter, and she never asked him for an ID. He was just about to light one when he felt a hand on the back of his shoulder.

"And just what do you think you're doing, young man?" Jamus's voice boomed from behind. Caught off guard, Nick spun around so fast he nearly lost his balance and fell into an oncoming cab. Jamus's grip went from light to iron, catching his brother and pulling him in off the curb.

"What the fuck'd you do that for?" Nick said, shrugging his older brother's hand off his shoulder.

"Didn't know you were gonna jump into the street, Nicky," Jamus said. "You gotta watch those cars."

"Fuck you."

Jamus cuffed him playfully on the back of the head. "Watch your mouth, have some respect for your elders."

"Or what?" Nick said, lighting the cigarette and trying to seem tough.

"Or I'll wash it out with soap," Jamus said. "Now, give us one of those, come on."

Nick handed him the pack of Marlboros. Even though it wasn't his brand, Jamus took one and leaned down to let his younger brother light it. "What'd I tell you about smoking?" Jamus said.

"That it's not a good idea, but if I'm going to do it, there's nothing you can do to stop me so I might as well learn how to look cool doing it," Nick said. Jamus could be cool about some things.

"Good boy." They both laughed.

Nick put the pack of smokes back into his bag, and they started down Dartmouth Street toward home. "How was church?" Nick asked.

"Same as," Jamus said.

"Did you go alone?"

"I did," Jamus said. "I was gonna take my kid brother, but he was out in the suburbs somewhere."

"I was at Matt's house," Nick said.

"I know where you were," Jamus said.

"Did you check in on me? Call Matt's ma?" Nick asked.

"Nah." Jamus ashed his cigarette on the brick sidewalk. "I trust you're going to be where you say you're going to be."

"You do not," Nick said.

"Do, too."

"Then why won't you let me go out any other time of the week?" Nick asked.

Jamus smiled. This wasn't the first time the two brothers had had this conversation. "You know the answer to that, Nicky. When you're a sophomore, you can go out one night during the week."

"Yeah, but why not now?"

"Because you're fourteen years old, that's why." Jamus took a long drag on the cigarette and chucked it, half finished, down through a drainage grate on the street.

"That's bullshit."

"Sorry bub, that's life." Jamus pulled out his keys as they neared the house. "How much homework you got?"

"None."

"Oh, come on. Seriously? What do you have?"

"Some English. A paper."

"Oh yeah?" Jamus smiled.

"I can do it. I don't need your help, Mr. Writer." Nick threw his cigarette into the street and followed Jamus up the brown steps to the front door. "I don't even need to start it till later this afternoon anyway."

Jamus unlocked the door and pushed it open. "How about an hour before the game, and you can finish up what's left later on?"

"No," Nick said. "I don't think so."

"Yes," Jamus said, imitating his brother's tone. "I think so."

"Man, why you gotta be such a hardass?" Nick tossed his bag onto the kitchen table. It slid almost all the way across the surface, coming to a stop just before falling off the edge.

"It's fun. It's a hobby of mine," Jamus said. "Easy on the wood, huh?"

"So, anything new at church?" Nick asked.

"Not really. There's a new priest, and he's a little weird, but overall it's pretty much the same."

"I don't see why you go," Nick said, starting to unpack his bag. "I mean, it's not like you can possibly believe in everything they say. Especially, you know, because you're…"

Jamus looked up toward the ceiling for a moment before responding. "I don't know how much of the specifics I believe," he finally said, "but I believe there is something up there, and I guess that's all I need to know."

"So why do you keep going?" Nick asked. "That's hardly what the priest would want to hear. Either you take it all or none of it according to him, right?"

"I don't know about that. I expect they're glad to have anybody who wants to be there, especially when the basket goes around," Jamus said. "But honestly, it's not the priest's business why I go to Mass."

"Seriously? It seems like they think everything is their business."

Jamus looked at his younger brother. "You're a little down on the Catholics today."

"And you're not?" Nick sat down at the table. "I mean seriously, how can you not be? You know how they feel about you, right?"

"There's more to it than that," Jamus said.

"Okay, fine. Why do you go?" Nick persisted.

"I like it," Jamus said. "I like the music and light, and I don't know, I guess I like the sense of peace I get when I sit there. It gives me a chance to meditate or something like that. In a way, it gives me time to be with God."

"What do you think about there?"

Jamus turned away from Nick and to the sink. "Oh, I don't know. I think about my work, I think about you. I guess I think about a lot of stuff."

The silence in the room lasted for a few seconds, and each brother could feel the unspoken subject between them. Nick finally broke the silence. "You think about Mom and Dad when you're there, don't you?" he asked. "Can you feel them or anything?"

Jamus turned at the sink and quietly watched his younger brother. "Yeah, sometimes," he said slowly. "Sometimes I think of them a little bit." He took a deep breath. "Hey, you need to get upstairs and get started on that homework."

"Yeah, yeah," Nick said. "Can I at least eat first?"

"Why don't you go up to your room and get started? I'll make sandwiches."

"Peanut butter."

"You want peanut butter?"

"Uh-huh," Nick said. "And chips."

"It'll give you zits," Jamus said, his tone raised just enough to be annoying but not overbearing.

"I don't care."

"Okay," Jamus said. "Peanut butter and chips it is. I'll bring it up in a few minutes."

"Thanks, Jamus."

CHAPTER TWELVE

Hayfield Academy sat on the edge of Harvard Square in Cambridge, not far from the Charles River. It was a temporary home for kids from China to Finland to Ethiopia to Peru and many other places. Parents from all over the world sent their children there for high school, and just over half of the student body was from outside of the United States. Walking down the halls of the school's single dorm, a visitor would hear any number of languages or dialects as kids called home to talk to their families. And even though cooking in the dorm rooms was forbidden, the whole building smelled like a mixture of strange foods from curry and rice to pickled fish.

The same atmosphere spilled over into the academic buildings, where Nick and Matt were in the minority as local students who actually lived at home. This, plus the fact that they were part of a very small freshman class, made them outsiders. But the two Boston Boys, as they came to be called, had let it be known early on they wouldn't be targets for hazing.

When a group of three Peruvian upperclassmen tried to take part of Matt's lunch during the first week of school, Nick had stood up quietly and surprised the biggest of the Peruvians with a quick right hook to the left ear. The older boy had not been expecting it and went down like a sack of potatoes. Nick figured he would get his ass kicked by the other two Peruvians, but to his surprise, they had backed away. Of course, Nick landed in all sorts of trouble with the school and, worse, with Jamus. But at least they didn't get bullied again. He had gotten into one other fight when a week later, he caught another kid trying to break into his locker. Nick never found out why. He didn't ask. He ran up behind the kid, swung him around and landed a fist in the guy's nose. Again, Nick ended up in the principal's office and that time he got five days of detention at school and grounded for a week at home. After that, Jamus made him promise no more fights.

As freshmen, Nick and Matt were relegated to lower-level lockers close to the floor, but they had managed to at least get lockers next to each other. It hadn't taken them long to figure out the schedules of the upperclassmen whose lockers were above theirs, so they could avoid going to their lockers when they would have to duck and scrunch underneath the older students. This afternoon they were grabbing books for the last class of the day and getting ready to head over to Malloy's room.

"Hurry up," said Matt as Nick pried through the papers and notebooks jumbled into the bottom of his locker. While Matt's locker was spotlessly organized, Nick's was the exact opposite. The growing pile of sediment at the bottom of it consisted of old tests, graded assignments, Coke cans, and other odds and ends that were only sort of identifiable.

"I'm coming." He grabbed the three books he needed for the end of the day and slammed the locker shut. "Okay, what was the reading for last night?" he asked as they started off down the hall for class.

"What do you mean?" Matt asked. "It was your night to read. Don't tell me you forgot, Nick?"

"What? No way, dude. It was not my night to read, I read on Monday."

"No," said Matt. "I did English on Monday and math last night. The agreement was that you would do math on Monday—which you did—and English last night, which I'm guessing you didn't."

"Shit, no."

Matt and Nick had three classes together, and they usually split up the homework assignments and shared with each other. Most of the time, the system worked efficiently. If Nick did math and history homework one day, he could count on Matt to have the English assignment. Occasionally, they would switch off and trade assignments. But sometimes, like today, it didn't go as smoothly as planned.

"Great," Matt said. "Now we're both fucked. You know he's going to call on us." The boys approached the door to Malloy's room. He was already in the back of the room going through some papers in one of the cabinets. Nick briefly considered skipping out, but he knew better than that. He was already on thin ice with both the school and Jamus, and a missed class would not go unnoticed.

"It'll be fine," Nick said. "There are sixteen other kids in the class. He's not going to call on us."

"Uh-huh," Matt said as they wandered in and found their seats over by the window side of the classroom. The steam radiators were on full blast to fight off the crisp fall mornings, but nobody bothered to turn them down in the afternoon. Nick yawned before he even sat down. *It's going to be a struggle to stay awake today*, he thought.

As the classroom started to fill up, Mr. Malloy finished what he was doing at the back of the room and made his way toward the front. His button-down shirt and his khakis had probably been pressed that morning, but he was creased along the back with wrinkles from where he had sat or leaned against his desk.

"Okay," he said, turning to face the eighteen fourteen- and fifteen-year-olds sitting in four uneven rows across the room. "Who read the chapter from last night?"

The silence of those eighteen students filled the room in front of him. "Come on guys, don't be shy. It's only Tuesday, too early in the week not to want to participate in class."

Matt looked at Nick and shook his head, a look of dread in his eyes and a thin bead of sweat forming above his eyebrows. Nick sat coolly back, rolled his eyes and mouthed the words "chill out" to Matt. Sure enough, if the very thought of getting called on in class wasn't enough to catch Mr. Malloy's attention, the lip reading was. The young teacher homed in on Nick.

"Mr. Cork? Any thoughts on this chapter?"

Nick sat still. Matt looked directly at him and formed the word "busted" on his lips. Nick made a quick face at his friend as he felt his coolness fade away. Suddenly, he could feel the heat rising from beneath his collar, rushing up to color his face. He looked down at the blank notebook on his desk.

"Any thoughts on the book in general?" Malloy asked. "Maybe some thoughts from last week's reading assignment?"

And that was all the latitude Nick needed. He had read last week's assignment and actually enjoyed it. "Well, it's one of the better books we've read so far this year."

Something about that sparked a glint in Malloy's eye. "Really?" he said, looking out across the classroom at Nick. "That's all you've got?"

"No, I mean, I like *A Separate Peace* more than anything else we've read this year because I can actually get into it. I like the story and the characters, Finny and Gene. They're our age, so it's kind of like reading about people here."

Malloy nodded for him to continue.

"Last week," Nick's voice was low and croaky as he absorbed the stares from around the room, "I didn't agree with most of what we talked about in class last week."

"Go on," said Malloy. "What part didn't you agree with?"

"Well, the part when we talked about how Gene had caused the accident that broke his best friend, Finny's, leg. Everyone seemed sort of on the same page that it was just Gene being an a—" He quickly corrected himself as a couple of titters erupted around the room. "I mean a jerk. But no one seemed to say very much about what might have caused him to do it."

"What caused him to do it?" Malloy asked. "Do you mean what motivated him to shake the branch?"

"Well, yeah. He shook the tree that caused Finny to fall and break his leg, but nobody talked about how Finny had treated Gene in the months leading up to the accident. Finny treated him like a second-class citizen—Gene was always living in Finny's shadow. He never had a chance to be himself. He always felt like he had to compete."

Malloy was silent, raising his eyebrows as if he recognized Nick had more to say.

"Well," Nick continued. "I mean, don't you ever feel that way? Doesn't everyone? It sucks to feel like you're just a chump—and you just want to get yourself to some sort of level playing field, to catch up with the world. If you think about it like that, it kind of gives you a different perspective on, you know, Gene, and what he did."

"That's crap," came a voice from behind Nick.

"That's a very interesting perspective, Mr. Cork, and not at all unfounded." Malloy nodded his head approvingly at Nick, and then he raised his eyes to the girl sitting two seats behind him. "Anara, you have a different opinion?"

Anara Kenn, a short dark-haired girl that Matt had been interested in earlier in the semester, hadn't even bothered to raise her hand. "I disagree. I think that Gene caused the accident on purpose, and we need to evaluate his decision on that event alone. But even then, I don't think Finny did anything wrong. I think he was just a nice guy, and Gene was just jealous."

Matt perked up a little at the sound of her voice.

"Hmmph," Nick snorted.

Matt glared at him.

"What?" he said under his breath to Matt. "I'm not going to agree with her just because you like her."

"Shut up," said Matt.

Malloy was trying to swallow a chuckle. "Mr. Cork, what do you think about judging the character's actions in isolation?"

"I don't think you can do that. I think the point of the story is to judge the whole thing together, as one statement."

"Ha," Anara said. "Maybe if you had read the entire book, you'd know."

"I know because I have a brain, Anara," Nick said. "Which is more than I can say for you. You're just upchucking what you read on Wikipedia."

"Okay, well, I think we need to focus on the book, not each other," interjected Malloy. "Anara, I'm glad you're reading ahead and have a complete view and opinion on Finny and Gene. Nick, I'm excited to think about what we might be able to discuss next week when you've finished up with this week's assignment."

"Yes, sir." Nick looked down at the empty notebook on his desk again. It had been worth a try, at least, steering the conversation away from the fact that he hadn't done his homework assignment. He swallowed and began jotting notes down as Malloy called on another student at the front of the room, asking her opinion about the chapter they were supposed to have just read. It was obvious from her answers she hadn't read it either.

❖

Out of the corner of his eye, Jamus could see the dim light from the living room. Nick was in there lying on the couch and listening to God only knew what on his iPhone. Jamus had a rule—one night of television a week. Nick could choose whatever night he wanted, but only one. This semester it was Thursday nights, so every other night of the week it was homework and reading or board games and talking. Tonight, Nick had chosen to read, but Jamus sat at the kitchen table looking right at Nick's book, which was not in the same room as Nick.

Jamus sighed and thought about calling out to his brother to ask if he wanted it, but then he thought better of it. The kid had already spent an hour and a half working on algebra earlier that night. Jamus could afford him a little sympathy. After all, he thought, gazing at the blank computer screen in front of him, he wasn't setting any standards for productivity. He hadn't written a word all day.

Instead he'd spent the last twelve hours sitting at the kitchen table, accomplishing nothing except doubling his normal intake of coffee and alcohol. So, while yelling at Nick to take the earphones out and get to his reading was probably the right thing to do, he didn't feel he had the moral high ground required to do it.

Instead, he grabbed the pack of Lucky Strikes sitting next to the ashtray at the end of the table and lit one.

CHAPTER THIRTEEN

Sean Malloy willed the number 11 bus to go faster, but it was no use. He was late again. That made three nights so far this week, and it was only Wednesday. The commute from Hayfield to his house was simple enough—a quick walk from the red brick campus up to Harvard Square, where he would catch the Red Line. He'd get off the subway at the Broadway T stop on the edge of South Boston and board the number 11 bus right to his door. But one kink in the system and everything broke down. If Sean was late getting out the door in the morning, or if he needed to stay after at school for a meeting, it could throw his whole commute off. He'd had his fair share of late nights since school had started, but so far this week was turning out to be a record breaker for kinks.

The last part of the journey home was the worst. The bus lumbered up to every stop, taking forever to move on as hordes of people crammed into or fought to get off the bus. Sean almost never got a seat on the ride home, and tonight was no exception. He stood, waiting patiently for the bus to crawl up to his stop, with his back squished against a pole and his left shoulder pressed into the armpit of a business suit.

Sean could see his house through the bus windows from a couple blocks away, the familiar pale green clapboards of the house slowly getting closer and closer. When it finally did arrive, he shoved his way to the front of the bus and out the door. Supper at the Malloy house was at six each evening every day of the year except for Sundays, Christmas, Easter, and Thanksgiving when it was at three in the afternoon. With him and Kevin living at home again, dinner had become a big deal, and they were all expected to be there for it. He waited for the bus to pull away, and then he dashed across the street, heading through the side door and into the back hall, a short room that served as a pantry and mudroom as well as connecting the kitchen to the utility room and the dining room.

His sisters had made the trek from the apartment they shared on L Street a few blocks away, and most of the family was already seated at the table in the kitchen. Kevin sat on one side of the table next to an empty chair, already eating. His sisters, Siobhan and Aideen, sat on the other side of the table arguing about something that Aideen's new boyfriend had said earlier that week and pretty much ignoring the plates full of food sitting in front of them. Sean's dad sat at the head of the table eating and reading a folded up newspaper, oblivious to everyone. Only his ma was still standing up at the stove, spooning mashed potatoes onto a plate already crammed with canned peas, meat loaf and a piece of bread.

"Lucky I saw your bus pull up, Seany," said Ma, handing him the plate as he dumped his backpack on the edge of the counter. "I was about to sit down myself."

"Thanks, Ma." He grabbed the plate out of her hands and kissed her on the cheek, then sat down, squeezing in beside his brother. His mom finished putting together her own plate and sat down opposite his father. She put her napkin on her lap and looked around the table before taking her first bite.

"How was work today?" she asked Sean.

Sean finished chewing his bite of meatloaf, swallowed hard and wiped his mouth with his napkin. "Good. Slow this afternoon. We had a department meeting to talk about curriculum for next year."

"You want to talk about slow," said Kevin. "I spent the day searching through four thousand documents for the word 'Labrador.' That's a slow day."

Aideen snorted and smirked out of the side of her mouth, ignoring Kevin and focusing on what Sean had said. "Curriculum? That's a big word. I guess that's what eight years of college will get you."

"Yeah," Sean said, trying to ignore the ribbing from his sister. "We're trying to decide what books we want to teach for the freshman class next year. Kids are getting bored with the more traditional stuff.

Some of it can't be helped. I think you need to teach things like Mark Twain, but not necessarily *Tom Sawyer*. Why not something a little less traditional like *The Prince and the Pauper*? And then I want to add in a few newer books that will connect kids with the world they're living in today, but there is a lot of resistance to that."

His siblings were all quiet. They just sat there looking at him. His father, likewise, was staring at him, his paper laid gently down on the red and white checkered tablecloth, the corner of the sports section firmly pressed into the butter dish. His sisters looked at each other and then broke into laughter.

"You're such a bookworm, Seany, no wonder you don't have a girlfriend," said Aideen.

"Leave him alone," said Kevin, although laughter hung on the edges of his mouth in a smirk. "He's the brains. Every family needs one. We can't all be blue collar."

"There's nothing wrong with blue collar," Dad chimed in, his first words of the evening.

"No, Dad, that's not what I'm saying," said Kevin. "But there's nothing wrong with being a little book smart either. I'm just saying that it's good we've got a brain in the house."

"You've all got brains." Ma shot him a sideways glance.

"Yeah, but Sean just uses his," Kevin quipped.

"Or tries to. Maybe he's making up for something else," Aideen shot back.

"Why are you ranking on him, Aideen?" Siobhan broke her silence.

"I'm just laughing a little. I'm allowed to laugh. It's funny, that's all," said Aideen. "I'm not making fun of him."

"You were laughing at him," Kevin said.

"Can I have the applesauce?" Sean asked.

"I wasn't laughing at him." Aideen was starting to get red, her cheeks puffed up in a defensive pout.

"Yes, you were," Siobhan said. "You're always laughing at him. You try to play the big sister card, but when it comes down to it, you don't really like what he's doing with his life."

"That's bullshit," said Aideen. "I'm just watching out for him. I don't want him to be too much of a library fag."

"Language!" Ma interjected. "We're at the table."

"Can I have the applesauce, please?" Sean asked again, his hands flat on the table, his silverware laid down on the edge of his plate.

"I can say bullshit, Ma. I'm an adult," said Aideen.

"You will watch your mouth at this table," said Dad, "and you will not raise your voice to your mother."

"It's not bullshit." Siobhan wasn't giving up. "You think he's getting too good for himself."

"Maybe he is getting a little too high and mighty," Aideen said. "Who talks like that? Who talks about books and curriculum and shit." She glanced toward Ma. "Sorry—stuff—like that anyway."

"Applesauce, please, anyone?" Sean gritted his teeth. His hands, still on the table, were now clenched into fists.

"Look, he's not getting too good for anything," said Kevin. "He's just doing what he wants to do. He wants to make a difference in these kids' lives, and he's really focused on it."

"Bullshit. He's Ma's little prince," said Aideen. "And now he works at Harvard and pretty soon he's gonna move into some condo in Back Bay, and we'll never see him again because he's too good for us here in Southie."

"Language! Please. This is not a pub." Ma looked exasperated.

"He's just a teacher," said Kevin, laying down his fork. "Can't you just let him be what he wants to be? Why is this such a big deal for everyone? He's a teacher. He's not going anywhere. It's not about the money. Christ, he'd make more money at McDonald's."

"He just wants to do something with his life," Siobhan said.

"Or maybe he just doesn't want to face the real world, and it's easier to stay holed up with his books, the way he always was as a kid?" said Aideen. "Did you ever think of that?"

"You're so full of shit," said Kevin. "He wants to make a difference. He wants to help kids learn something. Why are you so down on him? All you ever do is bitch at other people about what they're doing wrong. Have you taken a look at yourself and tried to figure out why you're so fucked up?"

"We're not talking about me, asshole. And besides, what kind of a difference is he going to make talking like that so no one can understand what he's saying?" Aideen said, pointing her fork across the table at her brother.

Sean cleared his throat loudly, slammed his fist down on the table, and yelled as loudly as he could. "Can someone pass me the fucking applesauce!?" Forks clinked on plates as everyone stopped talking and looked at Sean in stunned silence. "Please?"

The applesauce was sitting next to his father's left hand, but passing condiments at the table never would have occurred to him. Instead, he sat staring at his youngest son. In the silence of the room, Siobhan reached over and picked up the jar and the spoon lying next to it and passed them over to Sean.

"Sorry, Ma," Sean said, looking down at his plate. "I didn't mean to use the F-word."

The rest of the meal passed in silence. Even later that evening after the meal had finished, everyone went their own way without much to say. Kevin still wasn't going out, so he went upstairs to his room. Siobhan and Aideen had gone back to their own apartment, and Dad had gone into the living room to watch television and reread the paper.

Sean stood next to his mother at the sink, drying the dishes as she washed them. "So, you're already trying to make your mark there?" she asked.

"Huh?" Sean was lost in his own world.

"At school. You don't agree with what they're teaching?"

"Oh. That. Well, I agree with some of it. And I agree with what we're trying to accomplish with Freshman Lit, as a class," Sean said. "It's just that I think it's time to bring in some new titles. There's a lot of great lit out there from more modern authors, and I think teaching things that are more accessible to the kids makes it easier for them to learn the key ideas we're trying to get across."

His mother paused for a moment and scraped at a particularly crusty spot of potato on one of the plates. "I think that sounds like you're trying to make your own mark on that school." She smiled at him. "And I couldn't be more proud of you."

Sean smiled back at her. "Thanks, Ma."

"And the others feel the same way, even if they don't express it."

Sean chuckled a little. "You sure about that?"

"Yes. They're your brother and sisters. They just have a funny way of showing you how they love you. It's too close in a house like this."

CHAPTER FOURTEEN

"Come on, Sean, you're coming with me." Kevin was standing at the door to his room in white Umbro shorts, black socks up to his knees, and an old gray and blue sweatshirt. He walked into Sean's bedroom and started rummaging around in the bottom of the closet. "You've been cooped up in here for two weekends in a row. Today, you're getting out." He threw out one cleat as he spoke, looking around for the other.

"Kev, I've got to get through about four more books in the next week. I can't."

"Found it," Kevin called from inside the closet, turning around and holding it up. "Look, Sean, you still have your soccer cleats. Remember when you used to like to play soccer? Oh, wait, you still do."

"Kevin, I can't."

"Yes, you can. One game, Seany. We haven't seen you down at the lot in months. Hop to it." He turned around. "I'm going downstairs to get breakfast, you're coming. I'll see you down there in five minutes. We're leaving in ten." He started to go and then turned back as if he forgot something. "Soccer. You know, the one with a big black and white ball and lots of kicking?"

Sean laughed at him and closed the book. "Okay, make me some toast," he called back as Kevin bounded down the stairs. Sean looked down at the cleats, and then got up and went through his drawers for shorts and a sweatshirt. The two of them had played soccer almost every Saturday morning in junior high and high school. It was one of the few times when they were both on the same side of something. They could spend the entire week fighting about everything from homework to chores, but on Saturday, they were an unstoppable pair on the soccer field—the Malloy brothers.

Sean sat on the edge of his bed and pulled on his socks. He'd selected a black pair like Kevin had on and pulled them up as high as they would go. He found his shin guards under his bed only to discover they were covered with a thick layer of dust. Oh well, he thought, they'd still work. He'd put them on down at the field. He stood up and called downstairs. "My toast better be ready!" He headed down to grab Kevin and get up to the field.

The brothers turned down First Street and walked along the beach in the direction of Moakley Park. Sean dribbled the ball for a few steps before toe-tipping it straight up into the air and catching it in both hands, the ribbed edges of the synthetic leather hexagons feeling like home in his palms. He took a deep breath; the ocean air was cool and dense, almost thick, with salt. But the sun was bright and warmed them up as they walked toward the park. Now that Kevin had pried him away from his work it felt good to be heading outside for the day. How had he let himself miss this for so long?

"How was work this week?" Sean asked, tossing the ball to Kevin, who caught it and palmed it with his left hand.

"So-so," Kevin said, shifting the ball to his right hand and tossing it back to Sean. "Trying to stay focused on the bigger picture."

"Still plowing through boxes of email printouts?" Sean asked.

"Yep," Kevin said. "It's not what I thought I'd be doing when I signed up for a temp job. I thought I'd be answering phones, so I'm not complaining. And it seems I'm pretty good at it."

"Yeah?" Sean asked, throwing the ball up into the air and catching it as they walked.

"Yep. I'm wicked fast. I can get through a file box of emails in about two hours. It takes a lot of the other guys twice as long."

"Nice." Sean tossed the ball back to his brother. "They going to hire you?"

"Not sure. I'd probably take it. I have to imagine there's more to a job than this, but for now it's a good start."

Sean nodded silently.

"How 'bout you? How's school going?"

"You know, it's not what I expected either," Sean said.

"How so?"

Sean walked a couple of steps running his hand gently along a cement wall they were passing. "I don't know. It's a lot of stress, I guess." He searched for the right words. "I expected to have some students who just didn't care about learning, but I get the feeling almost none of them do, and on top of that it sometimes feels like the faculty is pretty much over it."

"Over it?" Kevin asked.

"Yeah, just over the whole teaching thing."

"Cheer up, bro. Stay focused on what you started doing this for. You want to change lives, open minds, right?"

"Yeah."

"Seriously. Stay focused on what you set out to do, and you'll be fine," Kevin said. He tossed the soccer ball out in front of Sean as they rounded the corner. "But today, stay focused on the game. I've been missing you down here. The Malloy brothers are now officially back on the field."

Sean caught the ball in the inside arch of his foot and dribbled absentmindedly along the sidewalk. "Yes, we are," he said.

"It's been a busy couple of months down at the field, even without you," Kevin was saying as they jogged along. "Good weather for most of September, so we've had two or three on the bench most days."

"So, what are you saying? That I might not get to play?" Sean asked. "You dragged me away from my work to go and warm a bench?"

"You could have brought your book," Kevin said, landing a friendly punch on his brother's arm. "But I'm glad you didn't. Besides, there're usually a few skirts watching." He smiled.

"Oh, yeah?" said Sean, still dribbling. "That's nothing new. There's never much to look at."

"Well, you might be surprised," Kevin said. "Grace'll be there. I'll make sure to tell her you said that, though."

"Shut up," said Sean, one-upping Kevin on the friendly punch and giving his brother a full-fledged body check off the sidewalk and into a hedge, quickly sprinting ahead a few yards with the ball to avoid retribution.

Sean and Kevin found their group of friends scrimmaging on the far end of the park. Sean knew all of them. Some were from his high school class, a few were from Kevin's class, and one or two had gone to school with his sisters. The younger guys still had the look of the neighborhood boys they had once been. They sported the same close-cropped haircuts, and the required Boston College or UMass sweatshirt with cut-off arms over white or gray waffle shirts. A few had track pants on, but most still wore shorts and long black socks. It was cool but nowhere near winter cold for Boston. Shorts were a nod to the toughness that defined this neighborhood. The few older players milling around had a more hardened look about them. They were unshaven with spots of gray in their beards, their creased brows and slightly fuller jowls the future for the tight foreheads and red cheeks of the younger crowd. A few still sported the closely cropped haircuts, but many had let things get shaggy. It was the full spectrum of life in Southie.

"Hey, Sean," Grace said from the corner of the field amongst the blankets the spectators had spread on the grass.

"Hey, Gracie," Sean said over his shoulder as he shuffled up to the group of guys starting to circle at the edge of the field. Kevin nudged his arm as they walked.

"Hey, Gracie," Kevin called out, mimicking Sean. "Got a smile like that for me, too?"

"Sorry, Kevin." She laughed. "Not today, honey. Maybe if you were cuter."

"What? I am the better-looking one," he shouted back. "And smarter."

"Sure," she called from across the expanding distance between them. "I'll believe that...never."

"You're an idiot," Sean said to his brother. "Leave it alone."

"When are you going to move on that, Sean?" he asked as soon as they were out of earshot.

"She's not serious, you know," Sean shot back at him, trapping a soccer ball that someone had shot his way from across the field. He began to dribble and jog toward the others.

"The hell she's not," his brother said as he followed. "Hey, ball hog, aren't you going to pass it?"

"Do you think you can keep up?"

"Oh, I can keep up," he said, following Sean down the field.

Chapter Fifteen

Father Richards smiled as he stepped out into the apse. Jamus watched the old priest as he looked over the crowd and wondered what the old man saw. Did he see Sacred Heart Cathedral as just another mammoth gray stone church, the kind that peppers Boston's Irish and Italian neighborhoods, a collection of faux gothic architectural elements complete with stone spires and vaulted ceilings, giving it the appearance of being something from a different age?

Or did he see it as a place where generations of families had come week after week for more than a century to worship, to celebrate weddings, to honor the dead and welcome the new, to listen, and sometimes just to forget?

The clergy who inhabited this ancient choreography of rocks seemed suspended in time with the stones of the church itself. Like Father Richards, the deacons and church office staff were all bent over, hunched respectably into perpetual old age, except for the new priest, a young man who'd come to the church earlier in the year, not quite fresh out of seminary, but close. He was exceedingly fresh this morning, sitting straight-backed in the front row of pews.

The church was usually wedding or Easter full, and this Sunday was no exception. People sat shoulder to shoulder several rows past the middle of the church. After that, they dispersed a little, thinning out until the last couple of rows where a few gray heads dotted the pews.

The light streamed through the tops of the colorful, leaded windows, giving the whole room a feeling of cold quietness, as if light itself was only a whisper in this place. Jamus sat quietly with his hands folded in his lap, looking up at the familiar windows. When the service started, he sat motionless with his eyes fixed on the altar, staring steadily at the scene in front of him.

The young priest stood up from his spot in the front row and walked up to join Father Richards. It turned out the young priest would be giving the sermon today. Jamus racked his brain to think of the priest's name, but nothing came. He was starting out on a roll this morning, though, preaching about the dangers of the moral sea of life.

Jamus glanced down at his shoes and did his best to stifle a yawn. He played over the recent conversation with his brother about church. The truth was Jamus thought about a lot of different things in church, and one of them just happened to be sitting in the pew across the aisle from him. Tall, reddish blond, and sitting quietly, staring at his feet like almost every other Sunday, Malloy sat next to his two sisters and his parents. Jamus guessed he was somewhere in his late twenties or early thirties. He knew him only from their brief run-in a few months back when he was looking for the girl with the big black bag after the service.

"Amos 8:11 says 'Behold, the days come, saith the Lord God, that I will send a famine in the land, not a famine of bread, nor a thirst for water, but of hearing the words of the Lord.'" Jamus was sucked back into the sermon as the ambitious young priest raised his voice to a barely comfortable volume. He could have sworn that the priest was looking directly at him as he spoke. "Now what does this mean? A famine for the words of the Lord? Can it be that we are living in such a world? A world where millions are starving, and they don't even know it?"

The priest held up his hands together and paused for a few seconds. To Jamus's surprise, he noticed that the parishioners seemed captivated. He looked around to see most of them with their mouths firmly pursed, leaning forward, waiting for the young priest to continue. He meant to just scan the room, he really did, but he found his gaze stuck on the Malloys again. Just as he was going to shift his eyes back to the front of the church, Sean Malloy looked up from his shoes.

Their eyes met for a second, and you would have needed a stopwatch to know who blushed first. Jamus looked forward almost instantly and stared frozen-faced at the altar. But the priest was savoring his dramatic pause, and the entire church was suspended in a dream. What happened next had to be the work of his imagination, because

Jamus could have sworn that the priest looked directly at him and nodded. His cheeks burned with a mixture of feelings—separation and aloneness, yes, but not embarrassment. If anything, that feeling in the pit of his stomach carried a hint of defiance. Or at least that's what he told himself in those seconds when it felt as if all of South Boston had piled into that church to stare at him. Jamus kept his gaze on the priest as the priest stared back at him and ever so subtly lifted up his chin, just enough so that Jamus would know it was meant for him.

The priest held the silence for a few more seconds before he finally relented. "The most important word in that phrase is 'hearing.' You have to make your own decisions in life. You have your own moral compass, and that's what will direct you along your path. Only you can choose to hear the words of the Lord. They are all around us. They are sometimes not what you expect them to be."

He paused for a minute before continuing, waiting for the tension to build, riding on his silence. "It is not for us to judge others, only for us to listen for the words of the Lord and make decisions that take us to where we want to go. Matthew 7:1 states 'judge not, lest ye be judged.' Jesus is not saying don't use your best judgment along your path. He's saying that your moral compass belongs to you and only you. We all must be free from the judgment of others if we are to truly avoid the Famine that Amos speaks of..."

The rest of the sermon was a blur. Jamus registered almost none of it as he focused on the hymnals in the back of the pew in front of him, the candles burning over to the side of the church, the giant ivory white crucifix behind the altar. At the end of the Mass as everyone shuffled out, he looked up again to the place where Malloy had been sitting. He was gone now, and Jamus had missed his exit. Not that it mattered. He wouldn't have said anything to him anyway, especially now. Jamus shuffled out with the rest of the crowd, back into the crisp morning air. Time to get back home.

CHAPTER SIXTEEN

Sean sat on a bench facing the beach, head down in a book. The sun was on its way toward setting, but a silver-gray light was still out, giving the water a dull luster. The late September evenings had started turning cold, and Sean was bundled up in a parka and gloves. Every minute or so, he would reach a gloved hand up and fumble to turn the page. They'd stick together occasionally, and he would shake his head and pull his right glove off with his teeth. He'd shuffle the pages back to the right spot and lay the book upside down on his lap while pulling the glove back on and picking the book up again. He repeated this like clockwork every five minutes or so, to the point where he might as well have just left the gloves off.

"*A Separate Peace*," Grace said. "I remember that one. Didn't we read it in seventh grade?" Her voice came from behind him, warm, almost to the point of breathiness.

"I can't remember for sure, but this year I'm teaching it to our freshmen," he said back over his shoulder. "I hope they didn't have it in seventh grade, but that might explain why I've had eighteen very bored adolescents on my hands for the last two weeks." He tilted his head to the side and seemed to realize something. "Come to think of it, they'd probably be bored no matter what we read. Teenagers can be like that."

"Sounds like it's a challenge."

He smiled and turned around to face the red hair and freckles he knew would be there. "Hi, Grace," he said, putting down his book. "What brings you out tonight?"

She smiled. "Just out for a walk. That is okay, isn't it? I'm not intruding?"

"No," he said. "It's nice to see you. Plus my eyes are starting to cross. I've been reading this thing all day."

She picked the book out of Sean's hands. "Ah, yes, it's all coming back to me now." She handed it back to him. "A whole bunch of stuff about some boys pushing each other off a tree, right?"

"That's more or less the right book." Sean grinned up at her. "I've got to write up a test for the end of the week."

"Another book about boys," she sighed.

"Boys?"

"Yeah, all the good books are about boys, haven't you ever noticed? At least all the ones we had to read in school—*The Iliad*, *The Odyssey*, *Gatsby*, Mark Twain, and *Huckleberry Finn*."

"You mean *Tom Sawyer*."

"Huh?"

"You said Mark Twain and *Huckleberry Finn*. Mark Twain was the author—*The Adventures of Tom Sawyer* was the book we had to read," he said, the corner of his mouth pulling up in the edges of a smile.

"Whatever," she laughed, "you know what I mean."

"Yeah, I know what you mean. And to be honest, we struggle sometimes to find strong female roles in the older books we read, but they're there. *To Kill a Mockingbird*, the Jane Austen books, anything by Willa Cather."

"Okay, okay." Grace raised her hands in front of her. "I give up, I should have known better than to pick a fight about books with you, Sean Malloy."

"Sorry, I get passionate sometimes. Maybe too much."

Grace waved it away and, after a few seconds, leaned in toward him conspiratorially. "So, not to change the subject, but I heard a rumor." She let the word linger in the air between them.

Sean felt a chill down the base of his neck. He swallowed hard and shook his head slowly and tried to laugh. "Oh yeah? A rumor? I love a good rumor," Sean said, turning toward her.

"You might not like this one." She sat down on the bench next to him.

Sean stared directly out at the beach and the harbor beyond it as if he could see something there that no one else could.

She nudged him with her shoulder. "Wanna guess?"

"Not really," he said, eyes fixed straight ahead.

"You're no fun," she said. "Okay, I'll tell you straight then: more condos."

Sean frowned and let out a sigh. "That's it? That's all you've got for me?"

She turned her head slightly, looking into his eyes, something between a grin and a frown spread across her freckled cheeks. "What did you think I was going to say?"

"You got me thinking it was going to be real scandal," he said. "I was expecting a story about the priest or something."

"Oh." She made a face like she had bitten into a lemon. "I know. The new one?"

Sean laughed. "Yeah, he's a strange duck, huh?"

"Yeah he is," she said. "Something's not right about him. I don't know what it is, but he has bodies in the closet somewhere."

"I hate the way he takes your hand in between his when he greets you," Sean said. "It creeps me out."

"Me, too! Do you know why he's here?"

"Not sure," said Sean. "I assumed he'd be taking over for Father Richards."

"Ugh, I hope not. I love that old man," she said, looking back out at the ocean.

Sean nodded slowly but was silent for a few seconds. "So, where this time?" he asked.

"Sorry?" She snapped her eyes back to Sean.

He smiled. "The condos. Where are they going in this time?"

"Oh, right, sorry. That was the whole point of the story, wasn't it? Up on E Street. O'Leary's sold. Or so I hear, there's nothing confirmed yet."

Sean nodded. "Well, you never know for sure until it happens. Southie is full of these rumors now. I don't get it. Generations of families have tried to get out of this part of town. It was almost a ghetto in the '70s and '80s, from what my ma says. But snap, they start running out of room to build million-dollar condos in Back Bay and the South End, and the money shifts. Of course this doesn't hurt." He gestured toward the beach. "A waterfront always brings them in droves. The yuppies need another neighborhood to gentrify, and here they come. Where'd you hear about it?"

"Flynn down at Grumpy's Pub," she said, taking out a cigarette from her giant black bag. "Mind?" she asked, pausing for a second as she searched in the bag for her lighter.

Sean shook his head no. "It'll kill you, not me."

"Yeah, well, life is short." She found the lighter and ducked her head almost into her purse as she lit the cigarette. "So, Sean," she said after a few seconds, "can I ask you something?"

"About condos?" he asked.

She inhaled, then turned her head away from him and blew a thick stream of smoke out into the cold night air, trying ineffectively to wave it away with her other hand. "No, not about condos. More…" She hesitated for a few seconds. "More about us. Well, you and me."

He folded the edge of the page he was on and closed the book on his lap, sensing his reading was over for now. "About us? Sure."

"And you don't have to answer this if you don't want to. It's just that we've known each other for a long, long time." She paused for a moment, her eyes fixed first on the beach, and then slowly shifting over to Sean. "And I want you to be honest with me about this."

Sean's eyes widened considerably and he raised his eyebrows in wait.

"Do you think there's something wrong with me?"

"Wrong with you? How do you mean?"

"Damn it." She kept staring at him. "I don't know. Is there something wrong with me? Is there something about me that people don't like or…I don't know…something they don't *get* about me?"

He stumbled, reddening just a little bit. "I…I don't think so. I've never heard anyone say anything like that."

She nodded her head, keeping her eyes locked on him and not moving an inch. "What about you? Do you think there's something wrong with me?"

"No. No, I don't." He looked up to meet her gaze. "I think you're nice."

"Nice. Hmph, that figures." She took a final drag on the cigarette and flicked it out onto the sand. She gathered her bag and flipped the huge strap of it over her shoulder before standing up and straightening out her skirt. "I've got to be going, Sean. Nice running into you down here. Good luck with the book and all."

"Okay." Sean looked at her. "Is something wrong?"

"Wrong?" she said and seemed to bite her lower lip. "I don't know." She stood looking at him, or rather through him, for what seemed to be an uncomfortably long time for Sean. He had grown up with two sisters, but neither one of them was ever much like Grace. She had a different way about her—she was more disconnected from things.

"Do you want to take a walk?" he asked, standing up beside her and tucking the book into his breast pocket. "I was just thinking it might be nice to walk down to Castle Island. You up for it?"

She took a minute before responding. "You know, I think I would like that."

The sun had gone all the way down by the time they reached Castle Island, and it was colder than it had been during the day. Castle Island sat at the edge of Southie, a colonial-era fort that was now a park. The graceful stone of the battlements was bleached white by the surrounding spotlights contrasting with the purple sky lit from the city behind it. Far off in the distance, they could hear the hum and rumble of jet engines taking off and landing at Logan Airport. But the daytime crowds had abandoned the park, and it was just the two of them walking along the edge of the water in the stillness.

"I used to think this was my island when I was a little girl," Grace said.

"You did?" Sean looked at her.

"Yes, my ma used to tell me stories about all these princesses when I was little, you know, to get me to sleep. I was awful at bedtime. And one night when she was through with a story about a particularly glamorous Indian princess, I said that I wanted to be a princess. And she looked at me for a moment and it was the strangest thing because I thought she was going to cry, which for a little girl—I don't know, I must have been about five at the time—for a little five-year-old girl, thinking that your ma is going to cry is pretty traumatic. Well, she didn't cry. I don't know if she ever was going to really cry. But she said to me, 'Gracie, you are a princess. You're my princess.' And I said well, then Mommy, I need a castle. And she said she had one she had been saving special, just for me."

"Castle Island?"

"Exactly," Grace said, her voice small like a child's. "Well, I wanted to see it right away, but she said I would have to wait until the next day, and that meant I would have to go to bed so I wasn't too tired the next morning to go see my castle. Well, I was quiet as a mouse that night, but I didn't sleep a wink. The next day she took me here." Grace gestured to the fort with both hands. "It was my first time here, and she told me it was my castle, and I was the princess of South Boston."

"That's beautiful," Sean said, stopping and taking Grace's hand.

"Yeah, well, it was beautiful while it lasted," Grace said. "It didn't go over too well the next year when I went to school, and I told everyone in kindergarten that I was the princess of Southie. But hey," she said with a shrug, "you win some, you lose some, and that was not the most devastating discovery I've ever made about life."

They walked along in silence for several minutes after that, each digesting the story of the princess and searching to regain a comfortable distance that would allow them to continue the conversation.

"What did you think about that Mass today?" she asked after a while.

"The moral famine sermon?" he said. "I don't know. I didn't really think much about it, to be honest."

They walked a couple more steps together in silence.

"Too busy staring?" she finally asked. Her hands were tucked into her pockets, shoulders hunched together as much as she could without shrugging off the giant black bag. She looked directly ahead of herself, avoiding his eyes as she said it.

If it wasn't dark out, and if Grace had turned to look at Sean, she would have seen him go white. But he kept his eyes glued to the pavement ahead and didn't say anything for a couple of seconds.

"Staring?" he finally asked. "At what?"

"Oh, come on, Sean. The whole church saw you two staring. It was practically a love story during Mass today, the way you two were looking at each other. Do you know his name, anyway?"

"I wasn't staring," Sean said. "I don't know what you're talking about."

"Fine, play it that way." She pulled her hands out of her pockets and began to dig around in the bag again. "I know what I saw, and it was some definite staring." She fished out the pack of Marlboro Ultras and tapped one halfway out before grabbing it between her lips. "Even the priest noticed," she said out of the side of her mouth.

Sean slowed his pace to a halt. "You know, I think I have to go now," he said, turning back in the direction they had come from. "I really need to finish up with my work for tomorrow's class."

"Uh-huh." She lit the Marlboro and inhaled deeply. "Sean, you know who he is, don't you?"

"No," he said, "I don't."

"He's that author guy. He lives over in Back Bay or something, he's not even from here."

"How do you know that?" he asked.

"Everyone knows that. You would too if you pulled your head out of your books for a few minutes and socialized with any of us."

"I socialize."

"No, Sean, you don't."

He began to say something but she cut him off. "When was the last time you were down to Grumpy's? Huh?"

"I've been busy with the new school year."

"You were busy all summer. I run in to your sisters all the time, and they say you're barely home for Sunday dinner anymore. What's happening?"

"I'm working is all."

"And now you're sitting in Mass staring at queers?" The word hung between them, the air colder than it had been before. Sean stood still, mouth open, not saying anything. "Are you sure there's nothing you want to talk about?"

"He's gay?" Sean said. "How do you know that?"

"Jesus H. Christ, Sean. For someone who is supposed to be so freaking smart, sometimes you're an idiot. His name is Jamus Cork. Why don't you read one of his friggin' books?"

"I've really got to be getting back to the house," he said.

"Yeah, you do that, Sean." She stood where she was.

"I'll walk you back by your place?"

"No, I don't think so." In this light, her eyes hardened and her face took on a brittle quality that reminded him of a porcelain doll. "I'm going to walk out a bit farther."

"Okay, then." He swallowed hard. "See you."

"Yeah, see you, Sean."

He started to walk away and then turned back. "Grumpy's? This Friday?"

She stared at him and took another drag off her cigarette, then turned away from him and started to walk out toward the end of Castle Island. "Sure. See you then," she said. "The princess of Southie," she said under her breath as she walked away.

CHAPTER SEVENTEEN

Tuesday mornings could be the loudest part of the week, Jamus thought as he took a sip of his coffee and turned a page in the book he had been reading since six o'clock that morning.

The ceiling above his head thundered with heavy footsteps. Clang, something dropped. Thump, something else hit the floor. Thunk, thunk, thunk. Pipes. At least Jamus hoped it was only the pipes. An army could have been getting ready to mobilize from the second floor of the Corks' brownstone given the amount of noise coming from up there. But it was only a fourteen-year-old boy getting ready for school on a Tuesday morning.

Jamus got up from the table, still holding on to both the book and the coffee mug, and poked his head into the hall. "Hurry up, Nick, you're going to be late again," he yelled up the stairs at his brother. He wandered back toward the middle of the kitchen.

The smell of almost-burnt toast filled the kitchen and snapped Jamus out of his trance. He dropped the book onto the counter and reached down to open the toaster oven door before it was too late.

"Nick! Toast is ready," he shouted.

"Coming," came the first response of the day from upstairs.

"Now, Nick!"

Jamus pulled the toast out of the oven and onto a folded paper towel, slathering it with peanut butter. He drained his coffee and refilled it from the coffeepot, then grabbed a second cup out of the cupboard, filling it for Nick. In a quick swoop and twist, Jamus delivered the peanut butter toast and Nick's coffee onto the table just as Nick bounded down the stairs and rounded the corner into the kitchen.

"Ten minutes," Jamus said as he turned around again to grab his own coffee and sat across the table from Nick. "Book bag?" Jamus asked.

"It's at the bottom of the stairs."

"Homework?"

"In book bag."

"Don't forget your lunch, it's in the fridge."

"Uh-huh." Nick took a sip of the coffee and bit into the toast with a loud crunch. He pulled out his phone and started to text Matt.

"No phone at the table."

"What?"

"It's not a surprise. You know the rule—no phone at the table."

"But you're reading a book."

Jamus put the book down in front of him and looked at his younger brother. He smiled and sighed. "You're right. I'm sorry. Breaking my own rules first thing in the morning. What's ahead for you today?"

"Math, English, and Chemistry," Nick said.

"Sounds fun," said Jamus. "Any lunchroom drama?"

"No. Not yet anyway. Can I text Matt now?"

"What's so important you can't tell him when you see him in twenty minutes?"

Nick turned the phone off and shoved it in his pocket. "Nothing." He took another hulking bite of his peanut butter toast and glanced up at the clock behind the stove. "What's the book for?" he asked.

"For a project I'm working on with Eileen," Jamus said. "I want to do a story about the Big Dig, but she isn't so sure it has legs."

"The Big Dig?" Nick asked. "Isn't that what they used to call the tunnel?"

"Yes. When it was still just a construction project," he said. "I know you won't remember, but that entire highway used to be an elevated structure—a big six-lane bridge running right through the middle of the city."

"I remember the Expressway, Jamus," Nick said between bites of toast. "It's not like I'm a kid."

"Right," said Jamus, nodding solemnly. "Anyway, it destroyed entire neighborhoods and literally cut the city in half. I want to focus on how the tunnel idea got started and how the city has kind of healed itself since the bridge was torn down."

"Healing? How they started a highway? Sounds kind of boring." Nick slurped down another sip of his coffee.

"Yeah, the tunnel part of it's a little boring, but the amount of shit that went on behind the scenes to get it started was pretty amazing. They had to promise all kinds of things to make it happen. The original planners wanted to do something great for the city, but they knew if they were completely open about the cost, nobody would buy in."

"That's wrong," said Nick, finishing up his toast and swigging down the last bit of his coffee. "They should have been honest about it from the start. Lying to people about it isn't cool."

Jamus gave up. He could tell Nick had latched on to a particular part of the story, and his point of view wasn't going to change. "Yeah," he said. "You may be on to something there."

"Gotta go," Nick said, pushing back his chair and crumpling up the paper towel that his toast had sat on. He wiped the corners of his mouth with it.

"Dishwasher," Jamus said, pointing to Nick's empty coffee cup.

"Ugh. I'm gonna be late, Jamus."

"Should have thought of that when you were taking that ten-minute shower. Coffee cup in the dishwasher before you go."

Nick grabbed his cup and bounced over to the dishwasher in an exaggerated display of effort. He opened the dishwasher door up just far enough to shove the cup into the edge of the top tray, then gently closed the door, pushing the top rack of the dishwasher back in the same movement.

"Bye, bro, see you tonight," Nick said as he grabbed the paper bag with his lunch out of the refrigerator and loped out toward the hall.

"Bye, bro," Jamus called after him. "Love ya."

"Yeah, yeah, me, too," Nick said as he slammed the door.

Jamus picked up the book in front of him and started to read again. He would need to leave for Eileen's office in another half an hour if he wanted to be on time.

❖

"Yeah, but I don't get it, what does he do?" Matt was asking in between bites of barely identifiable cafeteria food. Not that the quality of the food had any effect on his ability to pile it away. He worked his way through the watery mashed potatoes, cold carrots, and something between a Salisbury steak and shoe leather as if it were a challenge.

"I don't know. He's a writer. He writes," said Nick, looking down at the table between them, quietly going through his lunch bag. Peanuts, sandwich, potato chips, apple. Nothing good.

"Yeah, but what does he write?" Matt asked.

"He wrote a bunch of books," said Nick. "And he writes for the *Boston Courier*. He's like a reporter or something, a columnist, I think is what he calls it."

"How come you live with him?" asked Robby.

Nick pretended to ignore the question. He'd never liked Robby very much, but somehow he always seemed to turn up at their table during lunch. He would sit on the sidelines, listening to a conversation until he picked up on something that made somebody uncomfortable. Then he would take center stage, homing in, driving in with a relentless string of questions in his singsong fake British accent until it drove whomever he was talking to insane, and they got up and left or broke down and answered his questions. The only thing Nick hated more than Robby sitting there was Robby talking.

Nick decided to turn the tables. "Why do you talk like that?" he asked.

"Like what?" Robby said.

"You know, with that fake accent? We all know you're a scholarship student from Worcester. Why do you pretend to have an English accent? You're not even doing it right."

"I'm not doing anything," he said, his face turning a deeper shade of reddish brown. "My parents are from Nigeria, and this is the way they talk."

"Yeah but you've been here your whole life, right? I mean you were born here, so what gives?" Nick continued to push. "You know you don't have to talk like that. My parents are from Ireland, but I don't talk like I'm from there."

"Yes, so back to your parents." Robby had found his way back off the hot seat. "How come you live with your brother instead of them?"

"Because his parents aren't around anymore, dickwad," Matt said.

"Did they die?" Robby asked, an excited lilt in his voice.

Nick's eyes blinked tight and hard. He hated it when people said that about his parents.

"No," Matt snarled. "They're on vacation in the North Pole. Why don't you shut up and quit being an asshole?"

Robby looked directly at Matt and shook his head "There's no need to get nasty about it, Matthew."

"Fuck off, Robby. Go find someplace else to sit before I kick your ass," Matt said, his face reddening in frustration.

"Have you read any of the books?" Robby asked, belligerent in the face of Matt's threats, even though Matt stood a good six inches taller.

"What books?" Matt asked.

"His brother's books." Robby nonchalantly attended to his slice of hot lunch pizza. "Have you read any of them?"

"No." Matt struggled for a comeback. "They're not on the reading list this year."

"It's no wonder why they're not," Robby said, a snide look crawling across his face. "Have you read them, Nick?"

Nick looked up slowly from his lunch bag. He wanted to grab the little fucker and punch him until his eyeballs fell out. "Yes," he lied. "I have."

"Then you know...?" Robby trailed off, Matt looking at him, curious at the question that hung in the air between the three boys. Nick stared at him, waiting for the right moment to rip into him. He couldn't really afford another fight. Jamus would kill him if he got a detention again. The last place he wanted to end up was in the principal's office with his brother.

"I know you better shut up," Nick said.

"Or what?" Robby said.

"Know what?" Matt asked. "What should we know?"

"Or I'll break your fucking face," said Nick.

"Fine," said Robby. "I'll shut up. Just tell me how your parents died."

"Car accident," Nick said through clenched teeth.

"What were they like?" Robby asked.

"I don't know." Nick could feel his face turning red now.

"You don't remember?" Robby asked.

"I don't know," Nick said. "It happened when I was three."

"What about the books?" Matt chimed in.

"And you've lived with him ever since?" Robby asked.

"Yes."

"Even though he's a fag? Did he ever..." Robby hesitated. "You know, try to—"

Whether or not Robby saw it coming, no one will ever know. One minute he was sitting at the lunch table, perched obnoxiously over his meal when Nick flew out of his chair, grabbed a fistful of Robby's sweater and plowed him out of his chair and straight onto the floor. The next thing anyone knew, Robby was laying on the ground with a plate full of pizza all over his brand new TJ Maxx sweater. Nick Cork was sitting on his chest with one hand raised and ready to go, but he couldn't quite do it, he couldn't bring himself to punch this scrawny little jerk.

"You got anything else to say?" Nick asked.

"Fuck you, faggot lover," Robby said, spitting up at Nick. A growing crowd of students circled the two of them. Nick could feel the heat of their eyes on him. A few peals of nervous laughter petered out into silence and, for a few seconds, Nick's world was focused in on Robby's face. He wanted to get up, to walk away and forget about this whole thing; forget he was perched on top of this mean little person; forget the entire cafeteria was now staring at him; forget he had lost his cool again, but most of all he wanted to forget the pain he felt in the pit of his stomach.

"It's not my fault you live with your queer brother because he killed your parents. He probably did that so he could have you all to himself. I bet—" He didn't know what Robby was going to say next, but it didn't matter. Robby only got partway through the second word before Nick snapped. Nick felt the soft crunch of bone and cartilage as his fist collided with Robby's nose.

Blood squirted everywhere, and Robby screamed. Nick felt the hot stain of tears streak down his own face as his anger continued to grow, fueled by Robby's screams and the stream of blood. Nick didn't want to be here. He wanted to be anywhere *but* here, but he wasn't through yet. He grabbed Robby by one ear and put a hand over his mouth. Nick could hear the commotion behind him now as chairs scraped the ground and the sound of running footsteps cut through the sound of voices. He knew he had only seconds before one of the lunch aides or teachers pulled him off Robby.

"You listen to me, you little bitch. Don't you ever, ever say another fucking word about my brother, or I'll fucking kill you."

Matt was at his back. "Come on, dude, get up. Nick, he's not worth it, dude, get up. Come on."

"Do you understand me, you little n—"

"Don't say it, Nick," Matt shouted, cutting him off.

Nick fumed as he looked down at Robby. "Am I clear?"

Robby looked up at him, eyes wide with rage, unable to control the hot, streaming tears. He nodded his head, and Nick stood up just in time to feel a rough hand on his shoulder.

"Come with me, Mr. Cork, I think we have some explaining to do on this one." It was Nick's English teacher, not one of the cafeteria aides. At least he had a chance. Mr. Malloy would be a lot easier to talk to than the principal.

CHAPTER EIGHTEEN

Eileen Mckenna's office was on the tenth floor of one of the taller brick and steel buildings that lined the north side of Copley Square. Her desk, a rococo oak monstrosity, looked out on an ancient limestone church and, beyond that, at the Hancock Building, a sleek glass skyscraper that towered over all of Boston's Back Bay. Jamus sat facing her, and a few moments into their conversation, he caught himself wondering just how thick the window glass was.

He loved her, but this morning, he was gritting his teeth trying to sit still. The meeting had gone all wrong from the first sentence. She had been looking for some sort of start to *The Rancher's Wife*. Instead, he had given her a couple of chapters on his Big Dig project. The result had been disastrous.

"Jamus, what did I tell you about this project?" she shouted, slamming a miniature balled-up fist on the oak desk with a surprisingly loud thump. "I told you to hold tight, didn't I?"

"Eileen, I don't want to hold tight on this book. This is what I want to write," he said.

But her mind was set the same as Nick's had been. It was as if she had called up his brother to discuss the idea right after breakfast. She had said the same things as he had. Why couldn't anyone see the point to his Big Dig story? "It's a story about the renewal of civic pride and public trust in this city."

"No, Jamus, it's not," she fumed. "It's no good without a relevant angle for today. If the politicians of the sixties and seventies planned this giant highway tunnel project, then swindled the public into paying for it, well that's too bad. But a story about it would just make everyone—

and by that I mean anyone who would read it—angry about something they could no longer do anything about except enjoy."

He knew he'd lost the argument thirty seconds into the discussion. The Big Dig story was off the table, and the meeting was over. "Fine," he said, collecting the papers from her desk. "I'll work on *The Rancher's Wife.*"

"Thank you," she said, smiling quietly up at him. "I look forward to seeing something next time we meet." She looked down at her calendar, summarily dismissing him.

Jamus stepped out of the building onto Boylston Street and immediately reached for a cigarette. The wind raced around the side of the square and buffeted his whole body, pushing him back toward the entrance of the building as he tried to light up. The feel of the wind against his face, the same as it had been that night all those years ago on Long Island brought the edges of the nightmare back to him again. He clenched and relaxed his right hand, squeezing the lighter tightly.

It was the same story he kept rewriting with every book, and now she wanted him to do it again. He would never get away from it, not as long as he lived. He forced himself to focus on the street, the sidewalk, the buildings in front of him, the cigarette in his hand—anything to keep his mind from delving into that part of his past.

He fiddled with the lighter, turning his back to the wind and gently flicking it a couple of times before it finally caught. He brought the cigarette to his mouth and inhaled deeply, coaxing the tiny red ember to life. The ember was good to focus on. It kept him here, or rather it kept his mind here. He glanced at his watch and took a deep breath before sliding the lighter back into his jacket pocket. He had thirty minutes to get downtown for his next meeting. Jamus weighed the option of taking the T or jumping in a cab. Normally he would walk, but it had dropped into the low forties, and his fingers began to ache from the cold.

He shrugged after a couple of seconds and decided to brave the walk instead, heading off in the direction of the Boston Commons when he felt the buzzing of his cell phone in his pocket. He pulled it out and frowned as he looked at the incoming number. Hayfield Academy. He clicked the accept button on his phone. "Jamus Cork."

"Mr. Cork, this is Sean Malloy, Nick's English teacher at Hayfield."

"Yes?"

"Mr. Cork, could you come in to the school? There has been an incident we would like to talk to you about."

"What happened?" Jamus suddenly dropped the cigarette. "Is Nick all right?"

"Yes, Nick's fine. Everyone is fine. But we need to discuss a matter of discipline."

"Yes, of course," Jamus said. "I'll be right over." His downtown meeting would just have to wait. Tuesday was starting to throw him for a little bit of a loop.

Jamus had been to Hayfield Academy before, but he'd only met with the principal and a few of the teachers during the interview and application process for Nick's admission. He'd also met with the guidance counselor after one of Nick's fights. But he hadn't met with this Mr. Malloy. A cold wind blew off the Charles River, softer here than it had been in the city but colder, with clouds hanging low behind the school. As Jamus trudged up the front steps, he felt the pit in his stomach getting a little deeper with each stride. He opened the heavy doors and slowly made his way to the office to sign in.

The halls were empty, and when he reached the main office, he saw Malloy standing in front of a bulletin board with various student-made flyers about club meetings and sports. Jamus blinked and looked twice. The recognition wasn't hazy or distant. It was immediate and lightening clear. It was Malloy from church. The very same Malloy who sat a few rows in front of him each week with his sisters and mother. The same Malloy whom he had unwittingly locked eyes with and stared down through the moral famine sermon a few weeks back. Jamus locked eyes again with him in front of the principal's office at Hayfield and watched as his pale skin blushed a deep shade of reddish purple.

"Um, Mr. Cork?" Malloy had stuck his hand out as Jamus approached.

"Yes." Jamus felt his own cheeks burning. "Mr. Malloy?"

"Yes," said Sean.

"Do I know you from Sacred Heart?" Jamus asked.

"Um, yes," Sean said, blushing even deeper. "I think so. My family goes there."

"Ah." Jamus nodded, getting the message this was not what Malloy wanted to discuss. "I thought so."

Neither man spoke for an awkward few seconds, each shifting his weight from one leg to another in an almost identical pattern. "Anyway," Sean said, waving a hand apologetically toward the floor. "Sorry to have to ask you to come in today."

"Not at all, what's going on with Nick?"

"Could we head up to my classroom to talk?" Sean said, nodding toward the opposite end of the hall.

"Um, sure." Jamus looked around him, unsure of where to go.

"This way," Sean said, taking a step and leading the way down the corridor to a staircase.

Lockers lined the way and the hardwood floor creaked, announcing their march up to Mr. Malloy's room. The smell of something like lemon and wax enveloped them as they moved down the hall and up the stairs. Everything seemed peaceful and strangely quiet. Jamus looked at his watch to check the time. It was only two o'clock, just a hair too early for school to be out for the day. "Where is everyone?" he asked.

"Lacrosse game at home today. Everyone was excused early to go to the game."

"Ah," Jamus said as they came to the top of the stairs and headed down the hall, taking a right at the first door. "I guess they don't do that for cross-country meets."

Mr. Malloy's room was a giant, airy space, lined on one side with windows facing the front of the building, which meant they overlooked the Charles River at a distance. Jamus surveyed the room. "Nice view."

"Yes, we're lucky," said Malloy. "It's a good environment for learning."

Jamus shrugged, but declined to take the small talk any further. He was here for a reason, and the sooner he found out what that was, the better. "Mr. Malloy, what's going on with Nick?"

"Call me Sean, please." Malloy took a deep breath and sat down on the edge of his desk, facing Jamus. "Nick got in a pretty serious fight today."

"What does pretty serious mean?" Jamus sat down in one of the student desks.

"He started the physical fight, but we have reason to believe he was provoked. But the bigger issue is that he used some language we cannot condone here."

Jamus noticed Malloy's hands as he spoke. He held them out in front of him as if he expected Jamus to lunge toward him. They were not what he would have expected from a teacher. They weren't smooth and soft, they were rough and slightly calloused. The left index finger was crooked and swollen at the knuckle. They were very practical hands, Jamus thought, with very practical fingers and no ring.

"Language?"

Malloy recounted the story of the cafeteria fight earlier in the day. Jamus squirmed in his seat as he listened to the details of Nick pulling Robby up by the collar and the sequence of events leading up to the bloody nose.

"So let me get this straight," Jamus finally spoke. "He actually said the N-word?"

"Well, it depends on who you ask. His friend, Matt Spence, claimed he did not, but Robby, the kid he punched, claims he did. Like I said, I have reason to believe he was provoked by Robby. That kid has a way of going after his classmates that runs just under the radar of adult supervision."

"Robby?" Jamus asked.

"The kid that Nick hit."

"Right, sorry," said Jamus.

"Mr. Cork…" Malloy paused for a minute. "Is everything all right at home?"

"Yes," Jamus said, leaning forward onto the desk, the creak of the wood groaning against his full weight. "I know he's had a little trouble keeping up with some of his studies lately, but I have been helping him with that. I figured it was just tougher courses as a freshman. I…" He paused, shaking his head and staring at the chalk board behind Malloy, suddenly unable to look at him without remembering the moment in church a few weeks back. "I don't know why he would use that word."

"Is his mother in the picture?" Malloy asked. "Would it be worth talking to her about this?"

The muscles around Jamus's mouth tightened, and he shifted his gaze from the chalkboard to Sean Malloy's eyes. He realized how little Malloy must know about their family. He felt a vacant pressure behind his forehead, and he focused on staying in the present conversation even though he wanted to let his mind drift. "Our mother," Jamus said, slowing his speech down so that Sean would not miss a syllable, "passed away when Nick was three, as did our father."

Sean was silent.

"It has been tough sometimes." Jamus felt the ebb of the memory. That night was waiting just below the surface of his mind to reach up and flood him out again. He focused on the desk in front of him, clinging to it to help him stay in the present. "It's been tough for Nick not to know his ma and dad sometimes." He stopped for a moment, forcing the words out. "It's been tough for me sometimes, too, but there hasn't been anything recently that has changed at home or in our family."

The two men sat facing each other for a few seconds, neither one speaking or even shifting in his seat. An uneasy energy in the room slowly settled into something that felt like understanding. It was Sean's turn to look away, seemingly unable to meet the eyes of the appointed parent in front of him.

"I didn't know," he finally said. "I'm sorry."

"Don't be sorry," Jamus shot back at him. "We are a strong family, and he's a normal kid. I'll talk to him about that word."

"And the fights," added Sean.

"Of course, the fights." Jamus turned to look out the windows. The clouds in the autumn sky had started to clear just a little, and a few rays of sun pushed through, turning patches of the gray river to blue. In the distance the traffic had slowed, and he could hear the voices of a crew team through the closed glass, calling out a steady cadence as the slim boat moved down the river toward the mouth of the Charles. "Will he have detention or something for this?"

"An extra assignment, actually," Sean said. "I've asked him to read a biography of Martin Luther King Junior and do a report on it."

"When is it due?" Jamus asked. "I'll make sure he has it in on time."

Chapter Nineteen

You can't call people by that word," Jamus said. "Why would you think you could use that word?" He drew a cigarette out of the pack in front of him. They were sitting at the kitchen table in the Dartmouth Street house.

"He called you a—"

"I don't care what he called me." Jamus lit the cigarette.

"But," Nick said.

"But nothing," Jamus said. He let out a deep breath of smoke. "Nicky, what's going on?"

Nick glared at his brother. "Nothing's going on. He was just disrespecting my family. He was talking about Mom and Dad."

"That's the third fight this year." Jamus let out a stream of smoke.

"He read your fucking books," Nick said.

"What books?"

"The books you wrote," Nick said.

"Which ones?" Jamus asked.

"What the fuck! I don't know. All of them."

"Hey, watch the mouth, Nick, I'm not sitting here swearing at you. Could you clean it up a little?"

Nick rolled his eyes and looked away from his brother.

Jamus tried to overlook the eye roll and instead took a deep drag off the Lucky. "Six books is a lot of reading for a fourteen-year-old."

Nick continued staring at the wall, tapping a toe against the floor. Finally, he looked back at his brother. "Jamus, can I ask you something?"

Jamus ashed his cigarette in the ashtray on the table. "You know you can."

"Did Mom and Dad know you were gay?"

Jamus crushed out the cigarette. "Oh, come on, Nick." Jamus sat back and crossed his left leg over his right. "What does that matter?"

"I want to know. Would they have cared?" he asked.

"I don't know," he said, the words slowing down as he spoke. "I never told them. I was going to, but I never had the chance."

"What the fuck? Why?" Nick's face darkened. "How come you never told them? That seems like a pretty big deal."

"I never had the chance to," Jamus practically shouted across the empty kitchen. Nick winced. "Nick, what is this about? You've known this for years. We've had this talk half a dozen times. You know who I am, and it's not going to change. It doesn't make me a bad person, just a little different. And it doesn't affect you."

"It does when that's what started the fight." A flash of anger arced across Nick's face, his nose flaring dramatically. "They're never going to stop, you know."

"Stop what?" Jamus asked.

"They'll never stop making fun of me because of it. Because you're, you know…"

"How do they know anything about the fact that I'm gay—which, by the way, I am not ashamed of?"

"Well, it's kind of obvious," Nick said his voice rising steadily. "You always show up to things alone, we live in the gayborhood and you're, you know…"

"No, I guess I don't know." Jamus crushed out the cigarette. "What am I, Nick?"

"Well, you're too…I don't know how to say it. You *dress* gay."

"You got in a fight today because I'm too stylish?" Jamus pulled another cigarette out of the pack and lit it. "Is that what you're telling me?"

"No, I'm telling you that this asshole Robby asked me what it was like when my parents died, and if you ever tried anything on me because you're gay."

Jamus dropped the lighter. "He said what?"

Nick recounted the story of the fight and the conversation leading up to it word for word, as Jamus listened without moving a muscle. When he was done, Jamus reached over and brushed a greasy lock of hair out of his brother's eyes. "You can't ever use the N-word, Nick.

There is too much hate behind that word, and it's not okay to perpetuate that hate." Jamus hesitated for a few seconds. "But look, Nick, honestly, I don't blame you for losing your cool. He sounds like a little shit."

"Duh," Nick said. "That's what I've been saying, but thanks for the verification. I needed that."

"Verification?" Jamus raised an eyebrow. "That's not one of your words."

"I learned it in school." Nick reached over for the pack of cigarettes.

"Ah." Jamus drummed his fingers on the table a few times. "Don't you think you've had enough of those for one day?"

"No, I don't," Nick said.

"Mr. Malloy said you're going to have to do an extra report on Martin Luther King Junior," Jamus said after a few minutes. The energy in the room had changed, and the tension had started to dissolve.

Nick nodded. "He gave me a biography of MLK Junior to read, and I need to write a paper about his life. As if I don't already have enough homework to do." Nick looked down at the table. "Are you going to ground me or something?"

Jamus shook his head slowly. "No, I don't think I can ground you for that," he said.

A look of relief spread across Nick's face. "Jamus, can I ask you another question?"

Jamus narrowed his eyes, shooting his brother a look of suspicion. "What?"

"Well, are you ever going to have a—you know—boyfriend or whatever?"

Jamus shook his head and tried, unsuccessfully, not to turn red. "I don't know," he said after a few minutes. "I guess I really hadn't thought much about it. At least not lately."

"How come?"

"Don't know." Jamus crushed the remainder of his half-finished cigarette in the ashtray.

"Is it because of me?" Nick asked.

"Is it what?" Jamus said.

"Is it because of me?" Nick repeated. "Am I the reason you don't have a boyfriend? Are you afraid it would be a bad influence or something?"

"Don't be crazy," Jamus said. "The only reason I don't have a boyfriend is because I haven't met anyone I like."

"In ten years?" Nick's voice raised an octave in disbelief.

Jamus shrugged. "Yeah, more or less."

"Ten years? Are you gay or a priest?" Nick lowered the tone of his voice, thrusting his hands out in front of him, palms up in disbelief. Jamus chuckled at the Delsarte gesture. Nick had been doing it since he was a toddler, and it reminded him of the little boy that his brother used to be.

"Interesting question," Jamus said.

"Shut up." Nick lowered his hands. "You know what I mean."

"Well, what about you?" Jamus asked.

"What about me?"

"Do you have a girlfriend yet?" Jamus asked.

"No." Nick wrinkled his nose and turned his head slightly away, just a hint of red rising in his cheeks.

"Why not?"

"I don't want a girlfriend," Nick said.

"Okay, fine," Jamus said. "Then you know how I feel. I don't want a boyfriend."

They were at an impasse, and Jamus watched as Nick's face narrowed in concentration. "What if you meet someone?" he finally asked.

"Good question," Jamus said. "How would you feel about that?"

Nick shrugged and finally pulled a cigarette out of the package. He grabbed the lighter off the table and lit it. "I think it'd be cool."

"You do?" Jamus asked.

"Yeah, I do," Nick said. "I think it'd be cool to have another guy around the house. Then maybe we could get a real TV."

"Fair enough," Jamus said. "I've got a deal for you."

"A deal?" Nick asked.

"Yeah, a deal," Jamus repeated. "You get all As and no more fights, and I'll think about getting a big TV come June."

"What do you mean 'think' about it?"

"I mean you get all As and no more fights, you'll get to see what I mean."

"What about a boyfriend?" Nick asked.

"You can have a boyfriend if you want."

"No. I mean for you."

"That's not part of the deal."

"Fine," Nick said.

"No more fights?" Jamus looked directly into his brother's eyes, trying to make sure that Nick understood the gravity of the situation.

"No more fights," Nick said.

"All As?"

"What about mostly As?" Nick asked.

"Define mostly," Jamus said.

"Two Bs?" Nick asked.

"Two Bs tops," said Jamus.

"Deal." Nick smiled. "Finally, a real TV."

❖

Later that night, Nick lay awake in his bed thinking about the day's events, and wondering how he was ever going to get all As and Bs this semester, given that it was almost halfway through the term. As he played over the conversation in the cafeteria, one thing kept bugging him—Robby's reference to Jamus's books. He'd never read any of them. Not one. And Jamus never kept any of them in the house. He'd never thought about it before, but now that he did, it seemed strange.

CHAPTER TWENTY

Grumpy's Pub was one of those bars that people talk about when they tell stories about the places they come from. The bar reflected the complexion of the neighborhood, which meant it was a place for construction workers and bus drivers, the guys who worked at Boston Edison down the street, and store clerks and grocers who worked in the small shops along Broadway, and sometimes, like tonight, a schoolteacher.

A long oak bar ran the length of the single room. Behind it were a couple of tap handles and a shelf full of liquor, mostly whiskey. On the other side of the room from the bar was a line of booths, each with a perpetually sticky tabletop despite the best efforts of Flynn the bartender to keep them wiped down, and a line of windows looking out onto the street.

The windows were a mixed blessing. It gave Grumpy's less of a cave-like feeling, but it also meant that you could almost always be seen from the street. Anyone passing by would know where you were. So Grumpy's was where you went if you wanted to be witnessed; if you wanted the world to know that you weren't lost somewhere or stuck at home in the kitchen.

Sean was early that night, as always. He sat at the end of the bar in Grumpy's sipping a pint of Newcastle, captivated by the open book in front of him. This time it wasn't one of the books on the current reading list for Hayfield Academy. It was a different book, a new one he'd picked up after his last conversation with Grace about the strange author who attended their church, the same person that turned up at the parent-teacher meeting this week to discuss Nick Cork's most recent fight. The book, *Angel of New York*, made his stomach just a little queasy. He kept looking up every time Flynn moved closer or he heard the door open behind him. He was expecting Grace, but he knew she wouldn't show up for at least another half an hour.

> *They kept moving, all of them, bodies writhing together to a rhythm so primal, so intense that they barely felt the floor beneath their feet. Angel watched from the corner of the room, a bottle of water in one hand. He stared, silent as stone, a bored cigarette in his other hand, the ash so long it was just about to fall off. The dancers continued, edging closer and closer to something they could feel just beyond the horizon of consciousness. They chased it together, a pack of wild, half-naked dogs after something they would never quite catch but nonetheless were driven beyond the deepest urge to pursue.*
>
> *Then it started, at first like nothing more than a mist. It seemed to Angel someone might have spat on him or sprayed their drink out. But after a few seconds, he realized that it was the club. It was coming from the ceiling of the club. The dancers realized it around the same time as he did. It was snowing—little glittering flakes of synthetic snow floated down from the strobe lit sky of the club. The dancers went insane as the snow came down and the music sped up, blending into another song with a faster beat. They moved together, together as one, writhing in syncopated, artificial ecstasy.*

The dim light coming from the low-watt bulbs above his head and the two televisions behind the bar gave him enough light to see the page, but only barely. His eyes were starting to hurt. He rubbed the bridge of his nose and looked back down at the book. It was only a moment before Sean had gotten lost in the words again, so absorbed that he didn't notice when someone came in and sat next to him. Grace leaned into the bar and dragged her giant black bag up on it. The sound of the bag was what roused Sean out of his book. He looked up quickly, startled in the way that airplane passengers and students are surprised to find that they've dozed off for a short period of time during takeoff or lectures.

"Grace," he said, quickly folding the book closed and putting it back in his coat pocket.

"Surprised?" she asked, reaching into her bag and pulling out a tube of ChapStick.

"No, no," he said. "I just lost track of time."

"Still into *A Separate Peace*?" she asked, gesturing toward the book that he had slipped away.

"Um, yes, that's right," he lied. "We have the first test on it next week."

"You sound like you're still a student yourself."

"In a way, I guess I am," he said, taking a sip of the now lukewarm Newcastle. "I feel like I'm still learning how to teach."

"Isn't that what your college was for?"

"College is crap," he said, and she burst out laughing.

"College is crap?" she repeated. "The great Sean Malloy, professor of Southie, has spoken and college is crap? Well, I'm glad I didn't waste my time then."

He smiled at her and didn't say anything. It was better to leave it alone before it turned into a bigger discussion on college. He couldn't take another conversation like the one at the dinner table last week. "What'd you do today?" he asked instead.

"Well, let's see," she said, slipping the ChapStick back into her bag. "This morning I made several very important phone calls. Mostly setting up appointments for clients to come in and tell us how badly they've been injured by whiplash or something equally gruesome." She smiled and nodded slowly to him as if he was a small child. He nodded back. "Want to hear more?" she asked.

"Yeah, actually I do," Sean said. "I don't really know anything about what you do."

"Well, I'm officially an 'office manager' for the Law Offices of McCarthy and Tell," she said. "But really I'm a secretary. I answer the phone a lot, I get the mail, I file, I do payroll, which means cutting everyone's paychecks and doing their insurance."

"I know what payroll means." He smiled.

"Ease up." She poked him in the arm. "I didn't want to assume anything. I don't know much about what you do, Mr. Teacher."

"I teach," he said, draining his beer. "That's about it. It hasn't changed much since you and I were sitting in the classroom."

"Do you like it?" she asked.

"I try to." He rolled his eyes. "But some days it's hard."

"What do you love about it?"

Sean paused for a moment, signaling to the bartender that he would take another Newcastle and pointing to Grace. "Guinness?" he asked. She nodded, and he ordered her one.

"What do I like about teaching?" He rubbed his chin and tilted his head in his best mock-professor. "I guess I like the energy in the room," he said.

"The energy?" she repeated. "How very new age of you."

"Nah, not like that," he said. "I like that eighteen to twenty-five young people are sitting there actively learning from me each period of the day. Yeah, there's always somebody goofing off and throwing wads of paper or passing notes, but mostly they're watching and listening and just absorbing information from me. I know it sounds corny, but—"

"No." She cut him off. "It doesn't sound corny at all. It sounds wonderful, actually. It sounds amazing when you say it like that."

"It does?"

"Yeah, it does," she said. "It never felt like that for me when I was in a classroom. It was always this huge pressure cooker. I had to know all these facts and figures, and I never felt like I did. At the same time, I felt like there was this constant message pounded into me that I had to fit this mold, that I had to learn, or I would somehow get left behind in the giant race of adulthood just around the corner."

The bartender had slipped in and delivered their drinks while they were talking. The two glasses now sat in front of them, and Sean was grateful for something new to focus on. He reached out and put his hand around the cold pint glass of Newcastle, grasping and releasing it a few times before he spoke again. "Why did you ask me that thing the other night on the beach?" he asked, finally picking up the beer and taking a long sip.

"Ask you what?" she said, tapping her index finger softly on the side of her pint glass and looking just slightly away from him.

"You asked me if I thought something was wrong with you?" Sean turned his stool so he could look straight at her, searching her eyes for any remnants of the emotion she had shown during that conversation. "Why do you care what I think?"

She hesitated a moment and finally let out a sigh. "Isn't that what it's all about?" she said, facing Sean directly.

"What what's all about?"

"What life's all about." Her face went a slight shade of pink as she spoke. "Doesn't it all boil down to what everyone else thinks about you? Really?"

"I don't think so," he said. "I think life is about whatever you want it to be about."

"Really? What about when life doesn't turn out to be what you want it to be about?"

"I guess it depends on how you look at it," Sean said. "I know I've got a lot of things in my life I need to straighten out—hell, I'm twenty-six years old, and I still live at home with my brother and my parents. I could focus on what a loser that makes me, or I can focus on how I'm trying to change lives every day."

"What about when you don't even have that?" She twisted a little bit in her seat, and she briefly looked at her bag on the bar, as if she wanted a cigarette. "What about when you go to work every day and file things, and you know that is probably the best job you're ever going to get? And you go home to the same house you've always lived in, and you know you won't ever live anywhere else until you get married—if you even ever get married. And the most adventurous thing you've ever done is go to the Cape for a week after high school? What is life about then, Sean?"

Sean said nothing.

"What then? Huh, Sean?" She continued. "You don't get it. You can get out of here. You've got a good job and an education."

She looked away from him. Flynn the bartender stood a few feet from them wiping the bar down. She lifted her finger at him. "Flynn, honey," she said, "can I have a whiskey, please? Neat." The bartender moved silently to pour her drink.

Sean finally spoke. "I'm not going anywhere, Grace. You should see my student loan bills." He put his hand on her shoulder. "I'm here for a while, Grace."

"Oh, well," she said, looking up at him. "Everyone likes a pity party, right? God, listen to me, huh? You'd think I had it bad the way I'm talking. I'm just stuck, but it sucks trying to figure out what it all means. What do you do when you're stuck in a rut?"

"You go to Grumpy's and you have a drink, and you figure out some way to change things," he said.

"Uh-huh?" she said. The whiskey arrived, Flynn making no noise at all sliding it in front of her. "Okay then." She lifted her glass, and Sean raised his beer to meet it. "Here is to life being about whatever the hell you want it to be about."

"I'll drink to that," he said, and they clinked glasses.

CHAPTER TWENTY-ONE

K evin Malloy sat on the kitchen counter finishing the last of his cup of coffee and reading the Sunday comics section of the *Boston Courier*, when Sean trudged around the corner into the kitchen.

"Was that a date?" Kevin hopped off the counter as Sean walked in.

"Was what a date?" Sean snapped, turning his back to his brother as he ducked into the Kelvinator.

"Uh, you know what I'm talking about, Seany. In fact, most of Southie knows what I'm talking about."

"Christ, I hate Grumpy's." Sean pulled a container of strawberry yogurt out of the fridge and peeled the aluminum foil lid off it. "It was just a friggin' drink, Kevin. Nothing more than that. Jesus." Sean spotted the empty coffeemaker on the counter. "Would it have killed you to leave me a cup?"

"Chill, bro." Kevin pulled down the coffee and the filters from the cabinet behind him. "I'll make more. But don't think you can get me off track that easily. What happened on the date?"

"It wasn't a date."

"Grace thinks it was." Kevin busied himself with taking out the old coffee grinds and placing a fresh filter into the Mr. Coffee.

"What? How would you even know what Grace thinks? You haven't been to Grumpy's in months." Sean reached into the drawer and pulled out a spoon, then made his way to the kitchen table and sat down.

"Because, Sherlock, the first thing she did this morning was text her best friend Aideen. And Aideen texted me and Siobhan."

"What?" Sean said. "Do you think my life is some sort of reality show? Why can't you guys just lay off the twenty-four-hour surveillance thing?"

"Ha, that's funny. Who are you kidding? Besides, we're just looking after you, Seany. Anyway, Aideen said Grace told her the date was great. You guys talked for hours, and you really opened up to her. She said you were also really interested in her work, and you're a great listener. She said she always wondered why you were so quiet, but now she figures it's because you're so good at letting other people talk. She said she felt like she was the only person in the room with you."

"Oh, God." Sean put his head into his hands, dropping his yogurt spoon onto the table in the process. "Oh, God, she thinks that was a date. Shit."

"What are you sweating, man? You should be happy."

"I'm not interested in her, Kevin."

"Look, Sean, bro, I know you think she's a townie, but she's not. She's got class. A lot of girls we grew up with, they let themselves go, but Grace, she's got it going on. She takes care of herself, she doesn't have a trashy mouth, she's okay, Sean."

"I don't think she's a fucking townie, Kevin."

"Then what's the problem with her?"

Sean reached down and picked up his spoon. A streak of strawberry yogurt had slopped on the table in front of him and he rubbed at it with his finger, trying to pick it up but instead just spreading it around. He was quiet for a few minutes, maybe a few minutes too long because when he didn't say anything, Kevin repeated his question. "What's wrong with her, Sean?"

He shook his head silently, staring down at the tablecloth. Finally he managed a single phrase: "It's not her."

"Well of course it's her," Kevin said. "It's not you. You're a Malloy. You're perfect, bro." He punched Sean playfully in the arm, then as if realizing something for the first time, he stepped back and put a hand on his forehead. "Oh, hey. Hey, are you worried that I'm still into her? Because I'm not. I'm totally cool with this. She's obviously into you, and I think that's great."

"I'm not feeling so good," Sean said, pushing back from the table. "I think I'm going to just go back up to bed."

"Hey, what about your coffee?" Kevin said, but Sean was already gone. "Hey, I just made a whole pot of fresh coffee, what the hell?" he yelled up the stairs.

Chapter Twenty-two

The run-in with Nick turned out to be just what Robby needed to escape his position in the lower social ranks of the freshman class at Hayfield. His revelation of Nick's brother as not only gay, but a scandalous gay author had catapulted him from low-life frosh to the top of the social strata in a matter of days. The black eye Nick had given him didn't hurt his cause either.

Swarms of girls now hung around his locker between classes, more girls offering to help him out to his next class than he had ever spoken to before in his life. He had no need to sit with Matt and Nick again at lunch, not that he would have wanted to. His instant status made him a welcome fixture at several of the more popular lunch tables.

To make matters even worse, a few of the kids at Hayfield had asked if they could borrow Robby's copy of Jamus's book, *Angel of New York*. In less than a week, it seemed a copy of the book was tucked neatly into every backpack and handbag on the campus.

Nick's fortunes ran the opposite direction of Robby's at school. Nick didn't have a lot of friends before the incident, but afterward people went out of their way not to talk to him. In every class he had, kids slid their desks away from his and turned the other way when he sat down. The worst part was that his teachers pretended not to notice when kids poked, jabbed, and threw crumpled-up balls of paper at the back of Nick's head. Matt was a solid ally and sat next to him through it all, but they only had three classes together.

The one class that was an exception was English. Nick's English teacher, Mr. Malloy, wouldn't tolerate the kids behind Nick and Matt scooting their chairs back and snickering.

"Gentlemen," he said to the offending students, "please move your chairs back to their original position. If you have a problem with the arrangement of the furniture in this room then I am happy to discuss it with you after school at detention. And by 'discuss,' I mean that you will be copying word-for-word from one of my favorite volumes on social justice. Any questions?"

The kids behind them immediately moved their chairs back and Matt grinned ear to ear, turning around to give them a gloating glance. But when he looked over at Nick, Matt saw he wasn't smiling with him.

"Did you have anything to add, Mr. Spence?" Malloy addressed Matt directly.

"No sir," Matt said, looking back at Nick and then down at the notebook on his desk.

"Okay, good. Then let's get back to twentieth-century literature."

"I have a question about twentieth-century literature," said Anara Kenn, the girl that Nick had clashed with over *A Separate Peace* a few weeks back. Nick could sense that something was coming, just from the tone in her fragile-yet-super-annoying voice.

"Yes?" Mr. Malloy asked.

"Since we just finished *A Separate Peace*, and we haven't started reading anything else yet, I was wondering if maybe we could read this book as a class?" Nick turned around along with the rest of the class to see her holding up a brand-new copy of *Angel of New York*. The rest of the class, in on the joke for the past week, erupted in a fit of giggles. But Anara kept a straight face.

Mr. Malloy stared across the room at the book. "Anara, why don't you bring that up here?" he asked.

"Okay," she said, getting up from her chair and marching to the front of the room, smiling and acutely wrinkling her nose at Nick as she returned to her seat.

"Hmm." Mr. Malloy read the back cover of the book. "Do your parents know you're reading this?"

"No." She hesitated.

"Really?" Mr. Malloy smiled at her. "I think I'll keep this copy and send them a quick email letting them know you suggested it."

"Um…" Anara's smile was gone, and she seemed to be at a rare loss for words. "That's my only copy, Mr. Malloy."

"I'm sure your parents won't mind me keeping it for a little bit. At least until I've let them know you suggested it for the class reading."

She stared at him.

"Unless, of course, this is just some kind of joke to try and ostracize one of your classmates?" Mr. Malloy now stepped out from behind his desk and strode up to hers with the book in his hand. "I'm sure you wouldn't be doing that. I'm sure your parents wouldn't approve of that kind of thing. You wouldn't lower yourself to 'group think'—I think that's what you called it when we were discussing *A Separate Peace*, right? You wouldn't just be suggesting we read this novel for some trite reason like that?" He was standing right above her desk now, tapping the book in one hand.

"No sir" was the response.

"Good. I'm glad. Because that would be shallow and cheap and you'd immediately lose my respect." He shifted his gaze from Anara to the rest of the class.

Nick kept his head bowed deeply, staring at his hands. Matt had his mouth open, his eyes darting back and forth between Mr. Malloy and the look on Anara's face. A couple of kids in the room shoved their own copies of the book under notebooks or back into handbags.

"All the same," Mr. Malloy said, "I think I'll keep this copy."

The bell rang somewhere in the deadened silence of the room, and Mr. Malloy stood still as eighteen pairs of sneakers rushed out of his classroom in a stampede of adolescent drama. Nick and Matt were among the fast-moving group, neither speaking again until they reached their lockers.

As he approached his locker, Nick could see something was wrong. Thursday just wouldn't end. As he got closer, the word came into focus. Across the front of Nick's locker, someone had written in permanent marker "Faggot." Nick stood in front of the locker with his books in one hand and just stared at it.

"Come on, dude," Matt said, when he saw it. "Let's get out of here."

"Hold on. I've got to put my books away," was all that Nick could say. He walked up to the locker and ran his hand along the fresh ink. It was shiny and smooth, and Nick almost expected it to bleed onto his fingers when he touched it. He could hear the snickers and giggles of the other students behind him as they walked along in whispered footsteps.

"Hey," Matt said. "Don't let it get to you. They're just being assholes. It will blow over."

"Yeah," said Nick, remembering the conversation they'd had over the summer. "I guess you were right."

"Huh?" Matt cocked his head to one side. "About what?"

"We are pariahs."

Matt just shook his head. There was nothing left to say. As the two of them walked down the hallway and out the door for the day, all Nick could think about was how much he hated Robby and now Anara. Matt nudged him in the arm as they walked.

"Let it go," he said. "Don't let them have your day. Don't let them take it away from you. You'll never get it back."

Nick wasn't ready to let it go, but he smiled and shrugged. "You're right. Fuck them," he said.

CHAPTER TWENTY-THREE

Nick shrugged his backpack off as he entered the store. The smell of dust and old paper surrounded him. It was a little damp, but at least it wasn't sauna-level warm. Most of the other bookshops he had been to this morning were newer ones—Wordsworth, then Tower Books. They had those gigantic blowers right in front of the door, a hurricane of puke-inducing hot air that made Nick instantly uncomfortable in his jacket. It was early for a full-on winter coat, but Nick didn't want to take the risk of being cold. October in Boston could be unpredictable.

He also liked that no one made him check his bag at this place. The old guy behind the counter just nodded hello to him as he wiped his feet on the big gray mat in front of the door. Nick gestured to his bag, as if to ask if he should check it, but the guy just waved him in.

"Anything I can help you find?" he asked as Nick walked by.

"No," Nick said, trying to remain light and breezy. "Just looking."

Nick had been through this routine in four other bookstores so far this morning. He wasn't interested in anything except finding one of his brother's books. You would think he could have picked them up anywhere. It would have made sense for Jamus to keep a couple of copies around the house, but he didn't. Jamus was a vault when it came to his writing.

Nick had known a handful of Jamus's friends who'd asked about his writing over the years, but he wouldn't talk about his books with anyone, not even Nick. He would talk for days about the stuff he wrote for the newspaper, but when it came to his fiction, he shut everything down as quickly as a question could be asked.

But for all his silence on the subject of his writing, Jamus had been a fantastic storyteller. When Nick was little, Jamus would make up stories about fishing villages in Alaska or Zulu warriors in South Africa as Nick drifted off to sleep. Or he would weave together the bits and pieces of old Irish fairy tales with everyday things they ran into on the streets of their neighborhood. Nick was convinced at one point when he was six that a magic lake lay underneath the willow tree in the park down the street, but it disappeared the moment anyone set eyes on it.

Nick knew he and Jamus had a few relatives back in Ireland, but he had no memory of them. He'd heard that an aunt and uncle had come over for his parents' funeral, but he was three years old at the time. For the most part, Jamus and Nick were their own family. And so the characters of Jamus's stories had often filled that role of familiar acquaintances during dinner conversations and over the walks the brothers sometimes took around the Boston Public Garden or along the Charles in the warmer months.

Jamus would describe heroes and villains to Nick as if they were real people, talking about where they were from and explaining some of their idiosyncrasies. Nick listened and occasionally asked questions about what they looked like and how they knew each other.

But Jamus would never tell Nick about any of the characters in his books. Nick had asked about them once or twice, only to have Jamus snap at him that this was work, not a fun story. Time passed, and as Nick grew to be a teenager, the sleepless nights faded for him. The brothers spent less time walking around Boston as Nick was almost always hanging out with Matt. And so Jamus told fewer and fewer stories until somewhere over the last couple of years, that part of their relationship had gone completely silent.

And now, as Nick scoured the bookshops of Boston and Cambridge, it was almost as if the books might not exist at all. Nick walked around the small shop, looking for the fiction and literature section. He found it right against the back row. Looking down the spines of the books, he went through the Cs: Carol, Cather, Christie, Cone, Crane. *Crap, no Cork.* He looked back and forth again to be certain. *Oh well.* He took the crumpled list of bookstores out of his pocket and crossed this one off.

"Can I help you find something?" It was a different guy this time, younger than the guy at the front of the store. He was pasty with red blotches around his nose, and he wore a wool sweater that made Nick itch just looking at it.

"Um, I don't know," Nick said, almost under his breath.

"A specific author?" Pasty asked. "Or a title?"

"I'm looking for something by Jamus Cork," Nick finally said, his own brother's name sounding slightly foreign and metallic as he said it out loud to this stranger.

"Ah, okay," said the clerk, turning slightly blotchier and less pasty. "Jamus Cork, of course. Right over there." He pointed a pale, chubby finger toward a shelf halfway down the aisle from where they stood. Nick squinted his eyes to read the handwritten sign on the middle of the shelf.

"LGBT?" he said. "All of his books are over there?"

The clerk nodded.

"They're all gay books?" Nick shook his head.

"Well," Pasty stumbled, sounding unsure of what to say next. "Sort of…"

"Figures." Nick was vaguely surprised. Jamus had never mentioned any of his characters being gay.

"Let me know if you need anything else."

"Thanks, I'm all set." Nick turned away from the clerk and shuffled halfway up the aisle to the LGBT books and sat down on the floor in front of the "C" section. There were six of his brother's novels on the shelf in front of him. Nick frowned and pulled the first one off the shelf. This was what Jamus did, for the most part, when he wasn't writing for the newspaper or bothering Nick about homework. This was how he spent his days.

Nick looked at the cover of the first book and turned it over to find the summary on the back. He read it, surprised to realize how foreign it sounded. He didn't know exactly what he had expected the books to be about. Maybe, he thought, they should have been something like the real life he and Jamus lived, but the book didn't even take place in Boston. He read each one of the summaries, pulling all six of the books down from the shelf, one by one, and returning them after he had finished the back covers.

These stories were nothing like the fairy tales that Jamus had told him as a kid. It was plain to see why they were in this section of the bookstore; every single book was about a gay character. Most of them seemed to be stories about nightlife in New York or some underworld on the streets of New Orleans or LA.

"Edgy, raw and brilliant," read a quote from some newspaper in Austin.

"Hmmp," said Nick out loud. "Edgy, huh?"

There were six of them. One volume of each book Jamus had written, sitting there in front of Nick like a dare. "Read me," they seemed to say to him. He shook his head, unsure where to start.

"Have you read any of these," he asked Pasty. The clerk had been standing about seven feet away, reshelving some used science fiction paperbacks.

He looked over at Nick and then down at the bookshelf where all six Jamus Cork novels stood. "Yes, actually."

"Which ones?"

"Um, all of them, actually." The way he answered made the hairs on the back of Nick's neck stand up. The clerk's response was overly nice and, at the same time, a little embarrassed. Was this the way his brother's writing made people feel about themselves?

"Which one should I start with?" Nick asked.

The clerk tilted his head and thought for a second before walking over to the shelf. He stood next to Nick, staring at the six books and scrunching up his nose. "Hmm," he said. "How old are you?"

"Sixteen," Nick lied.

The clerk looked at him and rolled his eyes. "Uh-huh."

"Whatever." Nick turned to walk away. He was unaware of any law requiring a minimum age for purchasing literature in the Commonwealth of Massachusetts, but then again, he wasn't really sure and he didn't want to get in trouble for something like that, if it was a crime. He had more to think about than just himself now that Jamus had promised a big flat screen television if he didn't get in any fights for the rest of the year. While getting arrested wouldn't technically be a fight, Nick had a feeling his brother might just somehow categorize it as a disqualifying offense.

"This one," the clerk said, before Nick could walk away. "I'd start with this one if I were you. I'd tell you that it's a little graphic, but I'm guessing you don't want to hear it from me."

Nick looked down at the paperback cover. *Angel of New York*. Great. The book everybody at his school was already reading. "Thanks," he said and headed off to the register. But before he could get very far, he felt a hand on his shoulder.

It was Pasty. "Hey," he said, "if you need to talk to someone, here's a number you can call. I know things can be tough at your age, but don't worry, it gets better." He shoved a crinkled-up card into Nick's hand, facedown, before quickly walking off and disappearing into a storage room somewhere behind the register. When Nick turned the card over, he noticed the corners were folded down and some of the edges were frayed.

"Gay Teen Helpline" was written in rainbow-colored block letters above a telephone number. *Great*, he thought. *Just great.*

CHAPTER TWENTY-FOUR

At a different bookstore closer to home, Jamus stood with a dull, glazed expression on his face, looking through the shelves in the front of the store. He had worked at this bookstore when Nick was younger, and the owners had been good to him when he was just getting his writing career going. He often came in to say hello and chat with the few people he still knew there. But today Jamus was procrastinating, if he was honest with himself. If he wasn't being honest, he would rationalize this was research for *Rancher's Wife*.

Jamus wanted *The Rancher's Wife* to be different. He wanted it to be about older people in the suburbs, something he could write without baring his soul. But as he worked, he found details of his parents' lives creeping into these characters. It turned out to be harder to keep any distance from this project, and he was skating along that edge again, getting closer and closer to the hole that he fell in when he wrote. He was trying to stay clear of the same words and phrases that would drag him back into the nightmare visions of the past.

The morning had started off with so much promise. He had woken up that day with visions of finishing up a story for the paper and working on a couple of chapters of *The Rancher's Wife*, keeping it all at a distance. But the day had somehow gotten away from him. He'd made a coffee run first thing in the morning, which was a major transgression by his own standards. Jamus didn't let himself go out for coffee when he was working. He had a rule about making it himself. That kept him in the house and focused on whatever he was working on. But this morning, he was feeling an odd restlessness with his work.

If he could just get out of the house for a few minutes, maybe he would be able to concentrate. Perhaps a coffee run would do the trick.

The coffee run had led to what was supposed to be a short trip down to the bookstore, not that he needed to purchase any more books. He already had a stack of things in his reading pile. He just wanted to see what might be new in the display windows. Jamus's last book had come out two years ago and had long since made its way to the back of bookstores all around the country. Jamus knew his books didn't often make it to the display windows. A few did, but only in the larger cities with more progressive independent shops. He had never seen, nor ever expected to see a Cork novel in the front of a Barnes & Noble in someplace like Duluth.

But Jamus loved bookstores, and when he got stumped or bored with something he was working on, he could invent a thousand things that needed to be done, either chores at home or made-up research projects. He classified this morning's trip as research, perusing the shelves for inspiration.

He pulled down a new book by Chuck Palahniuk, skimming through the first chapter to see if the author's tone had changed much from the last book he'd put out, when a pair of worn suede saddle shoes caught his attention. They were the same shoes Malloy had been wearing a week or so earlier when Jamus had paid a visit to his classroom at Hayfield. He looked up to see Malloy a few feet away, engrossed in a volume of something that Jamus couldn't quite identify.

"Mr. Malloy?" he said, not completely sure if he was right.

Malloy blinked at the sound of his name, quickly putting the book down by his side as he looked up.

"Hi," said Jamus. "I thought that was you. Out doing a little research?"

"Oh, hi," said Sean, a look of embarrassed recognition flashed across his face. "Yes, actually, trying to rethink the syllabus for next year."

"You're reading *A Separate Peace* now, right?" asked Jamus.

"Er, yeah," Sean said. "We just finished it, actually."

"Nick and I were talking about it the other night," Jamus added. "It's not my favorite, but I can see why you chose it for the class."

The teacher looked at him sideways, Jamus's words seeming to jolt him a little. "Not your favorite? Why?" he asked.

"No offense," said Jamus, "it's just kind of boring. For me." He hesitated a few seconds before going on. "It's moral pabulum. Yes, it's clever how you can pull right and wrong out of both characters' actions, but please, it all breaks down to a moral code that is pretty simplistic for today's audiences."

Sean stared at him.

"I'm sorry. I've overstepped. I know it's a good book; it's a classic. Of course, I don't talk to Nick like this. I'm always very encouraging about his schoolwork."

"Always encouraging?" Sean repeated the words. "What does that mean?"

"I'm supportive. Of whatever he's reading or working on."

This seemed to spark a fire in Malloy. "But you don't want him to know your opinion about a piece? I don't care if my students don't like the things we read. In fact, I love it when they disagree with the things they read. As long as they read them, and it makes them think."

"Well, maybe you should give them stuff to read that's a little more provocative."

"That's exactly what I've been trying to do!" His voice was getting more passionate. Jamus was caught a little off guard by the turn their conversation had taken and the energy that had suddenly animated the teacher in front of him.

"Can I ask you something?" Sean said, cautiously holding up the book he'd been reading.

"Sure." Jamus nodded.

"This may sound crazy, but I noticed that your name is the same as the name of this new author I've been reading." He turned over the book in his hand. It was a copy of Jamus's most popular book, *Angel of New York*. Sean squinted his eyes and pulled the corners of his mouth back in a tight, almost embarrassed smile. "Is…this…you?"

Jamus took a deep breath and cleared his throat. "Um…" He held his breath for a minute, judging if the water was safe to enter. "Um, yeah. That's me."

Sean shook his head slowly from side to side. "Well, I guess I can see why you'd think that *Separate Peace* was boring."

"I didn't say boring," Jamus shrugged, "exactly."

"You said 'pabulum,'" Sean said. "That means 'boring.'"

"Yes…"

"I believe the exact definition is 'writing or speech that is insipid, simplistic, or bland.'"

"Okay." Jamus let out a brief laugh. "You got me. I guess I did say it was boring."

"Yes, you did," Sean said, "but that's okay. I'm not offended. I don't know if it's something I would have wanted the class to read if it was up to me."

"But it's not?" asked Jamus.

"Well, it hasn't been. That is, until now," Sean said. "We're in the process of reworking some of the curriculum, and I'm on the committee this time. Well, actually, I *am* the committee."

"I see." Jamus shot a glance at the book that Sean was still holding in his hands. "Please tell me you're not considering *Angel of New York* for your freshman class."

"What?" Sean smiled. "Too edgy for you? Really, Mr. Pabulum?"

"Well, maybe not for the seniors, but maybe something a little gentler for the freshman. How about *Naked Lunch*?"

"*Naked Lunch* might work." Sean laughed, putting the book down on the shelf.

Jamus reached out and touched the book that Sean had just put down, a trace of sadness registering on his face. Sean's laughter faded, and they were left awkwardly facing each other, neither knowing what to say next.

"How about a beer?" Jamus finally asked.

A heavy silence seeped out, flooding the space between them, shattering the cheerful rapport that had begun to play out. Jamus saw the smile evaporate from the teacher's face, and he instantly regretted asking. He could feel the back of his neck begin to sweat, and he knew that he had crossed the line. The seconds ticked away without a word. Somewhere in the background someone flipped noisily through a picture book and the roar of a far-off motorcycle hummed against the window of the shop. But Sean and Jamus had disconnected.

"Uh," Jamus stuttered to clean up the mess he had made of their conversation. "I'm sorry, that was…"

"A beer sounds great." Sean rushed the words out before Jamus could pull back his offer.

"It does?" Jamus asked.

"Yes. It sounds great. I could use an author to bounce some ideas off for the new curriculum. And I have a pretty good idea you're going to be honest with me about what you think."

Jamus smiled, thankful for the graceful peace Sean had restored to the conversation.

"When did you have in mind?" Sean asked.

Jamus looked toward the window, searching the air for the right day. "Thursday?"

"Sounds good. Seven?"

"Seven it is. Let's meet at the Snap Dragon on Boylston," Jamus said. "It's right off the Red Line from here."

Sean nodded. "The Snap Dragon. Sounds good. I'll look it up online for the address, and I'll see you there."

Jamus stumbled as he turned around to head toward the front of the store. He smiled and shrugged again to try and cover up the awkwardness of the move. Sean, in return, shrugged and smiled.

"Okay, see you then," said Jamus, offering a handshake good-bye.

"See you then." Sean clasped Jamus's hand, pumping it a few times before letting go. Jamus walked out of the front door of the shop and headed down the sidewalk in one direction before abruptly changing his mind, turning around, and heading off in the opposite direction.

Chapter Twenty-five

Nick shoved himself into the tiny second-floor bathroom behind Jamus. The upstairs of their house consisted of a front room, which belonged to Jamus and overlooked the small brick-sided street that they lived on; a back room, which was Nick's bedroom; and a six-by-eight bathroom that had originally been a closet. Wide pine plank floors ran the length of the upstairs, except in the bathroom, where Jamus had installed marble tile a few years back.

Its bright green walls only made it feel smaller, stuffed as it was with a commode, a shower, a sink, and a small cabinet where the two guys stored a variety of mostly unused sprays, ointments, and gels. The three things they mostly used—toothbrushes, floss, and toothpaste— lay stuffed on the back ledge of the sink behind the hot and cold faucets.

"You have a date?" asked Nick.

"It's less of a date and more just hanging out and having a beer," said Jamus, reaching into the medicine cabinet for the small brown jar of Crew pomade. "Nick, can you hand me that towel?" he asked, pointing to the damp green towel hanging on the back of the bathroom door.

"It's a date. Oh. My. God. You have a date. You've never had a date."

"I've had dates."

"I thought you said this wasn't a date? Huh, huh? So it's a date now?"

"Chill, Nick." Jamus smiled to blunt the unintentional roughness of his tone. "Yeah, I guess it's sort of a date, but I don't want to call it that."

"Why not?" Nick said, leaning in and fixing a clump of pomade that Jamus had failed to massage into his wet hair. "You know you're not supposed to put this stuff in until your hair is dry, bro."

"What?" Jamus glanced at the back of the pomade jar. "How do you know that?"

"It's pomade, duh."

"Right," Jamus said, looking at himself in the mirror and contemplating rinsing his hair out again.

"It'll be okay," Nick said, fixing a few more clumps of the stuff that had stuck around Jamus's ears. "It'll just look a little damp. It's not gonna make that much of a difference. So, now, why don't you want to call this a date?"

"I don't know, I just asked the guy out for a beer. No big deal."

"Well," Nick said, standing back from Jamus to evaluate his work. "He's into dudes, right?"

"Um…" Jamus screwed the cap onto the pomade jar and tossed it into the cabinet below the sink.

"What do you mean, 'um'?" Nick pressed.

"Well, I don't know for sure."

Nick rolled his eyes and let out an exaggerated sigh. "God! Jamus! What are you thinking?"

"I don't know. Like I said, it's just for a beer."

"Where are you going to meet him?"

"Down at the Snap Dragon."

Nick stared at him, scowling. "Well, you asked him out to a gay bar. That should sort of clear things up, right?"

Jamus searched through the cabinet, looking at all the creams and gels, shifting a few of the front bottles out of the way to see what lay in the depths of the shelves. "Do we have any cologne?"

Nick reached in front of him and rifled through a few things, grabbing a short black and red bottle he shoved at Jamus.

"I'm not wearing Axe." He smiled at his younger brother. "No way."

"What do you mean no way?" Nick said. "Don't you want to smell good?"

"I don't want to smell like a teenage boy," Jamus said. "I'll be fine without it." He leaned back a few inches from the mirror, which was all he could manage in the tiny room, and took stock. Light blue eyes looked back at him from above a once-broken nose that was broad without being big. His black hair, regularly trimmed with a number three clipper every four weeks, was just starting to get a little shaggy. His pale white skin reddened a shade at his cheeks and mouth where he had just shaved, and his pink, perpetually chapped lips hid a considerable gap between his teeth.

"Looking sharp, Jamus." Nick smiled and backed out of the room. "So, back to this guy."

"I took a risk. I don't know what's going to happen. I don't really even know if he's interested in anything but talking about books." Jamus slipped by Nick, out of the bathroom and toward his bedroom, anxious to change the subject.

"Books?" Nick echoed, turning to follow his brother. "What does he do?"

Jamus stopped in front of his closet. He closed his eyes for a second and tried to think. He hadn't considered this might be weird for Nick. He had to do something to get Nick off the subject. He pulled out a green Izod shirt. "Oh, I don't know, exactly," he said.

"Where did you meet him?" Nick pressed.

"Do you think you can iron this?" Jamus asked, shoving the shirt at his younger brother.

"What?" Nick looked at his brother as if he'd suddenly grown another head. "You crazy? I don't iron."

"Yes, you do. You iron better than I do." Jamus pulled the shirt off the hanger. "Come on, Nick. It'll take you two seconds, and it'll look like it's brand new. If I do it, it'll take a half hour, and it'll *still* look like a wet dog just rolled on it."

"Ugh," Nick exhaled loudly. "This is so not the way it's supposed to work." He grabbed the shirt from Jamus and headed down to the laundry room in the basement.

"Thank you," Jamus called after him. Jamus sat on the edge of the bed and took a deep breath.

Fifteen minutes later, Jamus stood at the bottom of the stairs in his freshly ironed Izod shirt and jeans. He wore the standard black Kenneth Cole shoes he always wore and a black scarf hung loosely around his neck. "Okay, the TV goes off at seven thirty, and you're working on homework until at least nine thirty, right?"

"Yep, got it," Nick yelled from the living room.

"Okay. No junk food."

"What the hell, Jamus?" Nick stomped out of the living room into the foyer. "We have junk food? Why didn't you tell me this? Now I can throw away this delicious celery stick with peanut butter on it. Where's the junk food?"

"Very funny, Nick."

"Now you're just being all nervous and it's really weirding me out," Nick said. "Just go."

"Bye, you." He grabbed Nick's head and gave him a kiss on the scalp. "I'll be home by ten."

"Yeah, yeah," Nick said. "Go get laid, will ya?"

"Mouth!" Jamus shouted. "I'm going to clean it out with soap."

"Yeah, yeah." Nick smiled at his brother. "I'm not waiting up."

CHAPTER TWENTY-SIX

"S ean, get out of the shower." Kevin banged on the bathroom door. "It's not a freaking YMCA, other people need to get in there."

"Christ, Kevin, lighten up, use the one downstairs," Sean shouted from inside the bathroom.

"I can't use the one downstairs, Dad's in it," Kevin said.

"What are you, ten? Hold it then, I'll be out in a minute."

"Come on, Sean, I really need to go."

"Fine." The door opened, and a cloud of shower steam poured out as Sean stepped dripping wet into the hallway, a towel wrapped around his waist. He headed into his room.

Kevin jumped into the bathroom, not bothering to close the door behind him as he relieved himself.

"What's up with you anyway?" asked Kevin, walking back down to his own room and shouting across the hall to his brother. "You never shower at night." Since he'd moved back, Kevin's room had become that weird collection of materials and objects that you only find in the bedrooms of adults living with their families, a situation not out of place in Southie. A poster of Larry Bird hung on one wall and across the room was a collection of Red Sox and Bruins posters. Two bureaus flanked the door, each piled with a collection of trophies, baseball cards, credit cards, and stacks of junk mail accumulated at various points over the span of the last decade. A monster heap of dirty laundry punctuated the end of Kevin's unmade double bed, giving the room a cramped feeling.

"Hey, did I tell you I got a job offer today?" Kevin shouted.

"No, congratulations," said Sean, rummaging through his bureau for a pair of boxers. "Where? At the law firm?"

"Uh-huh," Kevin said. "They said they've never seen anyone as efficient at discovery as me."

"Discovery?" Sean asked.

"Yeah, remember, that's what they call it when you have to read through a bunch of files to find stuff. I told you about it when I started."

"So they want to hire you?"

"Yep," said Kevin. "I have to go back to school to be a paralegal, but they said they'd pay for it if I do it while I'm working there."

"Kevin, that's awesome." Sean stuck his head into Kevin's room from the hallway. "You're going to take it, right?"

"Yeah," Kevin said. "I think so. It's good money, and I actually really like it there. I think the office manager has a crush on me."

"Yeah?" Sean said, turning and heading back into his room.

"Yeah," Kevin repeated. "Her name is Marina. I'm not into her, but she's at least nice to me. Actually, they're all kind of nice to me. So, you never answered me about the shower. You got a date or something?" yelled Kevin, changing the subject as he crashed down on his bed. "Maybe with Grace?" he added.

Sean was silent.

Kevin rolled onto his stomach and looked out the window as if that date might suddenly walk up to the front door below. "Sean?" said Kevin. When there was still no response from across the hall, he got up off his bed and walked over to Sean's room.

"Where're you headed?" Kevin asked again, this time a little more seriously.

"Nowhere," Sean said, shrugging and trying to look casual. While far from neat, Sean's room was a little bit less cramped than Kevin's. The bed was casually made, and the pile of dirty clothes was tucked neatly into a laundry basket in the corner.

"Tonight?" said Kevin. "You're going nowhere?"

"Nowhere special," Sean said back.

"Well, you're getting dressed up a bit for nowhere special," Kevin said.

"Didn't you need to get in the bathroom?" Sean asked, turning away and pretending to hunt for something on his bureau.

"Already went. I'm quick. Now don't try to change the subject," Kevin fired back. "Where are you going?"

"It's none of your business," Sean said, "Now get out of my room and let me finish getting ready."

"Fine," said Kevin. "I'll just text Grace and ask her what you guys are up to."

"Don't even think about it," Sean shot back, glaring at his brother.

"Okay." Kevin looked at Sean and sat down on the bed, showing no intention of leaving his brother alone. "So, it's not with Grace."

Silence.

"Which means," Kevin added, "that you're probably not going out in Southie."

"Seriously?" Sean turned toward the mirror over his bureau and fixed a couple of stray hairs. "You have nothing better to do tonight than harass me? What, are we twelve?"

The two brothers glanced at each other. Neither really knew who moved first. It was almost a reflex for them, set off by something in the tone of Sean's voice, some archaic, ingrown response that happened between brothers, maybe even without their own intention. But Kevin launched forward in a split second and grabbed Sean, tackling him on the bed.

"No, oh no, uh-huh," Sean shouted, but it was too late. He had already lost the advantage of timing, and Kevin had the edge in both size and speed. They wrestled for a couple of seconds, but Sean was outmatched. His older brother had him on the ground and pinned his arms, Kevin leaning heavily on Sean's chest and plowing an armpit over his head, both of them laughing as they went at it the way they had since they were kids.

"Where, where, where are you going?" shouted Kevin. "Tell me, or I'm not letting you up."

"I'm not telling," said Sean, his voice muffled by Kevin's armpit.

Sean thrashed for all he was worth, kicking and rolling around. The bed slid a few inches to the left, scraping loudly against the wooden floor. The rug scrunched up beneath them and something, probably a book, thudded to the floor from the nightstand. The whole house shook as the two Malloys thumped and rolled, tumbling over each other.

"You two knock it off up there, I'm trying to watch my shows."

Ma's voice bellowed up from the bottom of the stairs, reverberating through the walls and the furniture of the house. The boys froze for an instant before falling apart in gusts of laughter.

Sean took advantage of the break and rolled out of the scrum, slowly getting back to his feet. He looked down at his brother, carefully out of reach this time. He said, "It's not a date."

"It better not be, because you know who wouldn't be very happy about that? Grace Kinvara," Kevin said, winking as he got up. "Okay, I'll let you get ready." He started out the door back toward his own room but stopped short in the hallway. "But if it's not a date, why are you wearing cologne?"

Sean ignored him and turned back to the mirror. His hair was disheveled, and the shirt he had just pressed was completely wrinkled from cuff to collar. He sighed and pulled the shirt off and quickly looked through his closet for another. He was going to be late.

CHAPTER TWENTY-SEVEN

The Snap Dragon sat at the edge of Boston's Financial District, tucked between an ancient drugstore and a trendy furniture shop that sold sleek white sofas and dark pressed-wood tables. The front of the bar was a long façade of floor-to-ceiling windows looking out on Boylston Street. Inside, a few giant television screens scattered throughout the sea of tables and chairs drenched the room in the light of pop music divas and '70s-era disco videos.

The Club, as Boston locals sometimes called it, was a little bit past its prime. Even in the dim light of the autumn evening, the walls needed a coat of paint, and many of the tables showed signs of wear and tear with nicks and scratches and chips falling off them. All the same, the Snap Dragon was a common meeting place, and it was almost always packed after work and early on the weekend nights.

But that evening when Jamus walked in, the Snap Dragon was empty. Ten stools stood lined up against the bar in a zigzagged, uneven row, where an earlier crowd must have left them. The lights were dimmed for the evening, shading everything in a hazy glow, the crisp corners of daylight dulled to the rounded curves of night.

He let out a little sigh of relief at being the first to arrive, and he ran his fingers along the back of one of the stools as he walked down the bar, deciding where to sit. He registered the music playing in the background as something vaguely disco era, soothing in a strange sort of way. He gave Sharon, the bartender, a quiet smile and waved.

Jamus had known Sharon for almost a decade. She had been a fixture at the Snap Dragon since Jamus had come back from New York with Nick. He hadn't gone out much at first, just a night here and there when he could scrounge up the money for a Saturday-night babysitter. But gradually, as things improved for Jamus, he was able to make a weekly ritual of having a couple of drinks out on Saturdays.

Sharon had almost always been behind the bar when Jamus was there. She was one of the few people who had witnessed him as he cut loose, as he had a few drinks and didn't think about writing or homework or making ends meet. She knew his situation at home, and she watched throughout the years as he wrestled with it in different ways, never saying a word about it, although they had come to be chummy. She paid attention more than Jamus might have suspected, and she was the sole witness to the few times when he had let someone into his life, not because he cared if anyone else saw, but because no one else was watching.

For Jamus, letting someone in was rare, and it was always short, never lasting for more than one night at the bar. Tonight she stood behind the black glass bar stacking a pile of empty tumblers into the small square dishwasher. She nodded as he walked in and made his way slowly over to her.

"Hey, Jamus," she said, looking up as he sat down in one of the empty stools.

"Hey yourself," he said back, taking off his coat and folding it neatly over the back of the stool next to him. "Quiet night?"

"You just missed the work crowd." She put down the glasses she'd been stacking. "What a night for drama. We had a big fight earlier."

"A fight?" he asked.

"Yeah, nothing too serious, but a lot of shouting and fur flying. Two lawyers going at it." She chuckled.

"Fists?" he asked.

"No," she said, shaking her head. "No hair pulling. Just a lot of name calling and yelling. What can I get you tonight?" she asked, finishing up with the last of the dirty glasses. "The usual? Scotch rocks?"

"Um…" Jamus thought out loud. "I think I want it watered down today. Maybe about half water, half scotch over the rocks?"

"Oh? Switching it up tonight?" she asked.

"Well," he grinned slightly, "maybe a little. We'll see. I've got to keep my game face up tonight."

Sharon nodded and shot a look at Jamus that seemed at once inquisitive and accusative, but Jamus didn't respond. She poured the drink and placed it in front of him.

"Thanks." He took a short sip and frowned. "Wow, the water really kills it."

She smiled. "So, what brings you in tonight? It's not Saturday. Nick out at a friend's?"

"No." He waved his hand slightly. "No, I'm meeting someone out tonight. Nick's at home doing homework."

"Really?" she said.

"Or at least pretending to do homework."

She nudged his forearm. "No, I mean 'really' you're on a date? I've never known you to have a date." She wiped out another tumbler. "At least not here."

"No," he said, laying the palms of both hands down flat on the bar. "It is most definitely not a date. I'm just casually meeting an acquaintance out for drinks."

"Who is he?"

"Nick's English teacher."

"No!" Sharon's eyes went wide with surprise, a broad smile stretching across her face as she tried to stifle a fit of laughter. "Stop it."

"Shut up, it's just for a beer."

"Your baby brother's English teacher? Jamus, honey, you know that's a little weird."

"Why is it weird? We had a good conversation the other day, so I asked him if he wanted to get a drink."

"Does Nick know you hit on his teacher?"

"No. Not exactly."

"What do you mean, 'not exactly'?"

"Well, he knows I'm meeting someone out tonight." Jamus took a sip of his drink. "But he doesn't know who."

"And will you tell him?" She was still laughing a little.

"I can't imagine I will," Jamus said. "I don't think anything is going to come of it, so why bother?"

"Over already? Ending it before you've started it?" The smile still played on her lips, but it had lost some of its mirth, the corners of her mouth dipping just a little.

"You know me. It usually doesn't even get to this stage." Jamus pulled out his phone to check the time. "Fifteen minutes late already. What do you want to bet that he doesn't show?"

"Well, there's always the math teacher, right?" she said.

"Very funny." He drained his drink and put the glass down on the bar.

"Another?" she asked.

"Yes, please."

Sharon made the second drink and then slipped out from behind the bar to wipe down a few of the empty tables around the room and straighten some of the stools. Jamus quietly went about checking his phone for emails and a busy silence, underplayed by disco classics in the background, filled the bar as they waited for the arrival of the English teacher. But after another half an hour, the second scotch and water was about two-thirds gone and sat nested in a series of wet rings on the bar beside his phone. Jamus still sat there alone.

"You want me to freshen that up?" she asked.

"Yeah, might as well make it a real one this time," Jamus said. "He's not going to show up. I don't know what I was thinking."

"Thank God you've come to your senses," she said as she grabbed the bottle of Glenfiddich from the shelf above the bar. "Why anyone would want to water down good scotch is beyond me."

"I've been stood up, Sharon." Jamus lifted his head and looked at the bank of TVs playing music videos softly above his head. "By an English teacher, for fuck's sake."

"Don't sulk about it," she told him. "People run late. If it's meant to be, it'll happen. If it's not, well, so what. Fuck him."

Jamus settled into his third drink of the night when his phone buzzed and jumped to life on the bar. His eyes shot over to Sharon and she winked at him. "Told you so," she said.

"Nah." He shook his head, picking up the phone. "It's Nick."

How's the date going? The message from his brother came up in a blue bubble on the screen in front of him. He smiled, imagining Nick at home in front of the tiny television, trying to do his homework while watching a rerun of *Friends*.

Is ur homework done? Jamus texted back to him.

The phone buzzed with a response seconds later. *What homework? LOL*

Sharon watched the expression on Jamus's face. "Everything okay?" Sharon asked as Jamus clicked off the phone and put it in his pocket.

"Yeah, everything's fine. Nick is supposed to be doing his homework, but I'm guessing he's probably just engrossed in a rerun of some trashy sitcom."

"Oh, the joy of being a teenager."

Jamus threw back the glass of scotch and took a deep swallow, setting it down on the bar nearly empty. "Okay, I really can't finish that drink. I should be getting home or my ward is going to spend the rest of the night in front of the TV." He stood up and started to reach for his wallet when he felt someone slide onto the stool next to him. Glancing over, he saw a wide-eyed Sean Malloy staring back at him. Sean looked as if he had just run a sprint: red cheeks, a slight sheen on his brow, and something about his breathing suggested he was winded without him actually huffing and puffing.

"Sorry I'm late," he said.

"Oh, no worries." Jamus tried to sound casual. "I figured something had just come up, or well, you know." Behind the bar, Sharon rolled her eyes at him. He ignored her and looked at Sean.

Sean met his eyes for a couple of seconds, and then he looked away, scanning the rest of the empty bar. "You didn't tell me this was a gay bar." Jamus started to turn a pale red, but Sean laid out the words with such a smile that it was hard to find any malice in them.

"I know. I'm sorry," said Jamus. "I just assumed you would know about this place."

Sean's smile collapsed. "Because you think I'm...?" But he couldn't finish the sentence.

"No," Jamus quickly cut in, "because I thought it was a pretty well-known place."

Sharon, who had been standing back toward the opposite end of the bar, suddenly appeared in front of the two men, rescuing Jamus just in time. "You must be the English teacher. What can I get you, honey?" she asked Sean.

"Uh," he started out, as if deciding whether or not he would actually stay. "Do you have Newcastle?"

"We have it in a bottle," Sharon said.

"That's fine," said Sean. "I'll have one, please."

Jamus watched as Sean took a breath and waited for his beer to arrive. He was starting to get the feeling that he had made a horrible mistake. His gut had been wrong about the rookie teacher, and what had passed between them in the bookstore wasn't anything but wide-eyed admiration for Jamus Cork, the author. He took a deep breath and held it for a few seconds, trying not to get angry at himself.

"Look," Sean started as soon as Sharon had put the beer down in front of him. "I don't know what you think, but I'm not..."

"Not what?" Jamus looked directly at him, meeting his stare and prodding him, almost daring him to say the words himself.

Sean took a long sip of his beer. "Like I said, I don't know what you think—"

"I don't think anything," Jamus interrupted him. He dragged a pale finger along the rim of his glass. The ice had mostly melted, leaving a silky mix of booze and water in the bottom of the tumbler. "I don't presume you're gay, if that's what you're trying to say."

"You don't?" Sean sat up.

"No," Jamus lied. "I never presume anything about anyone."

"Then why did you ask me out tonight?"

"Why did you come?" Jamus shot him an accusing look, then swallowed the last sip of his drink and gently pushed the empty glass to the edge of the bar. Sharon caught his eye. He nodded to her, and she quickly refilled the glass and left it on the edge of the bar.

"Why did I come?" Sean stopped to think for a minute. "I, well, I wanted to clear this up."

"Yes, you did. But you didn't want to clear it up with me, did you? You wanted to clear it up with yourself."

"Look..." Sean's voice took on a hurried note, getting just a little bit louder. "I'm not..." He exhaled, unable to finish the sentence. "I mean, I don't want to be."

"Now that's a little bit closer to the truth, isn't it?" Jamus picked up the fresh scotch and took a decisive sip, placing it down again on the counter in precisely the same wet ring it had left when he picked it up.

Sean shook his head. "What's it like?"

"What's what like?"

"Being you? What's it like when everyone knows you're, you know."

"Gay?" Jamus finished his sentence.

"A single gay parent?" Sean added.

The thought of bringing Nick into the conversation gave Jamus a jolt. He hadn't expected that question, and it made the edges of his stomach sour. "Ah, well, came to see the animals in the zoo, did you?" Jamus took another sip of the scotch. He was starting to grow impatient with the conversation. "Look, Sean, I think this might have been a mistake."

"I'm sorry," Sean said.

"No, I'm sorry." Jamus tried to keep his tone civil, but the conversation was going all wrong, and everything about Sean was beginning to strike a nerve with him. "It's my fault. I should have known better." He took out his wallet and left a couple of bills on the counter. "I've got to be getting back. Nick's at home, and it's a school night."

"Wait," said Sean. "I wanted to talk."

"I know, you wanted to talk about your ninth-grade reading curriculum. You want to know what I think?" Jamus pulled his coat on and wrapped the scarf around his neck. "I think you should make them pick their own books."

"What?" Sean's eyes opened wide.

"I'm not kidding. I mean it. Who are we to tell people what to read? Give them a choice. Let them find the authors that speak to them, and you'll be teaching more than English, you'll be helping them find their own answers. You want to make a difference? Help them find their own way, don't just sit there preaching Dickens to them."

"They don't learn Dickens in ninth grade," Sean mumbled.

"Exactly."

Jamus looked down at where he'd been sitting, then gave Sharon a nod, turned around and walked out the door, leaving Sean to nurse the rest of his beer in solitude.

CHAPTER TWENTY-EIGHT

He stared out the window as the rain came pouring down, banging against the glass in huge panicked drops. He wasn't sure where he was; somewhere in the Meat Packing District, but he didn't know yet exactly where. His high was starting to wear off. With any luck, there would be one or two more little rolls and then he'd need to score again. He felt his pocket for the plastic bag, pulled it out, and confirmed what he'd known. It was empty. He nudged the body next to him. "Hey, get up," he said, pulling back the sweat-stained sheets. "Where am I?"

Nick closed the book for a moment, setting it down on his lap. He sat up on the bleachers and watched as Matt ran down the center of the field, one in a line of masked Hayfield lacrosse players whipping a ball across the field to one another. He cringed as the red-faced coach on the sidelines screamed at the top of his lungs, "Put it in his ear, come on. We need a little motivation out there, guys!" The good thing about cross-country practice, Nick thought, was that there wasn't much yelling. He pulled out his iPhone and looked at the time. They had another half hour of practice left. He tried to tune out the coach and went back to the book.

The story started off fast. It took place in a place called the Village in New York City, and the main character was indeed Angel. And Angel was a wreck. His life was full of parties and clubs and drugs—lots of drugs. By the end of the first chapter, Nick had learned all about how to score cocaine or ecstasy on the streets of New York. Jamus would have been horrified to know that Nick and most of the freshman class at Hayfield had inadvertently learned this from him. But Angel was somehow a good guy despite all his bad habits, although Nick couldn't put his finger on exactly what made him likable. Maybe that was the magic of Jamus's writing.

"Hey, Nick, no running practice today?" Matt shouted up from the sidelines as he lined up to rush the goalie in a new drill.

"Nah, Fridays are off," he yelled back down at the field. "How much longer?"

Matt shrugged. "Not sure. Half hour maybe." A player beside him nudged his arm, and Matt raised his stick, caught the ball, and rushed toward the goalie.

Daylight streamed into the room in eerie hues of blue and gray. Bottles left over from the night before were strewn around the floor. Angel's face glistened in the sheen of his own sweat. His head ached with a dull, banging passion, and his whole body convulsed as he tried to move.

By the second chapter, Nick learned about hustling—something that, until that point, he had thought meant going faster at cross-country practice. As he sat on the bleachers waiting for Matt, he started Chapter Three, and the book moved from the streets and clubs into the classrooms of New York University where a new character emerged, an art student who was working to put herself through school. She was totally different from Angel. Her name was Amy, and Jamus described her as "determined but emotionally distant."

He rolled his eyes to think of his brother describing someone that way. He could hear the words rolling off Jamus's lips. Emotionally distant. Nick turned up his nose slightly. Gone from the pages were the parties and drugs and sex of the Village. Nick found himself in a sea of page after page of libraries and art studios and student stress that made him start to worry about his own future and how freakishly difficult college might actually be.

"Hey, bookworm, you ready?" Matt sat down next to him, freshly showered and wearing the same clothes he'd had on in school earlier in the day.

"Yeah," said Nick, closing up the book and putting into his knapsack.

"Whatcha reading?" Matt asked.

"Nothing. Just something for Mr. Malloy's class," Nick lied.

"Uh-huh." If Matt detected anything weird or different in Nick's tone, he let it go. "What are we gonna see tonight at the movies?" He rummaged through a blue and red gym bag for his phone.

"I don't know. How about the new Batman movie?"

"Sounds good. We're still staying at your house tonight, right?" Matt asked.

"Yeah, if you don't mind sleeping on the floor."

"Nah, you've still got the sleeping bag, right?" Matt asked. "I'm cool with that. Should we call one of them to pick us up?"

"Screw that," said Nick. "Let's take the Red Line. It'll be way faster. We'll drop the stuff at my house, and then we can head over to the mall and hit the movies."

"Sounds like a plan." Matt grabbed his bag and the two kids headed away from Hayfield and up toward Mass Ave. to catch the subway.

❖

"Hey, Jamus," Nick said, rushing through the front door and quickly shedding his coat and backpack on the spot.

"Hey, Mr. Cork," came Matt's echo a few seconds later. He followed suit, hanging his coat on top of Nick's.

"Can I have some money for the mall?" Nick asked as the two boys piled into the kitchen and headed straight for the refrigerator. Nick stood in front of the open fridge door and looked in blankly. Matt dropped his bag by the table and joined Nick staring into the big stainless steel fridge as if something mystical inside might suddenly appear if they only stared hard enough and long enough to conjure it.

"Yeah, sure," said Jamus. He was seated at the kitchen table in front of his laptop with a couple of books spread out in front of him. "Just grab some out of the coffee can."

Nick abandoned his inspection of the fridge and abruptly shut the door without any warning to Matt. He reached up on top of the fridge, grabbing a red coffee can. It had always been, as long as he could remember, a magical source of constant petty cash. Nick reached in, pulled out two twenties, and put the can back on top of the fridge. "I'm taking forty," he said.

"Okay," said Jamus. "You guys still headed to the movies?"

"Uh-huh, a little later." said Nick, pulling out a couple of Diet Cokes from the fridge and handing one to Matt. He reached into the cupboard and pulled out a box of crackers. "We're going to get ready," he said, heading back out of the kitchen.

An hour or so later, as they walked out of the house to go to the movies, Nick looked at Jamus for an extra couple of seconds. He wanted to see if he noticed anything different about his older brother after having read the first few chapters in his book. How could Jamus have known all that stuff about being on the streets? He glanced at the books spread out on the kitchen table in front of Jamus, and he figured it must have been from research, secondhand stories from other books. That seemed to be the way that Jamus researched things. "Hmph," he said as he walked out of the front door, followed closely by Matt.

But Nick couldn't stop thinking about the book, and he had grown increasingly quiet as the night went on. Jamus met them after the movie and took the boys for dinner at Champions, a nearby diner. But even as they sat squeezed into a booth munching on fries and burgers, Nick had little to say. When Jamus asked about the movie, Matt told him all about it while Nick sat and nodded a few times.

"Are you okay, Nicky?" Jamus asked at one point during Matt's retelling of *Batman*.

"Yeah," Nick said with a shrug. "I guess so."

Jamus frowned slightly at his brother, and Matt looked uncomfortably from his friend to Jamus, not sure what to make of Nick's mood.

After a few seconds, Jamus looked over at Matt. "Well, what happened next, Matt?"

Matt went through the rest of the movie. Jamus interrupted at a couple of points, asking about costumes or sets. But Nick sat motionless for the most part.

Later that night, when Matt was snoring heavily in the sleeping bag on the floor of Nick's room, Nick flicked on the flashlight and grabbed the book out of his backpack. He read until he fell asleep sometime during Chapter Five with the flashlight still on. When he awoke early the next morning, his face was smushed onto the book, a giant pool of partially dried spittle welding his cheek to the pages and the flashlight batteries dead.

❖

The next morning, after a couple of bowls of Cheerios, the boys left the house and walked toward the Park Street T Station. The plan was to take the subway out to Alewife, where Matt's mom would pick them up, then they'd spend the rest of the weekend out at Matt's house in Arlington.

"Okay, okay, okay, here's the thing," Matt said, hands up in front of him making a box. They were almost halfway across the Boston Commons. "It's not like you can even compare the two superheroes. I mean, Batman doesn't even have any real powers."

"What do you mean, no real powers?" Nick said. "He uses his brains for everything, and that's a real power."

"Yeah." Matt drew out the word and tilted his head to one side in an exaggerated effort to pretend he was conceding a point. "But no, Nick, it's not a real power. Not like flying or x-ray vision. So if it was, like Batman versus Superman, then Superman would totally win."

"Not necessarily," Nick argued, more interested in being stubborn than anything else. "Batman's got a lot of tricks up his sleeve."

"Whatever, dude!"

But Nick wasn't as focused on the movie as Matt was. In the back of his mind, Nick kept turning over the few chapters he had read last night as he sat up in bed with the flashlight. In contrast to Batman, the characters in Jamus's book weren't heroes. They didn't want to save a city, and they didn't have the extra talents that the Dark Knight had. But things had taken a turn in the story. Angel had fallen in love with the art student, and he was struggling to be better for her. He'd tried to give up the drugs and the violence and the other stuff because he loved her, and he wanted to be good for her. But so far in the story, that was tough for Angel.

Matt yanked him out of his train of thought. "So, if Batman was real—and I'm not saying I think he is, because I'm not still ten years old—but if he was real, I don't think he'd be living in Chicago. I think it would be more like Boston. Don't you think?"

Nick shrugged. "I don't know, honestly," he said blankly, half in response to Matt and half to the dialogue playing out in the back of his mind about Angel.

Nick's deadpan response dashed cold water on Matt. Matt and Nick were still the kind of friends who could talk about superheroes to each other and not feel silly or stupid about it, the way they might in front of a bigger group. But Nick had just broken a cardinal rule of that relationship. He had made fun of the conversation. Not in a big way, but in a way that was bad enough. The shut down was almost instant between them. Matt shoved his hands into his pockets and looked down at the pavement in front of him as he walked.

"Well, I guess it would have to be Boston," Nick said, trying to rescue things.

"Forget it," Matt said. "It was stupid, I know."

"Dude, it wasn't stupid. I'm sorry, I was thinking about something else," Nick said.

They walked for a couple of minutes in silence as they crossed the Commons. The rain that started sometime earlier that morning was sticking around, drizzling just enough to keep them soggy. The trees sulked along the edges of the park, their wet, sludgy leaves littering the sidewalk as the two friends trudged along.

Nick's mind was still back on the book. The book. He had left the book on the kitchen table. He had to go back.

❖

That morning, Jamus had strategically waited until the boys had left the house before getting out of bed. Nick had yelled to him through the bedroom door that he and Matt were leaving for the day, and that had been his cue. He gave it another fifteen minutes just to be sure that neither of them had forgotten anything and doubled back.

Jamus had played Dad the night before and this morning was his. *Have fun, Matt's mom.* He stumbled into the kitchen and over to the sink. His priority was coffee. He grabbed the pot and put it under the tap, turning the water on and letting it fill up while he walked over to the table to grab a cigarette out of the pack. But where the pack should have been were two partially empty cereal bowls and a thin paperback book. The spine of the book had been bent back and a number of the pages were folded over, but it was a new volume. The original cover had been reimagined for a second pressing. Instead of the simple blue background and yellow lettering of the original, this volume's cover had a black-and-white photograph of broken glass as the backdrop with *Angel of New York* in bold red serif.

Jamus slumped down into a chair at the table and slowly reached over to pick up the book. He stared at the front of it, tracing his finger along the edges of the top. He opened it to the last dog-eared page.

> *Angel lay curled up in a ball in the middle of the room. A broken bottle of Jack Daniel's and his glass pipe littered the floor next to him. When he finally woke up, he had no idea how long he'd been unconscious. But the pain was still there. He hadn't been able to push that away. He'd slipped up and let her see him and the look in her face when she knew. It was like a mirror, and he was looking at himself for the first time. When you discover yourself like that, he thought, then it's over. Really, truly over.*

Jamus closed the book and put it back down on the table where it had been, running his fingers over the embossed letters of his own name underneath the title. He knew now why Nick had been so quiet last night. In the sink behind him, the water reached the brim of the coffeepot and flowed over. The gurgling sound of the drain pulled him out of his stupor. He stood up and turned off the tap, leaving the pot in the sink. He fished around on top of the refrigerator where he kept his cartons of Luckys. Grabbing a new pack and another lighter from the drawer beside the stove, he left the kitchen and made his way slowly back up to his bedroom.

A few minutes later, Nick quietly opened the front door of the house and tiptoed back to the kitchen. Matt followed him through the hallway, tripping over the rug on the way. Nick turned around and shushed him loudly.

"What, dude?" he said.

"Jamus is still asleep," Nick said. "Be quiet."

Matt rolled his eyes but made an effort to walk more quietly. The book was still on the table in the kitchen where Nick had left it. He grabbed it, stuffed it into his backpack, and then turned around and almost ran into Matt.

"You came back for a book, dude?"

"Shh," said Nick, holding his middle finger up to his lips and walking quietly back to the front door.

CHAPTER TWENTY-NINE

The Hayfield cross-country course started along the banks of the Charles River in front of the soccer fields and baseball diamonds, flanked by the old Polaroid building. The course ran down the Cambridge side of the river for about a mile, bisecting wooded parks and running alongside the traffic jams of Memorial Drive before turning right and crossing over to the Boston side of the river. It then ran west along Boston's Storrow Drive before crossing back to Cambridge to finish right in front of the school, about a quarter of a mile away from the starting line.

Jamus stood awkwardly apart from a group of parents at the edge of the starting line, looking over the small band of runners stretching and jogging in place. In the couple of months since Nick started at Hayfield, Jamus had been to every cross-country meet.

Jamus could feel the nervous energy of the waiting runners. He shifted his weight from left to right and pushed his hands deeper into his pockets against the cool air. He watched as a group of coaches conferred in a huddle a few yards away from everyone else. Jamus couldn't hear what they were talking about, but they seemed to be pointing to different spots along the route and arguing over something.

The meets were never crowded. No seating, no concessions, and no scoring made it a difficult sport for the student body and the friends and family of the team to really get into. And because it was primarily a boarding school, many of the families were spread out across the country and around the world. But a small group of spectators—mostly other runners who were injured, a few coaches from Hayfield and the other schools, and some of the local parents—huddled together in twos and fours at the starting line, bundled up in winter coats with paper cups full of hot coffees and lattes.

"I can't believe how cold it is," said a familiar voice beside him. Jamus turned to find Sean Malloy standing next him. "It seems almost cruel to make them stand out there in those uniforms."

"They're allowed to wear sweats up until the start, but none of them do." Jamus kept his focus on the runners milling about at the starting line. "Nick says it's because they make fun of the guys who do."

Sean nodded. "Makes sense."

Jamus rubbed his hands together and blew into them. "So what brings you out here?"

"Well," Sean said, pursing his lips together, "I got to thinking about what you said the other day when we were up in my classroom, about how nobody ever comes to support the cross-country team."

"Uh-huh." Jamus gave a slight nod. "And so you thought you'd find it in your heart to come down and show some school spirit?"

"I came down to see you," Sean said quietly. Then after a few seconds of silence, "Shit, why does this have to be so hard?"

"Why is it hard?" Jamus turned to him with a look of sour lemons on his face. "What's there to make hard?"

"Look, about the other night."

"There's nothing about the other night, it's fine."

"In the bar..."

"Forget about it, Sean. It doesn't matter."

"It does to me." Sean grabbed his sleeve. Jamus turned around in a shot, his eyes flaring with a temper seldom let loose, all the fiercer for its rarity. Sean backed up and let go of his shirt, looking around to see if anyone had noticed their interaction. "I'm sorry," he said softly. "I just wanted to say it was, um, difficult for me. The other night."

"Look, Sean. I am going to be pretty blunt with you. I wanted to get to know you, but I'm not going to rush you into anything you're not ready for, and I'm not going to play games. So, let's just leave it at that."

"Can we try again?"

Jamus saw his brother out on the field and waved. Nick responded with a discreet wave back, carried out at waist level so the other runners couldn't see. "You see that kid out there?" Jamus asked.

Sean looked in Nick's direction.

"The other night, you asked me what it was like to be a gay single parent. Well, I'm technically not. I'm not his parent. I'm his brother…"

"I know. I'm sorry. I didn't mean to…"

"It doesn't matter. I'm his guardian, and I'm answering the intent of the question. You see, it's like this." Jamus pulled the pack of Luckys out of his coat pocket and tapped on the back of it, drawing a single cigarette out with his lips. He ignored the stares he felt instantly boring into the back of his skull. "I don't do much else except look after him. I work and I play Dad, all day, every day. I don't have a life of my own, and I don't really know if I ever will. I spend every day worrying I'm doing something wrong, I'm not doing enough, or I won't have enough money to pay for something I'm supposed to do for him. I don't really have any friends, and at the rate I'm going, I am not making any new ones. So, that's what it's like."

"I see." Sean looked around. The other spectators were beginning to stare at the cloud of cigarette smoke forming around them.

"So, if you're done observing the car crash that is my life, I'm just going to finish watching my little brother run. It looks like we may be off to the races. Nice talking to you."

Sean started to walk away, but stopped after a couple of steps. "Could we try again on Thursday? Same place?"

Jamus kept his focus on the starting line and took a drag off his cigarette, exhaling a long stream of smoke. He waited for a moment until he could feel Sean getting ready to turn around for good and walk away. "Same place?" he said at last.

"Same place."

"Maybe," Jamus said.

Sean smiled. "I'll see you there." He turned and walked up toward the school building.

❖

Nick shivered as he carefully lifted up his left knee and pulled it to his chest, stretching out before the start of the race. He had watched out of the corner of his eye as Malloy walked over and talked to Jamus. Whatever it was, it couldn't be good. He could tell Jamus was pissed by the way he stood with his shoulders hunched. He set his leg down and pulled the other one up to his chest, stretching out that side of his body. He put it out of his mind. With five minutes to go until the start of the race, Nick glanced around at the different teams milling about, stretching and shaking and rubbing their hands together. For a fall sport, the cross-country uniforms were ridiculously lightweight.

The shorts were classic running splits and barely covered the tops of Nick's legs. The shirt was a singlet, not much more than a sleeveless T-shirt that kept absolutely no warmth in at all. Nick shivered in the brisk afternoon air and jumped in place a few times to try to warm up, but the wind off the river was ice on his skin. He would be thankful for the lightweight gear as soon as he started running, but right then he would have traded for a bulky pair of sweatpants and a hoodie.

He tried to clear his mind and focus on the race ahead. It was a flat course, with the only real hills being the steps up to the bridges across the river. Nick looked around and tried to take stock of the competition. He saw a few new faces out today—some upperclassmen and some transfers—but the other teams were from private schools around the area. Nick had raced many of the kids last year on junior high teams.

A couple of his teammates sauntered up beside him and reached down to stretch. "You gonna blow it out today, Cork?" asked Neil Thomas, one of the few Americans on the Hayfield team. He was a sophomore and had run on last year's team, but he wasn't especially fast. He was nice, though, and had been friendly to Nick since the start of the season, which wasn't the case with most of the upperclassmen on the team. Some felt it was their duty to make the freshmen suffer a little bit. Nick had demonstrated, through his fight with the Peruvians, that he had no interest in suffering at the hands of his older teammates, and this had made him unpopular with both the upperclassmen and the other freshmen on the team who had to absorb his share of the hazing.

"Hell, yeah," Nick said. "What about you, Thomas? You got a strategy for the run?"

Neil laughed. "Yeah, make it to the finish line." He pulled a lanky knee up to his chest and closed his arms tightly around it, balancing on one foot as he stretched. "Your parents here today?"

Nick looked around for Jamus. Malloy was gone, which was a relief. "Yeah," he said. "Yours?"

"Nah." Neil faked a smile. "They couldn't make it today. Gotta work, both of 'em. Plus it's a long drive. They live out in the western part of the state."

Nick didn't say anything. He shivered and thought about how nice it would feel to be wrapped up in one of those big fluffy coats on the sidelines.

One of the coaches called the group of runners to the starting line and began to go over the course again. "Follow the cones up to the Mass Ave. bridge. A Hayfield coach will be directing you over the bridge. On the other side at the cone, you will…"

Nick half listened to the course description for what seemed like the millionth time. He was ready to go; he squat stretched and bounced back up. "Come on," he said out loud, "let's go."

The starting gun popped two minutes later, and they were off. Nick jogged lightly to the head of the pack and let the first fast breakers wind themselves before breezing through them to the front of the race. The nerves in his stomach would take another half mile to settle down, but the release of finally running felt good. The skin on his arms and legs tingled as he started to warm up, and he felt an overwhelming sense of freedom as he cleared out in front of the pack of runners.

Nick was traditionally a front runner, meaning he would pace himself at the front of the pack from the outset. He would keep that pace until almost the end of the race, and then he would pull out all the stops in the last quarter of a mile or so. The problem with that strategy was it sometimes didn't leave much energy for that final sprint.

As they rounded a curve in the river, Nick could see back to the starting line. The coaches and spectators were already clearing out and making for the finish line back at Hayfield. But Jamus was still there, watching as the runners moved farther and farther away. Nick cleared his mind and focused on the race in front of him. He did a mental list of each segment and how he would tackle each part of the run.

❖

The few parents and coaches at the starting line had already begun piling into SUVs and minivans to move back to the finish line and await the runners. It was a three-and-a-quarter-mile course, and the first runners would start crossing the finish line in about fifteen minutes.

Jamus waited a few more minutes, watching Nick blur into the distance along the river. He was moving with the easy grace of a gazelle as he seemed to lope out ahead of the pack effortlessly.

Jamus smiled. As he walked up to his own car, he looked up to one of the Hayfield coaches. "He's been doing good? This is his first year running."

"Yeah, he's solid," the coach said. "Good runner so far this year."

"He looks like he loves it," Jamus said, looking back over his shoulder and trying to find the pack, but they had already vanished up the river and out of sight.

"He won't be that fast for long, though," the coach said.

"Why's that?" Jamus asked, knitting his eyebrows together at the comment.

"Well," the coach looked directly at Jamus, "you know he's smoking…a lot, right?"

"Ah." Jamus was on dangerous ground here. How much should he admit to knowing? He was never very good at covering up. His face showed everything. "I knew he'd tried it."

The coach stopped as they reached the student van. "Uh-huh," he said doubtfully. "Well, as his parent, you might want to let him know it's not a good idea."

There was that word again: parent. A feeling of inadequacy settled over Jamus. He wasn't a parent, not even close. He was a brother—a much older brother, but a brother nonetheless. Early in the year, one of the parents had approached Jamus about the issue of Nick smoking. They had driven by Nick on his walk to the subway after school and seen him with a cigarette. The parent took Jamus aside at an open house soon afterward and gave him the devastating news. Jamus didn't have the heart to tell her that while he didn't want Nick to smoke and he didn't think it was healthy, he couldn't tell him not to. Not when Jamus himself was a pack-and-a-half-a-day smoker. Jamus had enough battles to fight for Nick, and this was one the kid was going to have to fight himself. But he didn't say any of this to the helpful parent who stood across from him, telling him about the horrors of seeing a fourteen-year-old smoke. Jamus just thanked her and told her he would definitely speak to Nick, and harshly.

"Yeah, you make a good point. I should do more there," Jamus said, looking away uncomfortably.

"And you should consider quitting, too," the coach said. "It's not good for a kid like that to see his dad smoking, if I'm going to be honest with you. It doesn't really align with how we expect the parents of our athletes to behave."

Jamus turned and looked at the coach. He was a good fifty pounds overweight and was already winded from the brief walk up from the starting line. Something inside Jamus flipped. He shrugged off the feeling of inadequacy, and he was suddenly miffed. After all, who was this pompous, overweight graybeard to tell him what was right?

"Well, thank you, Coach. I'll make sure to check out your handbook before I make my next personal choice. Any regulations on weight?" said Jamus, looking down at the coach's bulging waistline. "I guess not," he added before turning quickly and getting into his own car. He cursed himself as he started the engine. He should not have done that. He should have just kept his mouth shut.

Fourteen minutes later at the finish line, Jamus waited and watched the horizon as the first runners started to emerge. A few seconds later he could make out Nick. He was at the head of the pack along with four other runners. He was pounding it, arms swinging deeply, legs bounding forward on great long strides. He was pushing as hard as he could. As he got closer, Jamus could make out the snarl on his face. He was in attack mode, completely focused, blocking out the rest of the world.

Jamus held his breath as they got closer to the finish. The runners were starting to fall into a line. The others were fast and Nick was fighting for third, but about fifty yards from the finish, Nick pulled out all the stops in a burst that surprised everyone and put him into second place as they crossed the line. Jamus jumped and let out a loud cheer as his brother finished. The rest of the parents clapped softly in polite disinterest. They were still mostly chatting among themselves, seeming more interested in whatever conversations they were having with each other than what was going on with the race.

Jamus stuck his thumb and forefinger in his mouth and whistled loudly. "Way to go, Nick!" he yelled, clapping vigorously. Nick was doubled over, breathing hard and making a face like he was about to throw up. He looked up and smiled briefly at his brother before dunking his head again in what looked like a wave of nausea.

"Walk it off," came one of the coaches' voices. "Walk it off, boys."

Jamus put his hands in his pockets and continued to watch Nick. He knew better than to cheer any more. He didn't want to embarrass him. It was so damn easy to embarrass kids at this age, he thought. The other parents had the cool, distant parenting thing down pat. He watched as they continued to ignore the kids who crossed the finish line. Some of the kids even looked up to see if their parents had noticed them cross the line.

Jamus thought they looked like they expected some acknowledgment, if not a full-blown yelling and screaming cheer. But what did he know? He wasn't really a "parent," after all, was he? He sighed and continued to watch as Nick finished a cool-down lap around the school's track and headed into the locker room.

Jamus stayed until the last kids crossed the finish line, which was only about ten minutes later. Then he headed back to the car and turned the heat on as he waited for Nick.

CHAPTER THIRTY

The cross-country meet had been on a Tuesday. Two days later, it was Sean who was sitting at the bar at the Snap Dragon by himself. He held a bottle of Newcastle in one hand and stared straight ahead of himself, trying not to feel awkward about being alone. Jamus wasn't late, at least not yet. Sean was early; he'd left a good half-hour buffer just in case anything went wrong. The same bartender was there again this week. She'd been polite enough, acknowledging him and even smiling when she said hello to him. But she had seen how things ended the week before, and she didn't seem inclined to go out of her way to be overly nice to him.

The place was almost empty again this week. A couple of guys in gray suits sat at the end of the bar. Sean had no idea who they were, but they looked like what he imagined investment bankers might look like. They both had broad, shiny brown shoes on, and their hair was still part-splitting perfect at the end of the day. He ran a tired hand through his own hair and realized it must look like a wild shrub sitting on top of his head.

"You look fine, don't mess with it." Sharon didn't bother to look up as she spoke. Instead she kept inspecting the levels of all the liquor bottles, making notes on a clipboard. "You meeting up with him again tonight?"

Sean nodded, then realizing she wasn't looking, he said out loud, "I think so. Not so sure, really."

"Not sure?" She put down the clipboard and turned to him. "What does that even mean?"

Sean took a swig of his beer. "It means I asked him, but I'm not sure he's going to come. He said 'maybe.' To be honest with you, I don't know if I would either after the way we left things last time."

"Yeah," she said, letting a low whistle out under her breath. "That was a doozy."

"Yeah, well, it's not easy, you know."

She rolled her eyes at him. "Please," she said. "What do you know about not easy?"

Sean could feel himself getting red. For a moment, he couldn't think of anything to say. "Are you gay?" he finally asked.

"That's none of your business." She wrinkled her nose at him and started to turn away.

"No, wait. I ask because I'm not sure what's going on in my head right now. I don't know what I'm supposed to feel, and I don't want to feel the way I do, because it means that I could probably get killed in my neighborhood."

She locked her eyes on him, but she was silent. After a few seconds, the quiet became awkward enough that he felt like he should say something else, but as he started to speak she cut him off by putting up her hand. "First, quit being so melodramatic. Do you think it's ever easy?" she asked.

He shrugged. "I don't know."

"Because it's not." She put down the clipboard she'd been marking up and walked over to where he was sitting. "It's never easy at first. Kids get killed all the time because of the things you're feeling. But you're not going to get killed, Sean."

He was surprised to hear her use his name. It brought a new depth and intimacy to the conversation. It was no longer just some lecture from a bartender at a gay club. It was now personal—to and about him.

"So don't sweat this, huh? Just chill out and get to know him, then worry about your feelings. But don't take it out on him. He's never been on a date in the ten years that I've known him."

"He hasn't?" Sean's eyes bulged out in surprise.

"No, he hasn't. So don't fuck with him, okay? Or when you do finally decide you want to come out of the closet, no gay bar in this town will serve you so much as a cup of ice." She winked at him and moved away from the bar, back to her clipboard and pen. "He's coming in now, I just saw him in the window."

"Thanks," he said, still figuring out how to process her threat. She must have sensed his confusion because she turned around and flashed a smile at him, as if to say it would be all right.

"It's okay," she said, winking at him. "Don't look so scared. You're going to be fine."

A few seconds later, Jamus walked across the room, slowly pulled out the bar stool next to where Sean was sitting, and sat down.

Chapter Thirty-one

The price of excitement is a tricky thing. It's invisible to
some. Angel knew this like he knew things people wouldn't
tell him. He could see through people sometimes. He could
feel what they were thinking before they could. It was a gift,
and it was a curse. He wasn't in control when he saw things.
The drugs helped that. They helped him be less him, and
tonight Angel was having trouble being Angel.

Angel reached back and put a hand on the back of his
head. He felt the damp sweat trickle down his neck. It was
a cold night for April, winter's last icy gasp at pulling back
spring, but still he was hot. His skin felt like a thousand tiny
little pins were pricking him from head to toe. Angel took a
breath and tried to relax while he waited. Her parents were
going to be here in minutes, and he could not screw this up.
He knew how much this meant to her, and he knew how much
the promise he'd made meant to her. He scratched at his
throat. He didn't know how he was going to get through this
night out without a fix.

Another Saturday came and went, and the fall weather had turned
gloomier. They had decided to spend the day at Matt's house, but
constant rain kept the two inside. Nick spent most of the day reading
the book. Matt had been disappointed at first at his friend's sudden
preoccupation with what he purported to be homework reading, but he
had soon occupied himself with the PlayStation in his bedroom. And
so the two boys had sat for most of a rainy Saturday, Matt playing war

games and Nick reading about a drug lord on the streets of New York who ended up killing everyone he loved.

On Sunday morning, Nick was already home when Jamus got back from church. "Who was Angel?" Nick demanded the minute Jamus stepped in the kitchen.

Jamus blinked. "Angel who?" he asked, setting his keys down on the kitchen counter. Since finding Nick's copy of *Angel of New York*, Jamus had done almost everything he could not to think about it. He'd spent most of Saturday in his bedroom, smoking and reading as much as he could find online about the origins of the Big Dig. Saturday night he had spent at the Snap Dragon, quietly nursing a warm scotch, thinking about the possible repercussions of Nick reading the one book he wished he could take back.

"Angel. Who was he in real life?" Nick sat, stone-faced, at the table.

"In the book? Yeah, I saw you had a copy." Jamus massaged the bridge of his nose between his thumb and his forefinger. He breathed in and tried to focus. "What are you doing reading that anyway?"

"In *your* book. Why don't you call it your book. It's not 'the' book—it's your book, and don't lie to me. I know there's an Angel, and I want to know who he was."

Jamus didn't move a muscle for what seemed like hours. He stood in the middle of the kitchen and looked down at the floor. Eventually, he finished pulling his jacket off and laid it over the back of one of the chairs. He walked over to the counter and grabbed a cigarette from the pack Nick had left there earlier that morning. Lighting it, he finally looked up at Nick.

"That's not true," Jamus said. "I didn't lie to you. I haven't ever lied to you." He sat down at the table across from his brother. "Now, why are you reading that book?"

"Tell me who he was. And who was Amy based on? Huh? And how come she lost her parents in a car accident just like us?" Nick's eyes were filled with rage. "Except that there was more to it with her, wasn't there? She fell in love with Angel, and Angel drove their car off a bridge when he was high, killing her and her mom and dad. Who was Angel, and what really happened to our mom and dad? I want to know. I have a right to know who killed our parents."

"Nick, it's fiction. Angel was—is—a composite character. I made him up based on a bunch of people I knew at school."

"You're lying," Nick said.

"Listen to me, Nick. It's fiction. There's nothing real about it," Jamus shouted, slamming his fist down on the table, shaking the ash off the cigarette he held clenched in his other hand. "Sorry. I didn't mean to yell, Nicky," he said, taking a deep breath.

Nick gathered himself up into a ball in the chair, arms around his knees. He'd never seen his brother like this before. Jamus had always been just Jamus, calm and steady, but today a cold, steel pain burned in his eyes, and a note in his voice warned Nick not to press on.

"Look," Jamus said. He was trying to steady himself, but a metallic tone in his voice cut through the air between them. "I was just so mad when Mom and Dad died. I had nothing to blame it on, and Angel was just a character that I could be angry at. It was a way of me dealing with things."

But Nick wasn't backing down. "That's not true. You're making that up, and I can tell. I can tell when you're lying, and you're lying now." Nick stopped for a moment and held his breath. "Why won't you tell me the truth?"

"That is the truth," Jamus said.

"Just not all of it," Nick shot back.

Jamus took a long drag off his cigarette and exhaled, blowing the smoke up toward the light. "No, Nicky, you're right. It's not all of it."

"Why won't you tell me?" Nick pleaded.

"Because I can't, Nicky. I just can't."

"You can't or you won't?"

"All right. You want to know the truth, fine. Someone else was in the car that night. It was me. I was driving."

The words settled in the space between the brothers, their meaning gradually coming through to clarity for Nick. Nick dropped his arms and put his feet on the floor. He leaned forward and started to speak, but nothing came out of his mouth. He shook his head feverishly back and forth and slowly the words formed on his lips. "No, Jamus. No, no, no. It wasn't you. Please."

"It didn't happen like in the book." Jamus took one last drag off the cigarette and crushed it out in the ashtray on the table. He reached out and put his hand on Nick's shoulder, but Nick shrugged away from him and just stared. Jamus took a breath. "We had been out to celebrate. Ma and Dad wanted to take me out to dinner because I had just finished grad school and a couple of editors had agreed to look at my first manuscript."

"*Angel?*"

"No, it was a different book. I didn't write *Angel* until later."

"Right," Nick said in a flat voice. "You were too busy living it."

"So," Jamus continued. "We were on our way out to dinner. Ma and Dad had picked me up in New York, and I remember wanting to drive so badly because I had been living in the city for so long and hadn't gotten to drive in almost a year." He paused for a second and reached for the pack of cigarettes, pulling one out and lighting it. The sound of the flint was the only noise in the silence of the room.

"We were going out to some place Dad had wanted to try on Long Island." Jamus's hands had begun to shake, and his eyes were glassy and wet. His voice sounded strained as he went on. "Nick, it happened so fast. I was in the right lane and some guy came out of the off-ramp going the wrong way." Jamus pinched the bridge of his nose, trying to stem the tears that were starting to flow.

"I wasn't high," he said. "It wasn't like that character in the book. But I couldn't do anything right that night. I swerved to try and miss the guy, but he broadsided us on the passenger side."

Nick was silent, unable to move. The look on his face had softened a little as he watched his brother and listened, for the first time, to the details of the accident that had changed so many lives.

"It was bad," Jamus continued. "Are you sure you want to hear this?"

Nick nodded his head quietly.

"Ma, she was in the front seat. She died almost instantly. Dad didn't. I was pinned behind the steering wheel, and I couldn't move. Something had hit me in the back of the head, and I couldn't feel much, but there was blood everywhere. We lay there for what seemed like an hour before help came. I..."

"You what?" Nick asked.

"I woke up a week later in the hospital. They were both gone, and Ma's sister had flown in from Ireland. I hadn't seen her in years and didn't know who she was, but she was the one who took care of you while all that was happening. When I finally got out of the hospital, she said she needed to go back to Ireland. She wanted to take you with her, but I didn't let her."

"Maybe you should have," Nick said, storming out of the room with tears in his eyes.

CHAPTER THIRTY-TWO

The rainy, gray October skies of the weekend had held over into Monday, casting a gloomy light over everything that day. Nick sat in math class with his chin lowered onto his fist, staring straight ahead at the chalkboard. He had remained that way, virtually catatonic, for the entire lesson. At one point, the teacher called on him to answer a question, but he barely bothered to respond, simply saying, "I don't know."

"And what about the homework assignment, Mr. Cork?" the teacher asked toward the end of the period. "I don't suppose you have that to hand in today?"

"Nope," Nick said, picking his head up slightly off the desk and shrugging. "I didn't get to it this weekend. Sorry."

The class had erupted into a sea of muffled giggles, but the teacher just frowned and looked from Nick to Matt and back. Matt, for his part, sat next to Nick with a confused look on his face. It had been his night to do math homework, and he had done it and left it in Nick's locker that morning to copy.

At lunchtime, Nick and Matt sat at a table by themselves. What seemed like miles of Formica lay between them, sticky with milk stains and leftover ketchup from the earlier lunch period. Nick had intentionally left the lunch Jamus packed for him at home on the kitchen counter that morning, so he sat staring at a fried chicken sandwich he had barely touched and probably wouldn't finish. Matt sat staring at Nick. He'd already finished his meal and had nothing else to do. Neither had spoken since math class, and because no one would sit with them or talk to them since the incident with Robby, they had nothing to break up the silence between them.

"Okay," Matt finally said. "What's up?"

"Nothing's up," said Nick, flipping the top bun off his chicken sandwich. "I'm fine."

"You're not fine." Matt waited a few seconds, trying to decide what he wanted to say. "You haven't been right for the whole weekend, and now you're even worse."

"I was fine this weekend, I just had some reading to do," said Nick.

"That wasn't homework," Matt said. Nick looked across the table at his friend, the chatter of the cafeteria evaporating as the conversation started to take on a more serious tone. "I'm not stupid, Nick. I know that wasn't assigned reading. We have the same classes, dude."

"I didn't say it was homework," Nick said.

"All right. Fine. What was it? And why are you so freaked out ever since you started reading it?"

"I'm not freaked out."

Matt tilted his head to the left with an exaggerated expression of exasperation. "Dude, you've been walking around looking like a zombie ate your brain. You didn't even like the Batman movie."

"Fuck, Matt, let it go."

"Fine, dude," Matt said, looking down at his empty tray. "Letting it go. Whatever."

After a few seconds, Nick let out a heavy breath. "Matt. I'm sorry. I didn't mean it like that," he said. "Look, can I tell you something?"

"Um, sure," said Matt. "I'd think you would know that by now. We've only been hanging out since, like third grade."

"Jamus wrote that book."

"Oh."

"Yeah." Nick ran Matt through the basic plot of the book and then the conversation he and Jamus had had on Sunday afternoon. Matt listened through the entire story, his jaw hanging open from the first, vivid description of the New York street life through the rest of Nick's replay. When Nick was done, Matt sat stone silent. When it became obvious to Matt from Nick's silence that he was supposed to speak, he was slow to say anything at all.

"So, let me get this straight...ish," he started. "You read a book about a sort of gay druggie that your brother wrote about seven years ago. You think that because one of the characters in that book got high and crashed a car that killed his parents, that Jamus is a bad person?"

"He did it." Nick slammed his fist on the cafeteria table, clanging his silverware.

"He did what?" Matt asked, straightening his own fork and knife on the tray in front of him.

"He crashed the car that actually did kill my parents."

"But it wasn't his fault. It was an accident, dude." Matt put his hands on either side of his tray and looked directly across the table at Nick. "You can't blame him for that."

"What if he's lying?" Nick said. "What if he was a druggie, and that's how he killed them?"

"He didn't kill them, Nick, and why would he lie?"

"He lied before about being in the car." Nick banged his fist on the table again, this time hard enough to send the silverware bouncing off his tray and crashing onto the floor. His voice was getting steadily louder now, and a couple of the kids at the table behind him were starting to listen in.

"He didn't lie," said Matt, lowering his own voice in what seemed like a vain attempt to quell the storm rising in Nick's eyes. "He just didn't tell you about it."

"No, Matt. It was more than just that. He didn't even tell me about how my parents really died. Why wouldn't he tell me that, huh? Why?"

"Because he was probably scared that you'd blame him, dude."

"What?" Nick looked dumbstruck.

"You're doing it now. You're blaming him. You know it wasn't his fault, and you're still blaming him."

"What the fuck, Matt?" Nick was full-fledged yelling now, and the hum of the cafeteria around them had deadened to silence. "Why are you taking his side? He fucking lied to me. I've got nobody, Matt—nobody. He killed my parents, and he's been lying about it for ten years and now you don't even see it. You're my best friend. You're supposed to be on my side." Nick rose out of his seat as he spoke, lifting his tray in front of him.

"Nick, dude, I'm on your side." He motioned for Nick to sit down. "I just think you might not be seeing the whole story."

"I see it," said Nick. "I see the whole story, I just don't see why you can't." He picked up the tray and slammed it down, storming out of the cafeteria.

Matt sat in silence, the rest of the cafeteria staring at him. Across from him was Nick's abandoned lunch. He looked around at the kids staring at him. "What are you animals staring at? Don't you have anything better to do? Go fuck yourselves." He picked up the untouched chicken sandwich and took a bite, chewing defiantly as the crowd looked on.

In the corner of the cafeteria, a figure in jeans and a white button-down Ralph Lauren shirt watched as Nick stormed out of the cafeteria. Mr. Malloy thought about going after him, but something changed his mind.

CHAPTER THIRTY-THREE

The next Sunday marked the first week of November, and days of steady rain had hastened the falling leaves. The bright reds and oranges of the early fall foliage had given way to the duller browns and yellows of the later season. But the clouds lifted that morning and the rain held off, suspending the gloom of the past week. A dull sun shone on the faded vinyl siding of the triple-deckers along the way, bathing everything in a lonely gray tint as Jamus walked down Broadway through the heart of South Boston toward Sacred Heart Church.

Jamus arrived a little later than usual, climbing the stone steps to the church as it was filling up for Mass. He tried not to look for Sean as he took his normal spot in a pew toward the back of the church. He even counted to fifty before allowing himself to glance up at the altar, but as soon as he did, his eyes had a mind of their own and went directly to the spot where Sean usually sat with his family. Jamus smiled to himself when he saw the back of Sean's head in its usual spot alongside the rest of the Malloys. As if on cue, as if Jamus had sent some invisible signal out, Sean turned around and saw him smiling. Jamus flushed red, and Sean winked at him, something Jamus had dared him to do over drinks the Thursday before.

Jamus's conversation with Sean over drinks at the Snap Dragon a few days earlier had been one of the bright spots in his week. He was originally skeptical about meeting the English teacher out for a second time after the disastrous first date, but it had been worth it. Sean had been more relaxed and the conversation, after the first few awkward lines, flowed easily between them. Sean actually had a playful side to him when he wasn't worried about his impending identity crisis.

All through the service, Jamus tried to concentrate on the sermon, but it was useless. The only thing he could focus on was the back of Sean's head. He stayed seated during communion, keeping his eyes down and flipping through the hymnal. Finally, after what seemed to Jamus like the longest Mass in the history of the Catholic Church, it was over. The dull murmur of people standing up and pulling on coats and sweaters filled the building.

As the church slowly emptied, Sean made a point of lingering, letting his family file out ahead of him. He told them he was going to run some errands and would see them later back at the house. His sister, Aideen, gave him a strange look but didn't say anything as she left. He watched carefully as Jamus wandered out the back door of the church after most of the crowd had dispersed. Sean waited a few minutes longer, and then he followed him out. Sure enough, Jamus was standing on the steps of the church smoking, like every Sunday.

"Hello," Sean said as he walked out beyond the shadow of the church doors and into the full sun of the November morning.

"Hey." Jamus returned the greeting with a nod, dropping the barely smoked cigarette to the ground and stepping on it. Silence slowly folded in around the two of them as the last of the crowd filtered out of the nave and clusters of regulars gathered together on the small lawn in front of the church.

Sean and Jamus stood looking at each other, each stealing short glances at the other's face, neither able to hold the other's eyes for more than a few seconds. Sean shuffled his feet back and forth and looked up and around at the crowd down on the church lawn. Jamus kept his eyes on the stomped-out cigarette at his feet in between quick glances up at Sean. They stood that way for a few moments before Jamus finally took his hands out of his pockets and waved one of them in the direction of the South End, as if gesturing that he needed to be going.

"Up for a walk?" Sean asked before Jamus could speak.

"Um, sure." Jamus's face seemed to relax just a little bit. "Walk me up toward the South End?"

Sean nodded, and they shuffled off in nervous steps, away from the church, staying on the edge of the crowd. Sean steered them in the opposite direction from his house, sidestepping any possible route his mom and sisters might be taking home. Neither of them spoke until they were a few blocks up from the church. Jamus finally broke the ice.

"I had a great time hanging out the other night," he said.

"Me, too," Sean said. "I didn't know that bar could be so much fun."

"What do you mean, that bar? It wasn't the bar. We were the only two people in it." They chuckled nervously in unison.

"Well, us and Sharon," Sean corrected him.

"That's true. She's a riot."

As they reached the top of the hill and turned right on Broadway, Sean grew quiet again. He kept his head down for a couple of blocks, cautiously watching on either side of the street but trying desperately to be discreet about it. For a while, Jamus kept quiet, too, and pretended not to notice Sean's guarded surveillance as they moved slowly away from the heart of South Boston, out toward the rest of the world.

"Nervous to be seen with an outsider?" Jamus finally asked.

"Nervous to be with you," Sean said after a few seconds. He shrugged. "Sorry, I didn't mean that how it sounded."

"Don't worry about it," Jamus said with a smile. "I know what it feels like." He lit a cigarette as they walked, his hand trembling slightly as he held the lighter. "It's a little weird for me, too."

"Is it?" Sean thought for a moment, stretching his fingers out in his pockets as they walked. "Why?"

Jamus didn't respond. He finished lighting his cigarette and slipped the lighter back into his pocket.

Sean continued, "I mean, you're out and everything. Why would you be nervous?"

Jamus laughed. "It's not that easy." The laugh faded as they walked a few more steps. "I'm not nervous about being seen with you. That's true."

"I see." Sean waved away a puff of smoke that wafted in his direction. "Then what are you nervous about?"

Jamus thought for a few minutes as they walked. When he spoke again, it wasn't to answer Sean. Instead, he asked a question. "Tell me about your family. They were there with you this morning, right?"

"My ma and my sisters were."

"Pretty girls, your sisters," Jamus said, taking a long drag off the Lucky.

"Pretty girls? Are you hitting on my sisters now?"

"I can't be hitting on them if they're not here," Jamus shot back, a smile in his eyes.

"Well, do you want me to go get them?" Sean pointed his thumb back over his shoulder. "It's just a few streets back. I'll do it, but I gotta tell you you're confusing the hell out of me."

Jamus laughed. "I'm not serious, you know."

"What, about them or me?"

Jamus gave Sean a look he usually reserved for Nick's more absurd moments. "Really? You have to ask?"

"You didn't answer my question," Sean said.

"Ah, the question about why I'm nervous? No, I guess I didn't." He hesitated before he spoke again. When he did, he had a different tone in his voice. "I guess I'm nervous because I don't know how to feel about you."

"Feel about me?"

"I'll be honest. I'm not good at being close to people."

"You mean friends?" Sean looked at him as they walked.

"Friends or anything else." Jamus raised his eyes to meet Sean's. "I have responsibilities that don't really make it easy for me to get close to people." He hesitated for a second. "To anyone."

"Besides Nick, do you have any family?" Sean asked. "Is there anyone else?"

"No, not besides Nick. Not here," Jamus said. "I think my parents were running from a few things back in Ireland, and they cut a lot of ties. Some aunts and uncles live back there, but we only hear from them every once in a while."

"IRA, huh?" Sean asked in a low voice.

"Not sure, really," said Jamus.

"That must be kind of hard on you guys."

"It hasn't been easy," Jamus said. "And lately it's getting worse."

"The fights at school?"

"Not just that," Jamus said, hesitating for a minute before deciding to tell Sean about how Nick had finished reading *Angel of New York*.

"I don't understand," said Sean. "Why shouldn't he read it? It's a good book. I mean, maybe the language is a little mature for him, but he's probably heard worse from the kids at Hayfield."

Jamus stopped for a second to flick his cigarette into a drainage grate. He immediately pulled another one out of the pack in his coat pocket and lit it. "He thinks I'm Angel."

Sean nodded, still looking a little unsure of the meaning behind Jamus's words. "Huh?"

"Right," said Jamus, looking up at a bank of clouds moving in from the harbor. "I forgot you don't know about this. Our parents died in a car accident when Nick was about three."

Sean nodded a little more deeply this time. "I remember you saying something about that when we met at Hayfield that first time."

"Yeah," said Jamus.

Sean's eyes suddenly bulged in surprise, as if just getting the gravity of the situation. "Angel kills his girlfriend's parents in a car accident because he was fucked up."

"Exactly." Jamus took a long drag off the cigarette. He wiped at the corner of his eyes. Sean looked up to see them watering. "It's the cold," Jamus said, "they always water in the cold."

"So," Sean hesitated, "how much of that's true?"

Jamus looked directly at him. "It's fiction. I didn't kill my parents."

"Sorry." Sean put his hand on Jamus's arm. "I didn't mean to imply that."

Jamus shook his head. "It's okay," he said. "I know. I'm just a little sensitive right now. It's been a week since we had that little blow-up. I can't wait to see what's waiting for me this afternoon."

They walked along in silence for a block, the buildings starting to subtly change as they crossed Dorchester Street and East Broadway became West Broadway. The triple-decker houses and smaller shops gave way to more brick and concrete buildings. "How is he doing in school?" Jamus asked.

"He seemed to have a rough week there, too," Sean said.

Jamus looked over at Sean while they walked. "He did?"

"Yeah, I almost called you on Monday," Sean said. "He had a minor problem with Matt at lunch."

"A fight?"

"No, not a fight. Just a heated conversation."

"About what?" Jamus could feel the skin on the back of his neck start to tighten.

"I don't know exactly. I wasn't that close to where they were sitting. But I think it was about you."

"He won't talk to me now," Jamus said. "We've always been so tight. It's weird. A week ago, we could talk about anything—even stupid things like what Ninja Turtle was the coolest—for hours. Now he's clamped down. He won't say a word."

"Give him time," Sean said, looking ahead as they walked. "He'll come around."

"That stupid book. I never should have written it. I hated it at the time, and I hate it even more now."

"What?" said Sean. "That is a brilliant book. Trust me, I just finished reading it."

"No, it's not. There is so much hatred in it. It's so dark. If I'd thought about how it would come back to bite me in the ass…If I'd thought about what that book was really about, I might have just gone to therapy instead of writing it all out."

"That's art, isn't it?" Sean asked.

Jamus laughed. "Don't go all artistic-intellectual on me," he said. "I'm feeling sorry for myself here. Can't you recognize a little healthy self-loathing when you see it?"

"Yeah, I can." Sean smiled. "You want to know what was waiting for me when I got home after Mass last week?"

Jamus took a drag off his cigarette. "Sure."

"Well, it was a typical Sunday after-church dinner at the Malloy residence. To start, my mom went home and finished cooking what she had started making at six o'clock that morning. My dad landed in front of some game that happened to be on the television. I went out to set the table, like I have done every Sunday without fail since I've been home, and my brother watched the game with my dad while my sisters helped my mom in the kitchen."

"That doesn't sound so bad," Jamus said.

"Oh, I haven't gotten to the good part."

Jamus smiled "Ah, there's a good part?"

"Oh yeah," said Sean. "It's called supper. We all sat down, and it started as soon as the last plate had been served. The latest installment of what is Sean doing with his life."

"Really? Sounds interesting."

"Oh, it's fascinating. It includes several topics, ranging from my job to my reading too much to how I don't spend enough time with my family."

"And you're missing that show this week?"

"I am."

"Will you tell them that you're skipping it to walk a gay junkie lit author home?" Jamus had meant for it to sound funny and light, but he was in the wrong frame of mind to be flip and the words fell out into the conversation with a thud.

"Ah, no." Sean said quietly. "No, I might leave that part out."

"Sorry," Jamus said. "I meant for that to come out differently."

Sean smiled, but he didn't laugh. "Sometimes at Malloy suppers we talk about my girlfriend."

Jamus nodded. "Uh-huh?"

"Yeah, or my lack of one. We talk about why I'm not seeing anyone, especially Grace Kinvara."

"Oooh, Grace Kinvara." Jamus stretched the last name out as he said it, giving it just a slight trace of a brogue. "She sounds mysterious."

"I don't know if I'd go with mysterious. But she's something all right."

"And are you interested in Miss Kinvara? I'm assuming it's Miss, but you never know. Maybe she's a widow—or better, still married."

"Very funny. We're trashy in Southie, but we're not that trashy. We're still Catholics."

"I know, I know," Jamus said. "Sorry." He waited for a few moments. "But you didn't answer my question now."

"I don't know what I'm interested in, to be honest with you."

"I see," Jamus said.

They walked on, the cadence of their strides softly falling into a single rhythm. Jamus gazed ahead as the outline of the expressway grew larger in front of them, blocking out the skyline of the city. He tried to remember what it was like when this raised highway cut through the entire city and not just this outer edge of it, how immense and final it seemed, cutting Boston into unalterable pieces. A few minutes passed before either of them spoke again.

"That's not exactly true." Sean looked thoughtfully down at his hands. "I know what I feel, and I can't help those emotions, but…" His words drifted off, and the silence hung in the air between them.

Jamus looked past Sean and took a deep breath, suppressing the urge to run that was building up inside his entire body. "But what?"

"But I'm afraid of it." Sean stopped, the edge of a nervous smile playing on the corners of his mouth. "I'm not sure if what I'm feeling is really me, or if it's something else. And I'm afraid of what it means to my job. What's going to happen if people find out about this? What if they fire me? And what if the people in my neighborhood find out? It could be a lot of trouble."

"What if, what if," said Jamus. "How much longer are you going to worry about what everyone else is going to do? It's your life." He stood facing Sean for a moment before continuing in silence. Sean moved in step with him as they headed under the concrete monstrosity of the expressway and up through the gray and red brick cube buildings of the Castle Square Apartment complex, known to locals as the Chinese projects.

Castle Square was an alien addition to the edge of the South End, inserted between neighborhoods in the 1960s by the city's redevelopment authority. It had become a haven for low- and middle-income Asian families. Snips of red and yellow curtains colored the windows, and here and there, a clothesline waiting for sunnier weather hung between the corners of the buildings or along a balcony.

Occasionally, the deep sweet and grainy odors hinting at other ways to prepare potatoes and peas and ham wafted down to Sean and Jamus. In the tiny yards along the street side of the building, an assortment of toys, lawn chairs, bikes and Big Wheels lay abandoned for the winter, revealing a glimpse at the lives of the residents huddled in front of televisions and computers inside the tiny rooms.

They finally reached the core of the South End as the last of the Castle Square buildings opened up onto Tremont Street, the main thoroughfare of Jamus's neighborhood. All around them, the sleepy Sunday was slowly coming to life. The brunch crowd, rough and ragged from the excesses of last night, meandered down the sidewalks of Tremont, headed to Hamersly's or some other mimosa-laden café where they would sit telling stories about the bars and clubs of the night before. A T bus rushed down the street and squealed to an abrupt stop, breaking through the quiet of their walk. It was the same bus, the 11, that Sean took to work on weekdays.

"I can walk the rest of the way on my own," Jamus said, facing Sean.

Sean looked up and frowned. "Jamus, I didn't mean—"

Jamus smiled and cut him off, putting a hand on his shoulder. "It's not you. I just don't want Nick to see you walking me home."

Sean laughed. "Your turn to be scared of being seen together?"

"Not scared," Jamus smiled. "He's got enough on his plate without wondering about why his English teacher and his evil older brother are hanging out together."

Sean relaxed and the creases in his forehead smoothed out. "Good point. I guess that wouldn't be the best thing for him to deal with right now."

"Hey, listen, are you up for another beer this week?" Jamus asked. "Or are you too busy deciding how to feel about your feelings?"

Sean smiled and let out a short, soft laugh. "I think I'll be able to take a break from that on Thursday."

"Oooh, Thursday again. Are we starting to have 'a night'?" Jamus teased.

Sean didn't say anything, but he leaned in and before Jamus knew what was happening, Sean kissed him very lightly and quickly on the lips. The kiss lasted only a second, and Sean had backed away even before it was over. He smiled shyly again and turned around to walk back toward home, leaving Jamus with a stunned look on his face.

"What the hell was that?" Jamus blurted out, his face turning an almost comic shade of red. "You know, you could give me a little more warning next time and I'll kiss you back." He tried to sound cool, to cover up his surprise, but he knew it was no use.

"That was good-bye for now," Sean said.

"Bye," Jamus called out after a few seconds, recovering himself just a little bit.

"See you on Thursday," Sean called as he walked away.

"Now I'm confused," Jamus said under his breath. He stood on the sidewalk watching Sean walk away, unsure exactly what to make of him. Out of the corner of his eye, he saw a woman stopping to check her cell phone, but he only noticed her because she was also watching Sean walk away. There was nothing remarkable about her except that she had stopped at an odd spot behind an awning, almost as if she was trying to hide. He turned around and headed for home.

CHAPTER THIRTY-FOUR

That doesn't look like the same book." The familiar voice came up on him from behind. Sean smiled, picturing her walking up to the beach in her big winter coat.

"Grace," he said, turning around to see her. He was right. She wore her big coat, knee-high leather boots, and a scarf around her neck, the same black bag slung loosely over her shoulder. But something about her had changed. A tired, almost gaunt expression settled around her mouth, and she kept her eyes locked on the ground, avoiding his gaze.

"I knew I'd find you here," she said, settling in beside him on the park bench.

"Pretty predictable, huh?"

"No, Sean, not really." She looked out across the dark water.

He let the comment settle before saying anything. "I've been meaning to call you."

She laughed. "No, Sean, you haven't. If you'd wanted to call me, you would have. You haven't returned my calls all week." Her voice was low, and she kept her eyes straight ahead as she spoke.

"No." He followed her gaze out to the water. "I guess I have been quiet." The book had been sitting on his lap up until now, his hands shielding the cover. This caught her attention, and she glanced down at it. Sean closed the book and tried to shuttle it into his jacket pocket, but she laid her hand down over his.

"Don't bother," she sighed. "I'll bet you fifty bucks I could guess what you're reading."

He slowly laid the book back down onto his lap.

"Yeah," she said, looking at the title. "That's what I figured."

They sat in silence for a while before she said, without turning to look at him, "What happened to *A Separate Peace*, Sean?"

He shrugged. "We're finished with it. Tests are over and we're on to the next book."

"Is that what happened with us?"

"What?" he asked, a catch in his throat.

She finally turned to look at him. "Did you get bored with us, Sean? Are you on to the next thing?"

"Grace, look, I don't..."

"Sean, don't." She laid her hand down on his. "I know."

"You know what?" he asked. "There's nothing to know."

"Sean, don't make me say it, and I won't make you." She pressed her hand a little more firmly on his and reached her fingers around the edge of his palm, gripping his hand but not tightly. "I followed you last Sunday, after Mass."

Sean felt the bottom of his stomach fall through the ground below him. He began to sweat, and his heart started to beat faster. "Grace..."

"Sean." She smiled. "You're pretending. And I don't care if you pretend. It's fine. But I can't play pretend with you because..." She held her breath for a minute, and Sean could see her eyes start to glisten. "Because it's breaking my heart."

She tried to smile, but her eyes were tearing up. She gripped his hand tightly and then let it go, abandoning him for the giant black bag. She thrashed about inside it for a minute, searching for something, and then pulled out a Marlboro Ultra and her lighter. She struck the lighter three times before shaking it furiously.

"Let me," Sean said, reaching over and taking it out of her hand. With one hand, he shielded it from the wind and rolled his thumb over the flint with the other, sparking it to life. He leaned in and lit her cigarette as she inhaled deeply.

"Fuck this," she said, letting out a billowing stream of smoke and a nervous laugh at the same time.

Sean smiled and handed her back the lighter.

"Tell me something, Sean, why you?"

"I'm sorry?" he said. "What do you mean?"

"I mean why you? Why do you have to be gay?"

"Uh, well..." Sean could feel himself starting to sweat again. "I don't know if I am gay, Grace."

"Oh, cut the crap, Sean. You're twenty-six years old. You're gay. You're too old for a phase."

"I see," he said.

"Please," she said, looking at him. "Don't sulk about it. I'm already going to be sulking enough for the both of us. The sooner you admit it to yourself, the easier it will be to get on with it and start building a real life instead of hiding out here on the beach in South Boston."

"I'm not hiding out."

"Yes, Sean, you are." She took another drag. "And the sad thing is that you need me to tell you that." She looked directly into his eyes and grabbed his hand again, spilling ash on his coat as she did. "Don't do this anymore, Sean. Don't hide behind your mother's skirt and your brother's barbs and the family fights that you guys have every night because it's easier to sit there and yell about things like you teaching instead of working in a construction site, and pretending like that's the real issue. It's not the real issue, Sean. But they're not going to deal with it until you do."

Sean couldn't meet her gaze. He kept looking straight ahead of himself, willing himself not to cry while the tears welled up in his eyes and spilled down over his cheeks and his trembling lips. "Grace," he finally said, taking a deep breath, "I don't know what to do."

"Start living, hon." She pulled her hand back and took one last drag on the cigarette before crushing it out on the sidewalk under the toe of her boot. "Move in with your writer."

He laughed.

"I'm serious. Do it, don't be afraid."

"No," he said. "I just met him."

"Sean, knock it off."

"No, seriously, I just met him a few weeks ago. His kid is in my class."

"He's got a kid?" Then, as if adding things up in her own head, "Wait, he's married?"

Sean laughed and rubbed his eyes with the back of his sleeves. "No, he doesn't have a wife."

"Does the kid know his dad's seeing his teacher?"

"Not exactly. I would say it's complicated, but it's really nothing. There's nothing to it. We went out once for beers."

"Beers, huh?" She glanced at him sideways. "Right."

"Well, I had a beer. He had a scotch." Sean had started to pull himself together a little. "I don't know what happened to me the other day. I just really liked him, and it came out of nowhere. I just..."

"Kissed him." She stopped. "I know," she said, tightening her lips into a deliberate smile. "I saw." She paused for a minute and drew a breath. "Look, Sean. I don't think we can hang out for a while." Silence filled the space between them.

"Oh," he finally said.

"Yeah, not for a while." She searched the air for the right words. "I just can't. I need to separate myself, until I can think about you as a friend. It's a little hard right now."

He nodded and reached for her hand, but she pulled back before he could touch her. "I love you, Sean, and I think someday we are going to be awesome friends, but right now I just gotta go." She stood up and lobbed the bag over her shoulder.

"Grace, look..."

"Bye, Sean. Good luck with him," she said, backing away from the bench and turning up toward the houses. "And I mean it—stop hiding. *Suigh ansin go foil.*"

He opened his mouth to say something, anything, to stop her, but no words came. Instead he stood up, not moving a muscle as he watched her walk away. A long time passed before he sat back down on the bench and stared out at the ocean. He wrapped his hands around the book in his lap and felt the night close in on him. The air seemed gray and heavy with the weight of her last words. After a while, he reached up and touched the hot damp stains on his cheeks. It was strange because he had forgotten he'd been crying. In that moment, he felt more alone than he had in his entire life.

Later that night after he had spent a few hours sitting on that park bench, staring out into the ocean and thinking about his life, Sean headed back to his parents' house. As he approached, he noticed the lights were all off except for one in the living room.

He walked in and took his boots off before tiptoeing in through the kitchen.

"Sean?" His mother's voice came in from the living room. "Is that you?"

"Yeah, Ma," he said, stopping at the kitchen table, out of view of the living room.

"You're out late."

"Just up the beach reading."

"Grace called at the house for you earlier tonight," she said. "I told her that's probably where you were."

"Thanks, Ma. Yeah, she came to say hi."

"Everything okay with you guys?"

"Yeah, Ma. Everything's fine." He paused for a second, wanting to go in the living room but not wanting his mom to see him. She would know he'd been crying and she'd ask why. "I'm gonna go up, Ma. I'm beat."

"Good night then, Seany," she said. "Love you."

"Love you, too, Ma." He bit his lower lip so he wouldn't start crying again, and he headed up the stairs as quickly and quietly as he could.

CHAPTER THIRTY-FIVE

For Jamus, Tuesday began much the same way as it did every week. Except that Nick wasn't talking to him, and the mix of anger and guilt had kept him from sleeping most of the night. That had been the case for over a week, and the situation didn't show any signs of getting better. Jamus started the day in the kitchen, reading. He yelled up for Nick to get down for breakfast at the ten-minute-warning mark, and Nick came thundering down the stairs like someone dumping a wheelbarrow of bricks down a trash shoot. He grabbed the piece of toast Jamus had laid out for him, but he didn't say anything. He left the cup of coffee untouched and headed out the door.

"Hey," said Jamus. "Good morning."

"Hey yourself." Nick turned briefly to his brother before heading back to the door.

Jamus slammed his coffee cup on the table and was up like a shot, making it to the door before Nick had his coat on. "Huh-uh. No, we are not going to do this anymore."

"What exactly aren't we going to do, Jamus?" Nick turned around to look at his brother, the tense pink of rage flooding his face.

"You are not going to mope around here and talk to me like that."

Nick just stared at him. Without saying a word, he reached around Jamus for his coat. "Then I just won't speak to you at all. Oh, wait. Maybe I ought to be more respectful. Maybe I should watch out, after all, you've killed before."

Jamus's hand jerked quickly. He wanted to cuff Nick across the back of the head, but he caught himself an instant before he did. He took a deep breath. "Nicholas Patrick Cork, you will not talk to me like that." His brother looked away from him, but Jamus took Nick's chin gently in his hand and turned the kid's face to look straight at him. "I don't talk to you like that, and you will not talk to me like that."

Nick just stared at him.

"Nick," he said, his jaw clenched. "I know you're mad at me, but their death was not my fault." Nick tried to jerk his head free, but Jamus held his grip. "If you don't think I have struggled with this every day of my life, and if you don't think I have missed them every second of every day, then you've got another think coming. Nick, they were my parents, too, and I loved them."

"And I didn't even get to know them," Nick said in slow, measured words. "Because of you."

Jamus let go of his brother's face and dropped his hand to his side. "I'll see you tonight," he said as he turned and walked back into the kitchen. "Don't forget your book bag."

❖

Jamus's meeting with Eileen went better this week. But that was mostly because he lied to her. He hadn't stopped reading everything he could about the Big Dig, but he didn't mention that. He brought in a few chapters from *Rancher's Wife*, handing them across the desk to her as he sat down. But she pushed them back toward him.

"Not today," she said. "I'm sure they're great, and besides, I know better than to interrupt your process."

He flashed an obviously fake smile back at her. "You love interrupting my process, as you call it, and you never like my first drafts. And this is what you asked for. It's the first few chapters of *Rancher's Wife*."

"Well, I want to talk about something else." She pulled a folder out of the top drawer of her desk. "What do you know about a company called Dexicont?"

Jamus frowned at her. "The technology company? What's their slogan—'Dexicont at the heart of the electronics you love,' or something like that?"

"That's the one," she said, a sly smile playing at the corner of her lips. Jamus thought she looked a little like a German shepherd about to pounce on an unsuspecting cat. "They want you to write a biography of their chief executive officer."

"Like a book biography?" he asked.

She nodded. "You do write books, last I knew," she said.

"Eileen, I'm not a biographer, I'm a novelist."

"And a reporter," she added.

"A columnist," he corrected her. "I write opinion pieces."

"One of their PR reps approached me a couple of weeks ago. They like your style. They think you're edgy and provocative, and they want your voice to tell their story."

"My voice? Have they read my books? I can hardly imagine they want their CEO portrayed like *Angel of New York*. Who is this executive, anyway? Computer designer by day, drug lord and junkie by night?"

"They like your column."

"Have they read my novels?"

"That's why I waited two weeks to tell you about it," she said. "When they first asked me, I sent them copies of all your books and told them to come back to me when they were done if they were still interested."

"And they were?"

"They were more than interested. This company wants to put these little chips it makes into all the gadgets the street urchins you write about are using. You know, the DVD players and i-prods, or whatever they're called. They want a Dexicont underneath the hood of the smartphones that those junkies are using. They loved the books."

He stared across the desk at her, taking in the expression of her pinched nose and small dark, passionate eyes he had stared into so many times over the past decade. At last he wet his lips and asked, "What's the project timeframe?"

"They want you out in California next week to interview their CEO, then over in Taiwan to talk to some of their partners there. There're a few other partners in Japan, a couple in the UK, and then I think one person in Germany."

"No. Sorry, Eileen. There's no way. I can't do that kind of travel right now." Jamus looked up at her. She was staring at him in disbelief. "Things are in a bad place with Nick. I need to be here with him right now."

"Why don't you take a look at this project scope? It's a great project—so much more to it than the Big Dig thing." She handed him the folder and reached into her drawer for another piece of paper. She looked over it and turned it face down on the desk before sliding it across to Jamus. "Here is an outline of the project budget."

Jamus searched her eyes for a few seconds before turning the paper over and looking down at it. The room was silent as he glanced through the lines of numbers until he reached the bottom of the page and let out a long slow whistle.

"That's a big number," she said.

"And a big margin for you," he said. "Does it include expenses?"

"No, expenses and stipend are separate." She smiled dollar bills. "You can bring Nick with you. Pull him out of school for a week. Maybe he would like the travel."

"Uh-huh," he said. "The Christmas break is coming up. I'll think about it. Can you see if you can push the dates back a little?"

"I'll try."

"Don't just try." He got up to leave. "Do it. If they want edgy, I'll give them edgy, but they might just have to wait a few weeks for it."

She smiled at him as he grabbed his bag, shoving in the chapters he had brought along with him, and headed out of her office.

"Call me," she said.

"I will. Don't worry."

Down in the lobby, his phone rang as soon as he stepped out of the elevator. He looked at the incoming call and noticed it was a Hayfield Academy number. He felt instantly nauseous, and a wave of fear passed through him as he pressed the button to accept the call. "Hello," he said, trying to hold the phone steady.

"Hi, Jamus. It's Sean."

"Hi, Sean, is it Nick? Is everything all right?"

"What?" Sean sounded surprised. "Oh, yeah, yes. Sorry, I'm calling you from the school line. I'm an idiot. No, everything is fine. I just wanted to say hi."

Jamus exhaled. After the conversation he and Nick had had this morning, he wouldn't be able to take it if anything had happened to his brother.

"Hi," he said back, unsure of what to say next. "Everything okay with you?"

"Yeah, just a little awkward, to tell you the truth," said Sean. "I felt a little weird about how I, er, left things last Sunday."

Jamus smiled and glanced around to see if anyone was watching. He lowered his head, cradling the phone to his ear, and headed over to the corner of the lobby where he was a little more out of the way. "Yeah, well I thought it was nice."

"Uh-huh. Me, too." Sean was quiet for a minute. "Look, Jamus, I'm sort of dealing with some things for the first time here."

Jamus sighed and leaned up against the burled walnut wall of the lobby. If this was going where he thought it was going, he really didn't want to hear any more. "First time, huh?"

"Yeah." Jamus heard a catch in his voice, as if he was trying to find the right words. "Someone said a couple of things to me yesterday that I needed to hear."

"Yeah?" Jamus asked.

"Yeah," Sean echoed. He started slowly relaying the conversation he and Grace had the other night on the beach. Jamus listened as the story poured out from Sean over the phone, occasionally shifting his position as people came and went through the lobby. Sean finally paused and sighed. "I guess I'm just trying to figure everything out."

"Out is the key word, huh?"

"Sorry?" Sean said. "What do you mean."

"Out, Sean," Jamus said. "This is what they call coming out."

"Oh." There was a long pause on the end of the phone. "Right, I guess I just haven't really thought about it from that perspective yet."

"Sean, you're going to be okay," Jamus said. "From what you've said, it sounds like that was a really, really positive conversation."

"Was it? I mean, she doesn't want to talk to me again."

"She just needs time," Jamus said. "And so do you. You'll get through this, and you'll find a whole other life waiting for you full of some pretty spectacular things."

Sean exhaled loudly into the phone, a sigh that sounded like it had been building up for some time. "Listen, my lunch break is just about up, I have to go."

"Okay," Jamus said. "See you Thursday. And, Sean?"

"Yeah?"

"Can you keep an eye on Nick today? We had…" He paused,

unsure of exactly what it was he was trying to describe. "We had some pretty tense words this morning. Just keep an eye out for him."

"Yeah, of course," Sean said. "I will. See you Thursday."

Jamus clicked the end button on his phone and stuffed it into his pocket. He reached into his coat for the pack of cigarettes and started to pull one out. But he didn't. He put the pack back into his pocket and headed out the door.

CHAPTER THIRTY-SIX

"Matt's family is going to Nantucket for Thanksgiving break," Nick said when Jamus came home that night.

"Hello to you, too," Jamus said, laying his briefcase in one of the chairs and tossing his keys on the table. He gently ruffled the top of Nick's head, messing up his hair on the way over to the sink to start dinner. It wasn't the playful gesture it usually was, but it was something toward connecting. "What do you feel like for supper?"

"I'm going with them," Nick said, combing back his hair with his hand.

"Oh, you are?" Jamus said. "Well, okay, let's have that conversation. Did his parents invite you?"

"Matt invited me."

"How are you doing on schoolwork?" Jamus asked.

"I know what you're doing, you're just looking for reasons not to let me go," Nick growled. "Well, I'm going, I'm not asking you, I'm telling you."

"Ah, okay." Jamus said. "Is that how you're going to play this?"

"I'm not playing anything, I'm telling you."

Jamus pulled a couple of pots up from one of the lower cabinets. "Okay, so you're telling me you're going to go. Pasta okay for you? I'm feeling like pasta tonight."

"I don't care. I'm not eating."

"You're eating," Jamus said. "And I didn't say you couldn't go, but the way you're headed, this conversation isn't looking good for you."

"You can't say I can't go."

"Oh yes, I can." Jamus filled the pot with water and placed it on the back burner of the stove. "I am your big brother and your guardian, and you're fourteen years old. I think that means I get to tell you what you can and can't do for now."

Nick slammed his fists on the table. Defiance raged behind his pale blue eyes, turning his face into a twisted mask of frustration that was at the same time very young and very old.

"Ah, no," Jamus said very calmly. "No fists, no yelling, no fighting. Tell me that you're caught up on your schoolwork, and then we'll talk about Nantucket."

Nick didn't say anything. He sat at the table and glared at his brother. Jamus ignored him and went about pulling things out of the cabinets and the refrigerator. The water boiled, and Jamus dumped in a handful of spaghetti. Nick sat motionless. "Hey, you." Jamus tried to rouse him. "You feel like setting the table?"

"Fine," Nick said. He stood up and grabbed the plates and napkins. The meal passed without a word and Nick asked to be excused when they were done.

"So, you're not going to tell me how it's going with your schoolwork?" Jamus asked. Nick shook his head and bounded up the stairs. Jamus waited for the bedroom door to slam before he got up to clear the table. He looked to the ceiling and let out a deep sigh. He had been doing this since he was twenty-two. He hadn't been an adult without taking care of a kid by himself. And though he had sworn never to let any of it show, he was scared to death he was doing it all wrong.

He went back to his briefcase and pulled out the file on the Dexicont project. He thumbed through it until he found the project calendar. Doing some calculations in his head around the holidays, he closed the file and put it back in his bag. Thanksgiving was this week, and while it was too late to try and wedge any travel in now, Jamus figured he and Nick could make the trip work over the Christmas holiday break from Hayfield.

The more he thought about it, the more it made sense. It would get them out of Boston for a couple of weeks and give them a little time together to decompress. The first stop would be San Francisco. Between the Embarcadero, Pier 39, and Alcatraz, there would be plenty for them to do. They could rent a car and head down Route One to Half Moon Bay; he could show Nick the California coast, and they could put some of Boston behind them. Of course, Jamus would have to work much of the time, but he was sure Nick wouldn't mind kicking back in front of the giant screen TV in the rooms at the Hyatt. Maybe this was exactly what they needed. He decided he would call Eileen in the morning and then talk to Nick after school.

❖

The Spences had decided to take the fast ferry from Hyannis Port to Nantucket. From the edge of the parking lot, the boat looked sleek and white, a crisp dream that promised escape for Nick. But as they walked down the dock, the boat came to life in a grungier, more dramatic way. It wasn't as new as it looked from afar. The paint was chipped, the railings rusty, and as they crossed the walkway to the boat, Nick noticed the deck smelled slightly of diesel fuel and puke. He held his breath as they boarded, Matt's mom handing the purser everyone's ticket as they walked down the gangplank and onto the boat.

Nick had told Matt the truth about sneaking out, but he had lied to Mrs. Spence, telling her that Jamus had okayed the trip. Nick had set his alarm to wake up an hour earlier than usual. On his way out of the house that morning, he'd packed his backpack, grabbed a pair of winter boots and sixty bucks from the coffee can stash above the fridge. Just before leaving, he wrote Jamus a short note telling him where he was going. He hadn't planned on doing that, but if Jamus freaked and called the cops, he'd really be in trouble. He didn't want to deal with that.

That day was the last day Hayfield was in session before the Thanksgiving holiday, and the halls and classrooms were nearly vacant. Most of the students were already gone, leaving early to beat the travel rush. Nobody even stopped to ask Nick if he'd been excused as he left school early that day, strolling casually out with Matt when Mrs. Spence arrived. Matt and Nick were always together, so Nick walking out the door with Matt wouldn't raise much, if any, suspicion. The only one who gave him a funny look was Mr. Malloy. They passed by his class on their way out, and Nick saw him glance up at them. Nick looked away and picked up the pace as they walked down the corridor.

On the boat, Matt's mom immediately staked out a booth near

the window, stuffing their bags underneath the table. She had brought food, olives and hummus and some stuffed grape leaves she had made the night before. Nick watched as she started to unpack lunch even before the boat was under way, and he wished that he had thought to bring some of the leftover pasta from the night before.

As they pulled away from the dock, Nick sat back in his seat and scrunched up his jacket into a pillow. He waved away something with feta on it that Mrs. Spence offered him with a polite no, thank you and turned to watch the little houses of the harbor recede into the horizon. He drifted off to sleep somewhere close to shore and didn't wake up until they were almost to the island.

❖

That morning Jamus woke up to an uncomfortably quiet house. Something was wrong. He was usually up before Nick, but the house sounded different that morning. He rolled out from underneath his covers and pulled on his bathrobe, trudging down to the kitchen, not bothering with his morning rituals of brushing his teeth and shaving. When he got to the bottom of the stairs, he found a note taped to the banister. Jamus stared at it for a few minutes before pulling it down. He didn't open it; he didn't need to. He knew without having to be told that Nick had gone with Matt's family to Nantucket.

He stood for a moment at the bottom of the stairs, looking up at the ceiling above his head. "I give up," he said out loud to nobody. He took the note and folded it up, dropping it on the kitchen table as he made his way to the sink. "I get it," he continued out loud, "and I am letting go."

He went into the kitchen, made some coffee, and sat down to work. He pulled out the Dexicont file and began reading the background the company had provided. At ten thirty, he put down the file and reached for his phone. He made a couple of calls and then decided to go for a walk.

CHAPTER THIRTY-SEVEN

It's not so bad, is it?" Sean said, trying to smile. It was the first time Kevin had been back to Grumpy's since his flashback episode over the summer.

"No." Kevin took a swig of his Guinness. "If you don't mind everyone staring at us, I'd say we're doing just fine." His older brother had been looking around nervously since they walked in, but Sean kept an eye open and didn't see that many stares.

"Come on, we're not outcasts here, Kevin."

"Really? Because I don't see anyone talking to us."

"That's not completely true, the O'Leary boys came over and talked to us," Sean said, referring to a couple of their high school friends who'd come up earlier in the evening to say hello.

"They were making fun of us," Kevin snorted into his beer. He was staring straight ahead at the door when his shoulders suddenly tightened, and his face went crooked. "Oh boy. Sean, we should really go." Kevin spilled a little of his beer as he rushed to put down his glass.

Sean shook his head. "No. You're doing fine. Right? No loud noises and hey, even if there is, you're going to be all right. I'm here, and you told me what to watch for, so we're good. Kevin, you can't be afraid of this place."

"Actually, it's not me I'm worried about just now." Kevin nodded over Sean's shoulder in the direction of the door.

"What?"

"Don't do it right now, but in a minute, casually turn your head and take a look at who just walked in."

Sean carefully turned his head a few degrees at first, then the full way, pretending to look for the bartender, and that's when he spotted the red hair, the gray coat, and the unmistakable giant black bag. Underneath the coat was the green dress, the same outfit she'd worn that day at church when they walked the old priest back to the cottage.

"Things aren't so great between you guys right now, are they?"

"How do you know?" Sean quipped.

Kevin winced, but he didn't back down. "Um, it's not rocket science, Seany." He pushed his empty pint glass to the inside edge of the bar. "You haven't seen her in weeks, and you've been out on other dates. Things can't be good."

Sean took a deep breath. The idea of getting up and walking out had occurred to him—more than occurred, actually. Every fiber of his being was screaming to get out of that bar. But he didn't budge. He told himself he needed to face this sometime. They lived in the same neighborhood, and he refused to spend the rest of his life avoiding places because of Grace Kinvara.

"Oh, shit," Kevin said. Sean started to turn around again, but Kevin put his hand on his arm, keeping him where he was. "Don't look now."

"What?" Sean scowled at his brother. "What do you mean don't look now. Why does it matter if I look?"

"Sean…" Kevin paused for a second, looking like he was trying to collect his thoughts and figure out a way to break bad news to Sean. "Uh, well, Sean…"

"God, Kevin." Sean's face took on a windblown look of exasperation. "What's the matter now? Did the Pope just walk in?"

"No, Sean. But you see, here's the thing. I think I know what's going on here, and I just want you to know that it's all right." Kevin's voice sounded strained.

"What's all right? What are you talking about?" Sean's stomach sank even as he spoke. He willed his face not to turn red, but he knew it was no use. He could already feel the sweat starting to bead across the top of his back.

"Your sisters Siobhan and Aideen just walked in." Kevin nodded in the direction of the door. "And I'll bet you dollars to donuts that they'll be chatting with your ex-girlfriend in a matter of minutes."

"That's the thing, Kevin," Sean exclaimed, throwing his hands up in the air. "She's not my ex-girlfriend."

"We live in Southie, Sean." Kevin leaned in, his hands out toward Sean, palms down. "And whether you like it or not, everyone in this bar thinks she's your ex-girlfriend."

Sean bit his lower lip and glared at his brother.

"Now," Kevin said, lowering his voice to almost a whisper. "We have two choices. We either leave now, or we stay here knowing you're going to have to talk to her."

Sean stared at his brother, evaluating the options he'd just laid out. The conversation with Grace had been clear. She needed space from him right now, but Sean thought about what could happen if she needed to vent, if she talked too much. Aideen would no doubt pry, if she hadn't already. And if anything came out, it was all over for him.

"I'm not going to run every time I see her." Sean looked over his shoulder and watched as Grace sat down with Aideen and Siobhan on either side of her.

"Well, for Christ's sake, you don't have to stare at them." Kevin gently knocked him on the side of the head, but it was too late. Siobhan had seen them and waved, her face lighting up in a smile. Her smile quickly faded as she motioned to the other two women, and Grace looked down at the bar and put her hands up to her head and gently massaged her temples. Both of the Malloy sisters leaned in, and Sean could only guess at what they were talking about. He swallowed the lump in his throat.

"Oh, man." Kevin shook his head. "This does not look good, Seany."

Sean had given up any effort of trying not to look at them. In the end, it was Aideen who got up first and tromped over to where Sean and Kevin were sitting. She arrived like a locomotive coming to a slow stop. Sean could almost see the steam seething from her ears. She stood in front of them for a few seconds, at first unable to focus on one or the other. But as she slowly got her bearings, she turned toward Sean.

"What happened with you and Grace?" she fumed.

Siobhan and Grace arrived a few seconds behind her. Kevin and Siobhan exchanged a quick glance, and Siobhan shrugged her shoulders and shook her head slightly.

"Beer, anyone?" Kevin leaned over the bar to order, but it was going to take a while. The place had filled up with Guinness drinkers, and it was a slow pour for each. He finally got the bartender's eye. "Hi, Flynn, two pints, please?"

He smiled and nodded. "Sure thing, Kevin. Just no taking down the bar again, eh?"

Sean winced, and Kevin shook his head. But Aideen drew their attention back. "Are you going to answer me, Sean?"

"I don't see how that's any of your business what happened between him and Grace," Kevin said, standing up from his seat at the bar and towering over his sister. "Now is it?"

"Aideen, leave it," Grace said. "You don't want to know about this. Let's just go back and have that drink, okay?"

Sean had had enough. Kevin had been right. It would be better to get out of here tonight. He didn't want to say anything he'd regret later. He stood up and backed his stool away from the bar, but he was trapped.

"Oh no," Aideen. "Flynn, honey—make that three more pints. We're going to have a little chat." She turned to Sean. "Why did you dump my friend?"

Grace shook her head. "You know, Aideen, this is really just between Sean and me."

"Oh no." She frowned and pushed out a pouty lower lip. "That bad, huh?"

"It's fine, really," Grace said. "But I just don't think anything is ever going to work out." She looked over at Sean.

"Too brainy for you?" Aideen asked.

"Not exactly," Grace said. "But close enough. Look…" She pulled a fiver out of the big black bag. "This is for the pint, but I've really gotta go."

Aideen pushed the five-dollar bill back to Grace. "What's going on, Grace? We're all worried about him. He's been sulking for weeks now."

"Hey," Sean said. "I'm right here. I can hear you."

"He's just going through some stuff he has to deal with on his own." Sean glared at her, but Grace was unable to meet his eyes. This was a close crowd, of course, but the tacit understanding was that you avoided the grit of the soul unless someone was being born, dying, getting married, or some combination of the three. "But he could probably use his family's support, so you might want to talk to him. Let him know you're there for him."

"No. Is he moving out?" Aideen turned to Sean. "You little barnie, are you moving out?" Her voice raised a few decibels in disbelief.

"Um, no," Sean said.

Grace took a deep breath and exhaled loudly. "You guys, you should just talk."

"He's gay, isn't he?" It was Kevin. Everyone got quiet when he said it, and Sean turned a deep shade of purple, unable to believe what he'd just heard. He fought back the urge to punch his brother. The bartender set down the first two pints in front of Sean, returning a few seconds later with the rest of the order. Even he must have sensed the tension in the group, because he glanced around at all the faces and made a quick exit.

All three women looked from Kevin to Sean and back, not saying anything. He took a sip of his beer. "Well, that's it, isn't it? That's what you're trying to say, or not say, Gracie?" He raised his chin in her direction.

She shook her head. "Nothing happened between us."

"I know, that's the problem here, isn't it? You kept pushing him, wouldn't let well enough alone." He shook his head. "It wasn't just you, we all pushed him. Hoped it would work. Maybe for this very reason."

Aideen stood dumbfounded, looking from her brother to Grace and back. "How long have you known?" she asked Kevin.

"I don't know." He cocked his head to one side. "Guess I've always sort of suspected. Well, at least since high school."

"I'm. Right. Here." Sean uttered the words through clenched teeth.

"I'm not having this conversation," Grace said and got up to go again.

"Grace, relax. It'll be okay," Kevin said. "Nobody's going to care. We all love him just fine."

"I care," Aideen shot back at him. "He's my little brother, too, and I'm not going to sit here and listen to you two call him a fag."

Kevin winced at the word, and Grace looked away from her. The bar around them had grown silent and everyone was watching them. Sean wished he could melt into the wooden floor.

"The word," Kevin said, "is 'gay.' Not 'fag.' You can't say that, Aideen, and he's your brother, so you better think twice before you talk like that about him—or to him." He nodded to Sean. "Sorry, Sean. I don't mean to keep talking over you."

"I don't believe this, both of you," Aideen virtually spat. "This is not okay, it's not right. I'm going home to talk to Dad about this." She turned to go, but Kevin grabbed her arm.

"Oh no, you don't," he said. "You're going to let him talk to them—and us—in his own time."

"The hell I am, let go of me." She pulled free from him and made her way to the door.

Grace looked up at Kevin. "Go talk to her," she said. "Don't let her go to your parents, not like this."

"You're right," Kevin said, and he grabbed his coat off the hook below the bar and went after his sister.

"What just happened?" Sean asked, staring out the door at Kevin and Aideen.

"Come on." Siobhan grabbed him. "We gotta get there before Aideen does."

"Get where?" He was almost in shock.

"Home, you idiot. Are you deaf? She's going to tell Dad."

❖

"Aideen, stop." Kevin's voice boomed behind her as she raced through the back door of the house, Sean and Siobhan followed closely behind them. It was late at night, and Ma and Dad were both sitting at the kitchen table. Dad was leaning forward in his chair a little unsteadily, trying to read the sports section of the paper. By the looks of it, he'd been out earlier in the evening with a couple of his friends and already had a few pints in him. Ma was playing solitaire, and they both had slightly bored, quiet looks on their faces when Aideen burst in.

"How long have you all known this?" she shouted at her parents, storming into the kitchen. They both looked at each other, puzzled expressions wiping away the bored looks on their faces.

"Aideen, nobody knows anything. Leave it alone," said Kevin, following her in through the door. Siobhan and Sean trailed a few seconds behind Kevin, catching their breath. Sean shut the door behind him.

"Know what?" said Ma, putting down a hand full of cards.

Sean stood behind Aideen, her hands balled up into angry fists, looking down at her parents.

"Sean, let's go upstairs," Kevin said, stepping out from behind Aideen and toward him.

"No." She grabbed Kevin's arm. "It's time for you stop protecting him." She looked at Sean. "Is it true?"

Sean blanched. His stomach suddenly felt as if it was going to implode, and he stepped backward as if yanked by some invisible string in the center of his spine. "Is what true?" he asked, swallowing slowly.

"Don't fuck with me, Sean." Aideen spat out the words.

"Language, please," Ma said, standing up.

"Do you know about this?" she asked her ma, still yelling. "Do you?"

"Aideen, this is not the time or place," Kevin said, stepping quietly away from Sean. "Come on, don't do this. Let's go." He tugged at her arm gently, pulling her toward the door.

"Leave me the fuck alone," she said, ripping her arm away from him.

"Are you queer?" she shouted at Sean. The room went silent for a moment as Ma looked across the table at Dad. Kevin looked at Sean and then down at the floor. Siobhan glanced from one of them to the other and back again. And Aideen stood still as a brick, staring at Sean. "Well?" she said, quietly this time, but with a razor-sharp anger still dripping from her words. "Are you?"

Sean stood where he was, not saying a word, shaking. Kevin stepped around Aideen, put one arm around Sean's shoulder, and stood solidly by his side. "It doesn't matter if he is or isn't," Kevin said. "He's one of us, and that's all there is to it."

"Answer me," Aideen screamed.

"Yes," Sean yelled back at her. "Yes, I am, all right?"

This time Aideen really did spit at him. "You are not my brother," she said. "You filthy queer."

"Fuck you, Aideen," Kevin shouted.

"That's enough," Dad said. He turned toward his youngest son. "Sean, are you sure about this? Do you know what you're saying?"

Before he could speak, Kevin jumped in. "Who cares, Dad? It's

Sean. It's not somebody else. Who cares? Just let him alone about this, okay?"

"It's not okay," his father snapped. He turned to look at Kevin. "Don't you understand this is a choice? We all make our choices and if this—whatever it is that he wants to be—if this is what Sean chooses, then there are going to be consequences."

"Oh, consequences, right?" said Kevin. "Well, he's my brother, and whatever consequences you think he's got to face, then I'll face them with him."

"Kevin, don't," Sean said. "It's okay."

"No." Kevin put his hand on Sean's arm. "It's not okay. He needs to hear this, and so do you. I know what it's like to lose who you are." He took a breath. The room around him had gone quiet. "I watched people die every day for years. And I almost didn't make it back. I lost who I was, and I will never, ever be able to find it again. I only have a few things now, but I know what they are and what they're worth. What I have left are the people in this room." Kevin took a breath, his eyes red and glossy. He turned to his father. "There isn't the same me in here anymore. And that's what you'll do to him if you take this any further." He stopped.

"We'll talk about this in the morning," Ma said, walking around the table to stand beside Dad. "Aideen, go home."

"I am not through here," Aideen said.

"Yes," Ma said, raising her voice in a way that none of them had ever heard their mother use before, "you are quite through here. You need to go. Siobhan, take your sister home. Get some sleep, both of you.

"Sean, Kevin—upstairs now. I don't want to hear from you until the morning, understood?"

All four of her children stood there, not moving, staring at her and at each other.

"Are you lot deaf?" Ma yelled after a few seconds, her voice piercing the air in the room like a banshee wailing. "I don't want to see a one of you in the next ten seconds, or I'm taking out the switch and I'll beat you all stiff. Move it!"

That final fiat sent them all moving. Kevin turned his brother around and headed him up the stairs. Siobhan put her hand on Aideen's shoulder, but Aideen jerked free of her.

RALPH JOSIAH BARDSLEY

"I'm going," she said, "but I won't be back while he's still here."
As she turned, Kevin caught her eye and shook his head. She gave him
the finger and walked out the back door.

❖

Later that night as Kevin lay in his silent attic room, his phone
buzzed. He somehow knew it would be Grace, and he lay still for a few
minutes before he answered the phone.

"Yeah." Kevin's voice was low and gravelly.

"Everything all right?" came Grace's muffled voice.

"I wouldn't say that," Kevin said, the bed creaking as he sat up.
"We had a bit of a fireworks here tonight."

"I'm sorry, I should have kept my mouth shut," Grace said. "I was
trying not to say anything."

"You didn't," Kevin said. "I did, actually, but it wouldn't have
mattered. It would have come out sooner or later, and we would have
had this show whenever it did. Did he actually tell you?"

"Yeah," Grace said. "After I confronted him about seeing him and
his boyfriend."

"Boyfriend?" Kevin winced at the word.

"Well, I guess they're not boyfriends," Grace said. "I guess they're
just sort of seeing each other."

"I didn't know he was seeing someone," said Kevin. "Who is it?"

"I don't know him, exactly," she said. "He goes to our church.
The author guy that always sits in the back and never talks to anyone."

"An author." Kevin laughed. "That figures. How do we know he's
into guys? It might just be that he's into books, you know."

"No, Kevin," she said. "I'm pretty sure he's into guys. I, um…I
saw them kiss."

"Okay," he said. "I don't need the details."

"Now, don't get squeamish, I didn't even give you any details. Is
he going to be okay?"

Kevin took a deep breath. "I don't know. I hope so. Aideen pretty
much lost it on him tonight in front of Ma and Dad. I mean really, really
lost it. Called him a bunch of names and just was not nice."

"Jesus," Grace said. "I'm sorry to hear that."

"Well, Ma broke it all up. Dad's not happy about it, but I'll talk to him tomorrow morning. I think he'll be okay after a while."

"They won't kick him out, will they?"

"No way," said Kevin. "He's still family. Even if they don't understand what he's doing with his life, they're not going to kick him out."

"Good," she said. "That makes me feel a little better."

"Go to sleep, Gracie," he said. "It's almost two in the morning. I'll call you tomorrow after we all talk, okay?"

"Okay," she said and hung up the phone.

❖

In the next room, Sean sat on his bed listening in to as much of his brother's phone call as he could hear. He flinched recalling the words that Aideen had said earlier that evening. A few seconds later, there was a knock at his door.

"Go away," he said.

"I just want to make sure you're okay, Seany."

"I'm fine."

Kevin was silent for a few seconds but didn't open the door. "Okay, then," he said. "I guess I'll see you in the morning."

Sean didn't answer. After a moment, he heard Kevin pad across the tiny hallway and back into his room. Sean pressed his eyes together and wondered how he was ever going to face his family again.

He drifted off to sleep for a while, waking up in the very early hours of the morning with the light still on. He pressed his eyes together and decided he couldn't deal with any of this. It just wasn't possible. He walked over to the closet and, moving as quietly as he could, he rummaged through some of his belongings, throwing a couple of books and a belt on the bed, along with some odds and ends.

CHAPTER THIRTY-EIGHT

The knock at the door took Jamus by surprise. With Nick gone for the past few days, an almost church-like silence had fallen over the house. He was sitting at the kitchen table working, still in his bathrobe and unshaven. The mug of cold coffee in front of him was the only thing he'd gotten up for all morning. He looked up at the clock; it was eleven thirty. He heard another knock at the door followed by the doorbell ringing. Jamus shut his laptop, pushed back from the table, and shuffled over to the front hall.

He opened the door to find Sean Malloy standing in front of him with a duffel bag in one hand and an arm full of books in the other. By the looks of it, he had dressed quickly. He wore a Dublin soccer T-shirt underneath an open ski jacket, and his jeans were worn thin in a couple of places. He looked as if he hadn't been home in a few days.

Jamus opened the door fully and gestured for Sean to come in, closing it after him. Inside the house, Sean dropped his bag and his books on the floor. His lower lip trembled as he tried to speak, but couldn't. Jamus looked him over from head to toe and back again.

"Sean, are you okay? Did something happen?"

Again, Sean tried to speak but nothing came out. Instead, he shook his head slowly from side to side.

"Your family?" Jamus asked. "Did you tell them?"

Sean nodded, and his shoulders began to shake as he looked down at the floor. He tried to hold back the tears, but they came anyway in great heaving sobs.

Jamus stepped toward him and put his arms around his shoulders. "Okay, okay," he said, "it's going to be okay."

Jamus held him for what seemed like forever, and in the front hall of that small town house in Boston, Sean Malloy cried. He cried for the family he had always been afraid to be a part of; he cried for the words he'd never said; he cried for the love his brother had shown him and for the cruelty his sister had revealed. He cried for not being who he thought he should have been and for being afraid of who he was. He cried for what he had done to Grace and for what he had done to himself. He cried for the lies and the voices and the pain he had never let himself feel. He stood there in the arms of a man he'd met only weeks ago but who was somehow not a stranger, and he let all of the pain and sorrow finally wash over him in great waves. And Jamus stood there and held him, through the eddies of tears and the great big huffing, heaving breaths and the streaming rivers of snot and drool, and he didn't let go.

When some time had passed, and Sean had started to breathe normally again, Jamus released him. He reached up and pushed a strand of hair out of Sean's eyes, running a thumb gently along the top of his cheek to push away some of the last of the tears. "How about something to eat?" he finally said. "You look like you could use something."

"Do you have any whiskey?" Sean asked, and they both laughed, breaking some of the tension that had built up around them in the room.

"I do have some whiskey," Jamus said. "And who cares if it's noon."

"Five o'clock somewhere," Sean added.

"Then it's five o'clock for us." Jamus walked him into the kitchen.

Sean, growing more aware of his surroundings, looked around the kitchen and carefully back out into the hall. "Oh, God," he said. "Where's Nick? I really don't want him to see me like this."

"Relax," said Jamus. "He ran away."

"What?" Sean looked around the room, as if to find any traces the kid might have left behind. "Ran away? Like seriously ran away?"

"Yeah," said Jamus. "As in, not here. But I gotta hand it to the kid, he did it in style. He ran off to Nantucket."

"With Matt?" Sean asked.

"Who else?" Jamus pulled a couple of glasses out of the cabinet and walked out into the living room to grab the whiskey.

"I saw them leave early the other day, and I knew something was wrong."

"You saw them leave?" Jamus said, walking back into the kitchen and putting the bottle and the glasses on the table. "You saw them, and you let my kid walk out of school like a truant? Great teacher you are. Ice?"

Sean shook his head. "Straight up for me. And yeah, I let him walk out. He does everything with Matt, so I figured it was okay. But it was funny; I could tell something was weird. He didn't quite look like himself when they were leaving."

"Yeah, he's been a pistol lately," Jamus said, plunking a couple of ice cubes into his glass and filling each halfway with whiskey.

"He wasn't supposed to go with them?"

"Nope," Jamus said. "I told him I'd think about it, but I wanted to know how his schoolwork was going."

"And he went anyway?"

"Yep, left the next morning before I got up," he said. "I came downstairs to make coffee and found a note on the banister. I didn't even bother to read it. I knew where he'd gone."

Sean's face had a pale, stunned look about it. "So that's it? You didn't check up on him, call Matt's parents?"

"Oh, I called Matt's mom. Actually, she had called me first and left a message. I called her back later that morning and told her I'd said it was okay for Nick to go, but that I'd forgotten to give him pocket money and could I pay her back if she could cover him for the few days they were gone."

"What did she say?"

"She said week and a half. She corrected me, afraid that I may have misunderstood they'd be gone for the full week and a half of break." Jamus raised his glass, and Sean did the same with his. "To Nantucket."

"To Nantucket," Sean echoed.

"I so suck at this parenting thing," Jamus said, a defeated look in his eyes as he sat down across the table from Sean. "I've never had any idea what the hell I'm doing. I've tried to be something in between a brother and a parent, and I've just ended up being no good at either."

"I wouldn't say that," Sean said. "I've seen a lot of fucked-up kids and a lot of parents who don't care. Nick's a pretty amazing kid, and I know how much you care about him."

"Anyway," Jamus said, waving a hand and taking another sip of his whiskey. "Enough about me and Nick. What's going on with you? I'm guessing this wasn't the best morning?"

❖

Two hundred miles away in a cedar-shingled beach house tucked behind the dunes of Sconset Bluff on Nantucket, Nick and Matt sat staring out through a huge sliding glass door as a frigid, sopping rain pelted the gray landscape. They had exhausted the house's supply of board games and had both grown bored with the few videos that Matt's mom had brought.

"So, do you think you're going to get grounded when you get back?" Matt asked.

"I don't know, and I don't care," said Nick.

"You know, you have to ease up on your brother," Matt said after a long silence. "I'd give anything to have a brother like that."

"Whatever," said Nick. "I hate him. He lies, he's overbearing, and he's always trying to control me. When he's not, he's trying to act like everything is okay and wonderful, but it's not. Because of him, we're nothing more than a couple of orphans."

"Really," said Matt. "Are you that stupid? You know he does everything for you, right? You do realize he was twenty-two when he started taking care of you. You know what most twenty-two-year-olds are doing? I'll give you a hint—not potty training."

Nick looked over at him as if thinking about this for the first time in his life.

"Dude," Matt continued. "Don't look so surprised. You mean you never thought about that? I'll tell you what I'm gonna be doing when I'm twenty-two. I'm gonna be getting laid and partying and playing professional lacrosse."

"They have professional lacrosse?"

"Of course they do, numb nuts." Matt rolled his eyes. "Don't you listen to anything? I've only been talking about it for years."

"You have not. You didn't even know about lacrosse before eighth grade."

"Whatever." Matt let out a heavy sigh. "You gotta lighten up on Jamus. He's actually pretty cool."

"You think he's cool?" asked Nick.

Matt just shook his head and got up off the floor where they had been lying down. "Do you want a pizza? I think I'm going to throw one in the microwave."

"Sure." Nick rolled over and sat up. "Hey, Matt, don't tell your ma that Jamus said I couldn't come, okay?"

He looked back down at Nick on his way to the kitchen. "I won't, dude, but I'd be surprised if she didn't already know."

"What?"

"She talked to Jamus the first day we were out here. She called him to let him know we got out okay."

Nick swallowed and said nothing.

CHAPTER THIRTY-NINE

Jamus's room smelled like linen mixed with ginger and just a hint of sweat. The autumn sun flooded in through the two bay windows that looked out onto Dartmouth Street, and tiny specks of dust floated past in the streams of light. Jamus rolled over in bed and stretched, luxuriating in the cool air of the early morning. After a few more minutes he reached up and rubbed his eyes. A braid of tangled sheets and blankets curled around the lower half of his body as he jostled his feet loose and swung his legs over the side of the bed.

"Coffee?" he asked as he got up.

"Mmm, yes please," said Sean, opening his eyes and rolling over to face Jamus.

The past few days had been hide-away days, as Jamus liked to call them, days when you locked yourself inside the house and didn't worry about the world outside or any of the people in it. It was exactly what both of them had needed. Sean had been more tired than he realized. The run-in with Grace and the scene with his family had left him exhausted, and he'd taken a good part of the last few days to sleep.

The first night had been a little awkward. That afternoon had rolled into one of those days when you feel like you've met your first best friend. They'd sat at the kitchen table over a couple more whiskies talking about everything. Sean talked about growing up with his brother and sisters in South Boston. He talked about the people he had known since he was a kid and how hard it was to feel different. Jamus talked about his parents and what they were like. He shared the story of the night of their death, telling it for only the second time in his life. They talked about the books they loved and the movies they'd seen.

When the whiskey got to be too much, they moved to coffee and then to tea. It was the kind of afternoon that went from noon to seven o'clock in half an hour. When they looked up at the clock in the small kitchen and realized what time it was, Jamus wobbled over to the cabinets beside the sink and pulled out the frying pan.

"Pancakes?" he offered.

And to Sean, nothing had ever sounded so perfect. They sat in front of the tiny television in the living room and ate stacks of pancakes drenched in syrup and butter and watched old movies until it was very, very late. When the movies were finally over and the plates had been cleared to the kitchen, they at last wrestled with the question of who was sleeping where.

Jamus surveyed the living room, looking down at the couch before asking Sean where he would like to sleep. But Sean didn't answer. He looked at the couch, too, and then up at Jamus, taking a step closer to him and lightly touching his fingertips to Jamus's hands. Jamus folded his fingers in with Sean's and raised their clasped hands until they were even with his chest. Then Sean leaned in and kissed him, gently at first and then deeply as if he were kissing someone for the very first time. Sean was overcome by the warmth of lips, the rush of stubble, the chaos of thunder that rolled around in his stomach as they embraced. He let out a breath, something between a moan and a sigh. It was, for him, like his body was waking up as a new being.

Sean slept in Jamus's room that night and each night after that for the duration of the hide-away days. They had lost track of time, Jamus writing and researching in the mornings while Sean read. In the afternoons, if the rain let up, they would slip outside for a short walk around the South End, Jamus pointing out little restaurants and shops he liked and Sean likening it to the parts of town he had grown up in. Once during the week, they talked about seeing a play at the little collection of theatres down on Tremont, but they lost the drive and settled into another night of dinner on the living room floor in front of the television.

And so the days cascaded over one another with the two men discovering a little bit more about each other and about themselves. For

Jamus, it was the first time he'd had the space to let someone into his heart. He knew love in theory and defined himself by what he wanted out of life, but it had been years since he had let himself open up to someone the way he felt himself opening up to Sean.

Sean, for his part, lay in bed that last morning having changed into a different person. He felt as if the first part of his life was finished, and he'd crossed over a threshold into some place where the future opened up for him. In that morning, and the few mornings before that, new things seemed possible for him in a way they'd never seemed possible before. As Jamus went down for coffee he lay in their still-warm bed and allowed himself to think about all the possibilities of having someone in his life.

Still, in the corners of his mind were the words he'd heard others say to him about this road, about the loneliness, about the coldness of it. But for the first time in his life, he knew he could make his own truth if he wanted to. He didn't know yet if that would be with Jamus. He hoped it would, but even if it wasn't, these last few days had given him the confidence to know it was possible.

Jamus arrived a few minutes later with two cups of coffee in one hand and the paper in the other. Sean closed his eyes briefly to capture the domesticity of the moment and savor its beauty. Tomorrow was the second Sunday since Sean's arrival, and though they didn't talk about when these hide-away days might end, each sensed at some level it would have to be soon. For Sean, school would start next week, and Jamus would have to travel for research on his new book. He'd told Sean about the Dexicont project that first day, but they hadn't spoken about it since.

"Can I ask you something?" Jamus said as he crawled back into bed and handed a coffee to Sean.

"Not if it's a math question," he said. "Other than that, yes, you can."

Jamus smiled. "You'll stay here? I mean," he stumbled for the right words, "when things go back to the normal routine?"

Sean took a sip of the coffee and slowly wiped the edge of the rim with his thumb where a drop had threatened to run down the outer edge of the cup. "Is that okay? I mean, you've got a lot going on, with Nick and everything."

"I would like for you to, but I understand if it's too much," Jamus said, searching Sean's face for an indication of what he might be thinking. "I'm sorry, I'm not trying to rush things."

"No," Sean said. "Don't be sorry. I'd like to stay. And I'm really glad you asked."

"Okay," Jamus said and left it at that. He had at least one more hide-away day, and he'd be dammed if he was going to miss it. He put down his coffee cup and took Sean's out of his hand and set it on the side of the bed. "Now, how do you suggest we spend the rest of this morning?"

❖

The wind howled across the gray Nantucket beach, spraying a mixture of sand and salt in their faces. Nick pushed his hair out of his eyes and looked out over the water. The waves crested farther out than they had the day before, leaving the water soft and foamy as it came ashore. Nick scanned the horizons for boats or other signs of life but saw nothing except for the white caps of the waves folding over one another in the distance as they came rushing toward the island.

"Which way is Boston?" he asked as they walked along the beach.

Matt pointed back across the island. "It's on the other side."

"The other side?" Nick asked. "So, what's out in this direction?" He pointed out and over the waves. "France?"

"Pretty much," said Matt. "Although I think you might hit Bermuda along the way."

"That would be nice," Nick said.

Matt laughed. "Yeah, it would. Think of all the babes in bikinis."

"Yeah," said Nick, but his mind was somewhere else as he walked along, staring out across the water.

"Nick, you still thinking about that book?"

Nick nodded. "I can't stop thinking about it," he said, without looking over at his friend. "All that stuff about New York. All the weird shit that was in that book. I just can't believe he would do all that stuff."

"Seriously, Nick? Do you really think he did?" Matt said. After a few minutes walking along in silence, Matt turned to him. "Look, I want my friend back, dude. This vacation sucks. Where are you, man? It's like you're not even here."

They took a few more steps. "Matt, you know when we were back in eighth grade?"

"It was, like, last year," Matt said. "Of course I remember."

"Do you remember at graduation how everyone had all these people there, all these moms and dads and stepmoms and aunts and grandparents," Nick said. "I think most of the kids in our grade had like seventeen people each to see them graduate."

"Yeah," said Matt. "I remember my mom and dad were both there, and they were fighting all morning. Then my grandma got there and she took over for my mom, having a go at my dad."

"Yeah, well I didn't have any of that," Nick said. "No one showed up for my graduation. No one."

"Dude, you're forgetting one pretty important person who showed up."

"Jamus?"

"Duh, yeah." Matt shook his head.

"He doesn't count," said Nick.

"Like hell he doesn't." Matt looked out into the ocean and then directly at Nick. "Don't you get it, numb nuts?"

Matt grabbed Nick's shoulder and shook him. "He counts more than any of them. You don't even see it, do you? You're so tied up in thinking about all the things missing from your life, aren't you? What do you want? A mom and dad that fight? Aunts and uncles who don't know who you are? Look around, Nick. There are lots of people who don't have anyone who loves them and takes care of them the way you and Jamus take care of each other.

"Look at me. Look at my family. We take trips to the beach in the summer, and my dad likes to play sports and we get to watch a huge television in seventeen rooms in our house." Matt stared at him and Nick looked back, mouth open, the sand pelting his face until it was red and sore and he wanted to cry.

"And you know what? Nobody gives a shit about what I do. All my mom cares about is making sure that my dad is miserable. Do you think we have all those televisions because we need them? No, it's so that she can make him pay. And him, all he's doing is fucking his twenty-two-year-old girlfriend. Where do you think he is now? Do you think he's got a weekend to spend with me? Do you think he makes it to a lacrosse game? Do you? My mom won't either, as soon as she doesn't have to drive me."

Matt was shouting now, his voice crashing in between the waves. It had started to drizzle, and Matt's hair and skin were damp, so Nick couldn't tell if he was crying or if it was just the rain in his eyes. "And that army of relatives. Do you know what it's like to not matter to anyone? Nick, you matter to Jamus. He is always there for you. In fact, he never misses a fucking thing—cross-country meets, graduations, after school, during school. Christ, he's always two steps behind you watching out for you.

"Do you know what my parents would do if I wanted to do something they didn't approve of, like, oh, I don't know, running away to some island on school break?" He looked Nick directly in the face. "If they noticed, which they probably wouldn't, they would chase me down and beat the living shit out of me.

"So, yeah. Maybe he did some of the shit in that book fifteen years ago. But who the fuck cares? Why do you care? You know he didn't kill your parents, Nick. It was a fucking accident. He told you that. So move on, crawl out from under the pity party tent and stop walking around like you're some wounded little bird. Everybody's got shit to deal with." Matt rubbed the snot away from his nose with a fist and wiped it on his jeans. "But you've got someone who cares about you and you shouldn't fucking forget that."

Nick was crying now, tears rolling down his cheeks as he tried to swallow the wad of phlegm that had risen up into his nose. It was the first he had cried in a long time and maybe the first time he had cried in front of Matt ever. It was starting to get dark out, and the edges of the beach were beginning to blur into the water.

"I guess when you put it like that," Nick said, heaving back the tears, "he is pretty awesome."

"Fuck yeah, he's pretty awesome," Matt said. "Now can you please call him and tell him you're okay and you're sorry and then can you come back to Earth?"

"Uh-huh," said Nick, nodding and sniffling.

"Because I'm really fucking bored here without my best friend."

"When did you start swearing so much?" Nick asked.

"Dude, we have to swear now. We're in high school."

"Oh," said Nick. "I didn't know that."

"Yeah, it's like in the bylaws or something."

"What are bylaws?" Nick asked.

"The rule book, you know, the thing they give you on your first day," Matt said, sounding smug and wiping at his face one last time.

"It had a section in there about swearing?"

"Just shut up, okay?"

Nick agreed to shut up, and the two of them decided it was time to head back to the house. Turning around, they realized how far they had walked. It was much more than they thought, and the beach walk they had taken out from the house through the dunes was just a speck in the distance.

"Shit," said Matt.

"Right?" said Nick. "When did we walk that far?"

They trudged back along the edge of the water where the sand was hard enough that they didn't sink. The return was against the wind, so it took a lot longer than the walk out. It was almost dark by the time they reached the little path that took them off the beach and to the house.

As they made their way over the dunes to the house, Nick noticed that their cottage was the only one along the entire beach with lights on in the windows.

CHAPTER FORTY

The last Sunday in November was crisp and sunny, ending weeks of gray rainy weather that had sat down over New England and seemed like it would stay forever. There had been a frost the night before, and the air was clear and cold in a way that hinted at the energy of the oncoming winter.

Jamus breathed in as he walked alone through the streets of South Boston toward Sacred Heart. Sean had decided not to join him this morning, and Jamus didn't blame him. It was still too soon, he'd told Jamus as he lay in bed watching him get dressed for Mass. Jamus had said he understood, but he wanted to go, if that was all right with Sean. "Yes, go," he'd said. "It will give me some time to grade the hundreds of term papers I've left sitting for the last week and a half."

Crossing under the Expressway from the South End to South Boston had a different feeling for Jamus this morning. With every step he took into Sean's old neighborhood, the easy warmth of the last few days ebbed away. He walked over the crest of the Thomas Park hill, and as he approached the church, his stomach started to tremble and turn over.

He could hear the sky and the ocean speaking to him as he walked, whispering to him, telling him, warning him to turn back. In his mind even the vinyl-sided houses along the street seemed to shut him out with locked doors and shuttered windows. He had taken a son of South Boston and not returned him. What had he come back here for? Of course, Jamus knew he was being paranoid; he knew this was some weird guilt bubbling up in the back of his brain. But the feeling was vivid. He squared his shoulders against his own imagination and continued along his walk.

Finally he reached the church, only to find himself standing for a quarter of an hour in front of the doors, unable to walk in. He traced the intricate figures of the stone saints above the door with his eyes, and he stared at the giant circular stained glass window. He tried to think back to his earliest memory of this church, but nothing came to him. He couldn't isolate a single memory. It was just a collage, a giant cluster of feelings and emotions and memories that were indistinguishable from one another.

"Until now," he said aloud to himself. He looked up at the cross that marked the top of this wall. "This will be my first memory of this church." With that, he stepped forward and went into Sacred Heart.

The cold sun streamed in through the stained glass windows and bathed the sanctuary in warm oranges and reds. Jamus took a deep breath and sat down in his usual seat. He looked around and let the familiar comfort of this place seep in through the nervousness of being here today after the week he'd just had with Sean.

This was still the place where he felt his parents the most. When he looked up at the crucifix and the pictures in the windows, he was eight years old again, sitting in this same place, only he was squished in safely on either side by his ma and his dad. He closed his eyes and remembered the way they smelled on those mornings: his dad of shaving soap and starch, and his ma vaguely of lavender powder. He would hold his dad's hand through the first part of the service, until they had to stand. He even remembered that he would stand on his tippy toes, and when his dad would let him, he would stand on his dad's feet so that he could see the priest, Father Richards, as a young man.

Jamus let these memories play in the edges of his mind as he sat there for a few minutes. But he opened his eyes as someone scooted into the pew and sat down right next to him just as the Mass was starting. Jamus went to slide down and make room for the guy, even though the pew was relatively open and there was plenty of room. But the stranger put his hand gently on Jamus's knee.

"Don't," he said. "I need to ask you something."

Jamus sat still. This man was somehow familiar, but he couldn't place him. Then it dawned on Jamus where he had seen the features—the blondish red hair, the lines of that face. He looked across the church to the pew where the Malloys sat, and Sean's parents and his sisters were looking back at Jamus and the stranger.

"Is he with you?" the stranger asked.

Jamus coughed.

"Please, just tell me if he is. I'm worried. They're worried." He tilted his head in the direction of his family.

"You're his brother?" Jamus asked in a hushed whisper.

"Yes," the stranger said. "Kevin."

"Oh." Jamus took his time answering, watching the priest at the front of the church and thinking through exactly what he would say. "He's fine. He's safe."

"He's with you, then?"

Jamus nodded.

Kevin looked down at his hands, his eyes starting to water. "Thank God," he said. "We were worried, the way he left."

"I don't know you," Jamus said. "I'm not really comfortable talking about him with you."

"Of course." Kevin flattened his palms on his lap. "I understand." The tears that had formed in the corners of his eyes started to roll down his cheeks.

Jamus glanced over and pulled out a tissue from inside his coat pocket and handed it to Kevin. "Only slightly used," he said, smiling.

Kevin looked at him carefully before seeing the smile and realizing Jamus was kidding. "Thank you," he said, and after wiping his nose roughly, he tucked it into his pocket.

They looked up to see the new priest had taken his place behind the lectern. He raised his hands dramatically above his head and looked toward the ceiling of the church and took a deep, loud breath as if he were about to call on the power of all the saints. The old priest, sitting on the other side of the altar, rolled his eyes and shook his head.

Jamus and Kevin each stifled a laugh, but not quietly enough. The new priest looked up, his solemnity interrupted, and he spotted them immediately, reprimanding them with his eyes. Maybe they had imagined that or maybe it was real, but they both sat quietly, trying not to laugh throughout the rest of the service.

❖

Sean sat by himself at the kitchen table in Jamus's house grading papers. The week or so spent with Jamus had included almost no work, and it was with a heavy heart that he sat down this morning with a cup of coffee to realize that he had a titanic job ahead of himself. He pulled four stacks of papers out of his bag and began to go through them class by class.

The house had a peaceful feeling to it alone. The front rooms on the first floor sat behind a wall of shrubs shielding some of the noise from the street. As he worked, Sean listened to the gentle rush of the wind through the trees outside the window, blowing away the few remaining leaves of autumn. Occasionally, he heard someone on the sidewalk talking on their cell phone or the hum and push of a truck lumbering along up the road.

He was about halfway through his first stack of papers when he heard the key in the lock. He looked up at the clock to see it was too early for Jamus to be home from church. His next thought was that it must be Nick, but he didn't panic or think to hide. He couldn't avoid some kind of run-in with Nick. Sean was so naturally at home in the house that he had shared with Jamus for the past several days, he felt as if it was okay to be there.

So it was Nick who walked into the kitchen to find his English teacher sitting at his kitchen table quietly grading papers and sipping coffee. He stopped short at the kitchen doorjamb and looked up at Sean and then down to the other end of the kitchen. He dropped his backpack on the floor by the table and headed over to the fridge.

"Hi, Mr. Malloy," he said as he opened the refrigerator door and pulled out the milk and organic peanut butter.

"Hi, Nick," he said, looking up briefly from his papers.

"Jamus at church?" he asked.

"Yep." Sean watched as Nick moved about the kitchen, putting bread into the toaster, pulling down a glass from the cabinet for his milk, and grabbing a paper towel off the roll to lay his toast on.

Nick looked up to see him watching. "Want a piece of toast?"

"Um." Sean thought about it for a second. "Sure, thanks."

"Peanut butter?"

"Yes, please," Sean said, looking back down at his papers.

If Nick was the least curious as to why Sean was there, he shrugged it off as only the very young are comfortable doing in uncomfortable situations. He finished moving about in the kitchen, sliding Sean's toast in front of him on a paper towel before grabbing his own toast and milk and sitting down opposite his teacher.

"My test in there?" he asked, casually crunching down on the toast.

"Oh yeah," Sean said. "Yes, it is."

"What did I get?"

"You'll have to wait until Tuesday to find out, now won't you?"

"You could tell me now, and I could just get it out of the way," Nick mumbled through a mouthful of peanut butter. "I've got a flat screen television riding on this semester's grades."

"Really?" Sean said. "That doesn't sound like such a bad idea for this place."

"Seriously," said Nick. "So how about it? How'd I do?"

"Nope." Sean took a bite of his own toast. "You'll have to wait. The torture of making you sweat is part of the fun of being a teacher." He grinned. "How was Nantucket?" he asked, changing the subject.

"Um…" Nick's tone darkened at the mention of Nantucket. "Mr. Malloy, you're not here for an intervention or anything like that, are you?"

Sean laughed. "No," he managed. "I'm not. But the next time I see you skipping out of class, I'm going to have to call you on it." Sean let it drop at that and went back to grading the papers in front of him, occasionally shielding a name if he thought Nick was surreptitiously glancing over at it.

Finally, after what seemed like a hundred years of sitting somewhat awkwardly across from each other, they heard the key in the lock. Sean and Nick looked up at each other as they listened to Jamus stop in the front hall to take off his coat and scarf and stomp off his boots on the welcome mat. He rounded the corner into the kitchen and stopped short when he saw Nick sitting at the table.

"Back from Nantucket?" he asked, before continuing to the stove and filling the kettle with water. Nick was silent, but when Jamus turned around from the sink, his brother was standing in front of him, hands down at his side, eyes cast down at the floor. A puzzled look on Jamus's face said he didn't know how this was going to go. But before he could say anything or even think anything, Nick wrapped his arms around him in a giant bear hug. Jamus put down the kettle and hugged him back.

It was several minutes before Nick let go, and when he finally did peel back, Jamus realized his brother had been crying. "I'm sorry," Nick said.

"It's okay," Jamus said, and pulled him back into his chest. "It's okay, Nicky, it's okay." The two brothers stood in the middle of the kitchen for a long time until Nick sniffed loudly and hiccupped. "Hey," Jamus said. "You're not getting peanut butter on my church clothes, are you?" He could feel Nick's muffled laughter on his shoulder.

"You're not mad?" Nick asked, backing away slightly.

"Mad?" Jamus repeated the word thoughtfully, putting his hands on Nick's shoulders. "No, I'm not mad, Nick. I was worried."

"But you knew where I was, right?" Nick asked.

"Yes, I knew where you were," Jamus said, looking straight into his brother's eyes as if to underscore what he was saying. "I was still worried, though."

"I'm so grounded, aren't I?" Nick asked. To which Jamus just shook his head.

"I don't know yet, we'll figure something out, but I'm definitely rethinking the flat screen TV."

"Hey," Nick protested, "that was about grades, not behavior."

"I don't know," Jamus said. He looked up at Sean. "And how are the grades looking, Mr. Malloy?"

"Like I said to Nick, you'll both have to wait until Tuesday to find out. I'm not saying a word. But I do need a break from these," he said, stacking the papers into a neat pile and getting up from the table. "I think I'll take a little walk. I'll be back in about an hour or so," he said, picking up the piles of papers as he left. "And I'll be sure to put these well out of sight." He looked at Nick and then at Jamus before slipping away through the kitchen door and out to the front hall. A few minutes later, they heard the front door open and close as he went out.

❖

Nick sat back down in front of his half-eaten peanut butter toast and watched as his brother reorganized some dishes in the cupboard and pulled down the teapot.

"Why is he here?" asked Nick, when he knew they were finally alone.

"He got kicked out of his house, I think," said Jamus. "Cup?" he asked as he set a few tea bags into the pot to steep.

"Oh," said Nick, nodding at the tea bags. "He still lives at home?"

"Well," Jamus shrugged, "I don't think he does anymore."

"Is he living here now?"

"Yeah, Nick, I think he is," Jamus said, grabbing a couple of mugs and the teapot and sitting down at the kitchen table. "Are you okay with that?"

"Do I still have my room?" Nick asked.

Jamus laughed. "Yes, Nick. You will always have your room."

After a few moments, Jamus looked across at his younger brother. "Nick, there are a few things I need to tell you."

"About what?" Nick asked, a note of caution creeping into his voice as he finished the last bite of his toast. "Can I get another piece of toast first?"

"You can get another piece in a minute," Jamus said, sitting down next to Nick. "But I want to tell you this first." He took a deep breath. "All right, look, I'm sorry I didn't tell you about how Mom and Dad died. I still have trouble with those memories, and it's hard for me to talk about it." Nick struggled to remain on his chair, fidgeting and curling one foot up underneath himself as his brother talked. "The truth is that I did blame myself for a long time."

"It's okay, Jamus, I know you didn't do it."

"I know, Nick, but it's still hard for me. And I should have told you sooner, because telling you…" Jamus stopped for a minute to catch his breath. "Well, when I told you, that was the first time I could really let it go and not feel like I had to keep it all inside. It's hard to explain, but I spent so many years trying to keep things in line and not talking about any of it. Because I felt like if I talked about it I wouldn't be able to handle it. But then when I did talk about it, it helped. It helped me sort some of it out in my head."

"When you told me?"

"Yeah, when you made me talk about it," he said. "No one else had ever made me talk about that night. I'd kept it all inside for so long, and it was just eating away at me. I was afraid to move on; afraid to do anything else in my life except write about it time after time after time in different stories, but always back to highways and car crashes. Nick, you could have read any one of the books I've written, and you would have walked away with the same thing. Because it's in all of them. That's why I don't keep copies of any of them around."

"But why?" Nick asked.

"Because I couldn't let it go. I just kept reliving it every time I sat down to write something. I even started to do it again with the last thing I was working on. I couldn't put my finger on it, but I was writing about a highway—again. I couldn't get away from it. I guess what I'm trying to say is no more secrets. All right? Not from me, and not from you. Okay?"

"Um, does that include school stuff?"

Jamus smiled. "Yes, that goes without saying."

"Well," Nick said, "does that also include boyfriend stuff?"

Jamus nodded slowly.

"Well, this is kind of weird, but are you and Mr. Malloy…"

"He got kicked out of his house, and he's staying here for a while."

"On the couch?" Nick asked.

"No, not on the couch." Jamus felt himself going red, but he was powerless to stop it.

"And not in my room?" Nick raised his eyebrows.

"No, not in your room," Jamus replied, lowering his voice.

"In your room?" Nick tilted his head and pointed toward the ceiling, making a surprisingly mature face.

"Um, yes. In my room." Jamus shifted uncomfortably in his seat.

"And there's nothing more you want to tell me?"

"Actually," Jamus said, his tone brightening slightly, "there is something I want to tell you."

Nick nodded expectantly, urging him to continue.

"Well," Jamus started cautiously, "I've taken a job writing a different kind of book. A biography, and there's going to be a lot of travel."

"Travel?" Nick's face lit up. "Like, travel to where? When?"

"A lot of it's going to be over Christmas break, and you're coming with me. How do you feel about California for Christmas?"

Nick's smile shone like a burst of sunlight. "California? Sweet. What part?"

"San Francisco," he said, "and then a couple stops after that. It'll be a surprise. But I expect it'll be pretty fun."

Chapter Forty-one

Angel raised his face to the sun and felt its warmth on his cheeks and on his neck. The first time he had seen the morning light on this city, it glowed crystal and golden, and to him it had seemed like anything in the world was possible here. This morning on his walk home from the club, he realized how small his world had become. He'd thought that it was getting bigger, but it had been shrinking. Every day since he'd arrived in this great lost city of magic, he had taken steps to make it smaller. He had lost everything today and he knew now that he had a choice to make. He could keep going or he could find a new path; a new sun to follow. He shut his eyes and breathed in the cool morning air and made his decision.

Nick took a deep breath before walking into the classroom. It had been a few weeks since Mr. Malloy, as Sean still required Nick to call him at school, had started living at the Dartmouth Street house with Jamus and Nick. For Nick, it turned out to be a lot less weird than he had expected. Matt was the only friend that he was allowed to tell about his brother's new roommate, and in characteristic Matt fashion, he thought it was "wicked cool."

Standing outside the classroom door, Nick shook his head and cleared his mind. Today was oral report day. This was the final project in the semester, and his performance today counted for a quarter of his grade in English. Oral reports were ten-minute discussions led by each student on a book of their choice. For the months of November and

December, book choice for oral reports was a major topic of discussion around the school, and consequently at home for Nick. But Nick had decided to keep his book a secret from everyone, including his brother and Sean. He had told only one other person—Matt. That was mostly because he needed Matt to have his back in class on the day of the report, and he didn't think it was fair to spring it on him at the last minute.

He felt someone behind him at the door to the classroom. Turning around, he came face-to-face with Matt.

"You ready?" he asked.

"No," said Nick, a petrified look on his face. "I think I've changed my mind. I can always just talk about Huck Finn or something we read last year, right?"

Matt shook his head. "Come on, dude. You wanted to do this, remember? Show those fuckers you don't care what they think."

Nick nodded slowly. "I don't know if I think it's such a good idea now."

"Hey, no wussing out. It's still a good idea. Besides, you kind of need to do this." He gave his best friend a smile and shoved Nick through the door into the classroom.

Nick took his seat and waited for his name to be called. He was one of four kids scheduled to go that day. Mr. Malloy always kept quiet about what order the students would present in, so Nick sat petrified and sweating for the first five minutes of class while Malloy took attendance, shuffled around some papers, and then took a seat in the back of the room.

But first up for the day wasn't Nick; it was a short chunky kid named Jeff. Jeff had read Ayn Rand's *The Fountainhead* for his report. He started out with a soft, shy, almost embarrassed ramble about the times the book was written in and what Rand's impact was on American culture. Nick could tell that he had prepared and wanted to do really well on this, but he was bombing.

Nick would have felt sorry for him if he wasn't scared to death that he also had to get up and present today, and his report might not even go as well as Jeff's. Nick sat stone still as the kid at the front of the classroom stumbled over every word out of his mouth, and the sweat started to bead on his forehead. Mercifully, the class seemed to get bored, and they largely tuned him out. Finally, at eight minutes and forty-five seconds, Mr. Malloy let him off the hook.

"Thank you, Jeff. That was very thorough." He made a few marks on a sheet of paper in front of him while Jeff continued to stand at the front of the classroom and drip. "You can have a seat, Jeff. Nick, you're up next."

Oh God, thought Nick. His stomach sank, and he could feel the back of his neck go cold. He slowly collected the set of index cards he had been shuffling nervously in front of him and stood up.

The passage of time had done nothing to improve Nick's life at school. After Thanksgiving break, the rest of the semester had passed in much the same way as every day since the fight with Robby. He walked down the hall day after day through a barrage of whispers and smirks. His locker had become a canvas for graffiti markers and the school custodian could barely keep up with all the scrubbing off and painting over required to keep it clear.

A wave of hushed whispers and giggles rolled across the class as he walked up to the front of the room. He turned around and faced the class, swallowing the butterflies in his stomach and softly clearing his throat. "The book that I chose for this report is *Angel of New York*, by my brother, Jamus Cork."

The class erupted in a fit of laughter. Mr. Malloy lost his cool, banging his fist loudly on the desk he was sitting in at the back of the classroom. "That's enough!" he shouted. "You will give this student the attention and respect you have given every other presenter in this class. Is that understood?"

The class quieted down, and Nick looked around before continuing. "I expected that reaction," he said, looking into the faces around the room. He stopped and smiled when he got to Anara. "I think someone suggested earlier this year that we read this book, but like everything else she thinks of, I thought it was kind of a stupid idea at the time. But she was right. It is a good book. It's a great book."

"Mr. Cork, back to your report, please," Mr. Malloy said softly.

"I chose this book because I had never read it, and it seemed like I probably should—not just because everyone else was reading it and making assumptions about me, but because the author is my brother, and I figured I should hear what he had to say about and to the world."

Nick leaned back on the teacher's desk behind him to steady himself. "The book takes place in New York City. It's about a world we know nothing about. It's an underworld where drugs are everywhere, and people do all sorts of cruel things to each other. But what's important about the book's setting is that we see the same themes here that we see in other stories, like *The Odyssey* or *A Separate Peace*. We see love, honor, friendship, and a struggle to get to a better place or be a better person. Like all of us here in this class, we struggle with the battle to be better but end up giving into the pressure of what other people think of us or expect us to do." The class was silent, but not in the same way they had been when Jeff was speaking. They were staring at Nick, listening to him rather than ignoring him.

"The main character in this book is a street kid named Angel. He's into all sorts of bad things—drugs, prostitution, stuff I can't even say in this class."

"Fag," someone mumbled in the back of the room, causing Malloy to snap his head around.

"No," Nick said calmly, looking at Mr. Malloy and then at the guy who had called out. "He's right. Angel does a lot of gay things in the book, and he does them for money. A lot of the other characters in the book are gay, too, and it deals with the prejudices that those characters face every day; prejudices that my brother probably faced a lot, too. That's not central to the plot. It's not about being gay, but I heard a lot of people talking about that this semester, and if my locker door is any way to judge, everybody got stuck on that part of the book. And by the way," he said, focusing first on the guy who had interrupted him, and then at every face in the room, "I don't care if you think I'm gay. The guy who has raised me since I was three is gay and there is nothing wrong with him. So go ahead and call me that all you want. It's not an insult." He smiled and watched for a response but heard only a deep, still silence. No one dared to speak. After a few seconds, the heater in the back of the room clicked on and broke the spell.

"But back to the book. What happens as you read this book is that you start to see pieces of yourself in these characters. You all read this book," he said to the class. "Couldn't you relate to the way that Angel wanted to get out of the world he was in? He hadn't created this world, but he lived it. He was trapped in it, and everything he did was a reaction to it. It's kind of like all of us here—we didn't create this, but we're kind of stuck here whether we like it or not.

"But then there is free will, right? That theme we see in Steinbeck's work and so many other books. But here free will is a little different. Here, Jamus—I mean the author—shows us that free will sometimes needs a little shove. You're not going to do something different just because. You need to be pushed into it, and what does it for Angel is falling in love. He falls in love with this beautiful girl who is in a whole different world than his. And he tries to be better. Not to fit into her world, but to be the kind of person he feels she should be with."

"But what about the end?" Anara said. All the sharpness was gone from her voice, and she seemed genuinely sad with what she was saying. "In the end, it didn't work."

"No, it didn't," said Nick. "And I'm not going to lie to you. That ending was hard for me to read. In the end, Angel lost his way, got high again, and crashed a car with the girl and her family in it. He ended up killing everything he loved because he couldn't quit the life he had come from."

"But isn't that the opposite of free will?" Mr. Malloy's voice surprised him. It was somehow less formal, less of the English teacher and more of Sean, the guy from Southie who had been crashing at his house for the past few weeks.

"The hardest thing for me was figuring out exactly what to take away from the ending of this book," said Nick. "But here's what I've chosen to walk away with. Free will is there. You can grab it and go after the things in life you want, and you should. It might not always turn out the way you want, but you have to try. The second is that quitting something and moving on isn't always easy. It takes time and many steps, and they're not smooth or pretty. It's grueling, and if you give up, there are consequences. Sliding back means you take others with you."

Nick was quiet for a moment before he continued. "Earlier this year, I got a fortune cookie message that said, 'We find the family we are meant to have.' And I guess that's part of it. You find the family you're supposed to have, but you also have to choose to be part of that family, to keep those people in your life. So in the end, make your life what you want. Know that it's up to you what you do with it, but be careful of other people and take care of them." He stood a minute and then took a deep breath and let out a loud sigh, all of the tension draining from his body.

"Anyway, that's pretty much all of my report," he said to a silent room. A few seconds passed, and no one said a word. Just when it was beginning to feel even more awkward for Nick, he heard a loud scraping of wood across the waxed floor, as someone pushed their chair back to get up. It was Matt, who stood up and started to clap slowly. The class stared at him for a minute, and then Anara stood up next to him and started to clap. A few seconds later, several others stood up—not all of the class, but most of them. Nick smiled. Matt had been right, he had needed to do this.

Chapter Forty-two

Sean and Jamus stood on the steps of Sacred Heart Church in South Boston. Jamus still fidgeted a little from time to time since he had quit smoking, but by and large the habit and most traces of it were gone. They were late and Mass had already started; they could hear the organ playing behind the great wooden doors of the church.

Sean looked at those giant doors, more foreboding today than they'd ever been in his entire life. Then he looked down the street, past the rows of houses to the beach on the horizon. "Is this going to work?" he asked.

"You and me?" Jamus asked.

Sean nodded. "Because if it's not, then I really don't want to go through with this part."

"I can't say it's going to be easy," Jamus said, following his stare from the beach back to the church doors. "But I'd like to try."

"Come on, you two," said Kevin, standing behind them. "Are you going to take all day on this? For crying out loud, it's just church."

"Yeah," said Nick. "You guys don't have to be such drama queens."

"Hey," said Sean, "that's a derogatory term, you can't use that."

"Drama queen," Nick said again.

"Jamus, did you hear that?" Sean said. "Are you going to let that go?"

"All of you, in," said Kevin, stepping up to the church door and pulling it open with one hand. With the other, he reached out and gestured for them all to walk in.

Acknowledgments

Thank you:

Dana, for your patience, love, and support in my pursuit of my dream of writing. Ma, Dad, and Mike for being such a great core. All the Callahans, Cordners, Groses, Emerys, Rossiters and Bardsleys—for giving me something to write about. Erin Bush, Janet Short, Kate Bardsley, Carolyn Callahan, Tanya Ricci, Eleanora Paciulan, Mary Squires, and Randy Susan Meyers for your help with the writing process. Carol Simmons for your help in navigating the world of publishing. The Splinters—a never-to-be-forgotten group of fearless writers who gave me my start on this journey.

Thank you, Jerry Wheeler, for being such a great editor, and the whole crew at Bold Strokes Books for being amazing to work with.

About the Author

Born into an Irish American family in a small town outside of Boston, Ralph Josiah grew up as a Coast Guard brat, wandering around helicopter hangars in New Orleans, Cape Cod, coastal North Carolina, and Sitka, Alaska. He currently resides in San Francisco and Boston with his husband and partner of more than fourteen years, Dana Short.

Ralph Josiah holds a bachelor's degree from Greensboro College and a master's in communication from Emerson College. He has a passion for good books, exciting travel, and long runs—where he happens to do most of his thinking. He is inspired by things that are different and believes that grace happens when and where we least expect it.

Contact Ralph at rjbardsley@gmail.com or ralphjosiahbardsley.com.

Books Available From Bold Strokes Books

Corpus Calvin by David Swatling. Cloverkist Inn may be haunted, but a ghost materializes from Jason Dekker's past and Calvin's canine instinct kicks in to protect a young boy from mortal danger. (978-1-62639-428-5)

Brothers by Ralph Josiah Bardsley. Blood is thicker than water, but you can drown in either. Jamus Cork and Sean Malloy struggle against tradition to find love in the Irish enclave of South Boston. (978-1-62639-538-1)

Every Unworthy Thing by Jon Wilson. Gang wars, racial tensions, a kidnapped girl, and a lone PI! What could go wrong? (978-1-62639-514-5)

Puppet Boy by Christian Baines. Budding filmmaker Eric can't stop thinking about the handsome young actor that's transferred to his class. Could Julien be his muse? Even his first boyfriend? Or something far more sinister? (978-1-62639-510-7)

The Prophecy by Jerry Rabushka. Religion and revolution threaten to bring an ancient civilization to its knees...unless love does it first. (978-1-62639-440-7)

Heart of the Liliko'i by Dena Hankins. Secrets, sabotage, and grisly human remains stall construction on an ancient Hawaiian burial ground, but the sexual connection between Kerala and Ravi keeps building toward a volcanic explosion. (978-1-62639-556-5)

Lethal Elements by Joel Gomez-Dossi. When geologist Tom Burrell is hired to perform mineral studies in the Adirondack Mountains, he finds himself lost in the wilderness and being chased by a hired gun. (978-1-62639-368-4)

The Heart's Eternal Desire by David Holly. Sinister conspiracies threaten Seaton French and his lover, Dusty Marley, and only by tracking the source of the conspiracy can Seaton and Dusty hold true to the heart's eternal desire. (978-1-62639-412-4)

The Orion Mask by Greg Herren. After his father's death, Heath comes to Louisiana to meet his mother's family and learn the truth about her death—but some secrets can prove deadly. (978-1-62639-355-4)

The Strange Case of the Big Sur Benefactor by Jess Faraday. Billiwack, CA, 1884. All Rosetta Stein wanted to do was test her new invention. Now she has a mystery, a stalker, and worst of all, a partner. (978-1-62639-516-9)

One Hot Summer Month by Donald Webb. Damien, an avid cockhound, flits from one sexual encounter to the next until he finally meets someone who assuages his sexual libido. (978-1-62639-409-4)

The Indivisible Heart by Patrick Roscoe. An investigation into a gruesome psycho-sexual murder and an account of the victim's final days are interwoven in this dark detective story of the human heart. (978-1-62639-341-7)

Fool's Gold by Jess Faraday. 1895. Overworked secretary Ira Adler thinks a trip to America will be relaxing. But rattlesnakes, train robbers, and the U.S. Marshals Service have other ideas. (978-1-62639-340-0)

Big Hair and a Little Honey by Russ Gregory. Boyfriend troubles abound as Willa and Grandmother land new ones and Greg tries to hold on to Matt while chasing down a shipment of stolen hair extensions. (978-1-62639-331-8)

Death by Sin by Lyle Blake Smythers. Two supernatural private detectives in Washington, D.C., battle a psychotic supervillain spreading a new sex drug that only works on gay men, increasing the male orgasm and killing them. (978-1-62639-332-5)

Buddha's Bad Boys by Alan Chin. Six stories, six gay men trudging down the road to enlightenment. What they each find is the last thing in the world they expected. (978-1-62639-244-1)

Play It Forward by Frederick Smith. When the worlds of a community activist and a pro basketball player collide, little do they know that their dirty little secrets can lead to a public scandal…and an unexpected love affair. (978-1-62639-235-9)

GingerDead Man by Logan Zachary. Paavo Wolfe sells horror but isn't prepared for what he finds in the oven or the bathhouse; he's in hot water again, and the killer is turning up the heat. (978-1-62639-236-6)

Myth and Magic: Queer Fairy Tales, edited by Radclyffe and Stacia Seaman. Myth, magic, and monsters—the stuff of childhood dreams (or nightmares) and adult fantasies. (978-1-62639-225-0)

Balls & Chain by Eric Andrews-Katz. In protest of the marriage equality bill, the son of Florida's governor has been kidnapped. Agent Buck 98 is back, and the alligators aren't the only things biting. (978-1-62639-218-2)

Blackthorn by Simon Hawk. Rian Blackthorn, Master of the Hall of Swords, vowed he would not give in to the advances of Prince Corin, but he finds himself dueling with more than swords as Corin pursues him with determined passion. (978-1-62639-226-7)

Café Eisenhower by Richard Natale. A grieving young man who travels to Eastern Europe to claim an inheritance finds friendship, romance, and betrayal, as well as a moving document relating a secret lifelong love affair. (978-1-62639-217-5)

Murder in the Arts District by Greg Herren. An investigation into a new and possibly shady art gallery in New Orleans' fabled Arts District soon leads Chanse into a dangerous world of forgery, theft...and murder. A Chanse MacLeod mystery. (978-1-62639-206-9)

Calvin's Head by David Swatling. Jason Dekker and his dog, Calvin, are homeless in Amsterdam when they stumble on the victim of a grisly murder—and become targets for the calculating killer, Gadget. (978-1-62639-193-2)

The Return of Jake Slater by Zavo. Jake Slater mistakenly believes his lover, Ben Masters, is dead. Now a wanted man in Abilene, Jake rides to Mexico to begin a new life and heal his broken heart. (978-1-62639-194-9)

First Exposure by Alan Chin. Navy Petty Officer Skyler Thompson battles homophobia from his shipmates, the military, and his wife when he takes a second job at a gay-owned florist. Rather than yield to pressure to quit, he battles homophobia in order to nurture his artistic talents. (978-1-62639-082-9)